299 Days IX: T

by

Glen Tate

Book Nine in the ten book 299 Days series.

Your Survival Library

www.PrepperPress.com

299 Days IX: The Restoration

ISBN 978-0692264461

Copyright © 2014 by Glen Tate

All rights reserved.

Printed in the United States of America.

Prepper Press Trade Paperback Edition: July 2014

Prepper Press is a division of Kennebec Publishing, LLC

- This book is dedicated to people I don't know yet. Although, in all honesty, I have a pretty good idea who some of them are. These are the people who will rebuild our areas after the Collapse. Some will do exciting and heroic things, others will do mundane things like getting water systems and electrical grids working again. Some will restart hospitals, others will write constitutions and new laws to prevent this from happening again. This book is dedicated to them: the rebuilders.

This ten-book series follows Grant Matson and others as they navigate through a partial collapse of society. Set in Washington State, this series depicts the conflicting worlds of preppers, those who don't understand them, and those who fear and resent them.

The Restoration is the ninth book in the *299 Days* series

When the Patriots finally launch their strike against the Loyalists, Grant Matson's leadership, bravery, and training are put to the ultimate test. The 17th Irregulars are teamed up with regular military units and they must put their differences aside in order to successfully overthrow the Limas.

While the battle rages on, the Loyalists outside of Olympia start to pay the price for their allegiances to the wrong side of the Collapse, while well-intentioned others welcome the beginning of New Washington that recognizes fairness and hard work.

The battle winds down and a new day begins as the Team recognizes that victory does not come without loss. Grant, now a celebrated war hero, is not without his own personal hardships, and fears facing a new life without his family.

Books from the 299 Days series published to date:

For more about this series, free bonus chapters, and to be notified about future releases, please visit **www.299days.com**.

About the Author:

Glen Tate has a front row seat to the corruption in government and writes the *299 Days* series from his first-hand observations of why a collapse is coming and predictions on how it will unfold. Much like the main character in the series, Grant Matson, the author grew up in a rural and remote part of Washington State. He is now a forty-something resident of Olympia, Washington, and is a very active prepper. "Glen" keeps his real identity a secret so he won't lose his job because, in his line of work, being a prepper and questioning the motives of the government is not appreciated.

Chapter 291

Used

(January 1)

Nancy Ringman was wobbly from all the wine, but felt like her legs were encased in concrete. She could barely move them. Each step was a struggle, requiring all her strength and then a long rest. There was nothing physically restraining her; it was all mental. She held the box with the pistol in her hands. She knew that once she got out to the football field, she had to do it – and she really didn't want to do it. She wondered if it would hurt to shoot herself. She kept wondering if she shot herself in the head, would the brain shut down instantly and prevent it from registering pain. Or, would she feel pain before she died?

Each step was taking longer and longer. During her brief rests, she looked at where she was, the Clover Park Temporary Detention Facility. Remembering the people who used to be there, many of them just a few hours ago. Now they were gone. Everyone was gone. The staff had melted away as the explosions and gunfire got closer and the prisoners … they were … gone.

"Under my feet," Nancy said softly as she stepped onto the first of the fresh dirt at the football field. "Under my feet," she repeated. She smiled. It wasn't a happy smile; it was an ironic and tragic smile. She realized that, throughout her life, she desperately wanted to have people under her – in her job, in her marriage, in everything – and now she had succeeded.

"Success," she whispered to herself as she took another step on the fresh dirt. "I've been so successful," she said sarcastically. "Look at me! I'm a success," she said out loud in the empty football field.

She started to feel something under her feet and quickly jumped back onto the grass and away from the dirt. There wasn't anything physically moving under the dirt; there was a very faint sense of … something … under the dirt. She felt like lots and lots of things were under that dirt. Not bodies, although she knew they were down there, but … lives. Under that dirt were lives. Fathers who would never see their wives and children. Brothers and sisters who would never see their siblings. Weddings that never would happen, lives that never would go on. It had all stopped and those incomplete lives were under the dirt.

And she had done it. She could have stopped it. She could have let them go. She let out that same ironic and tragic laugh as a moment before. "I could have just done a bad job," she said to no one, except the faint things under her. "I could have failed – for once," she said, without a laugh this time. "But no," she said, "I'm Nancy Ringman. I never fail. I get the job done. 'You can count on me, Linda'," she said, repeating her answer to her boss, Linda, when she was told to "make room" for the new arrivals at Clover Park by getting rid of the prisoners. "You can count on me," she mumbled again.

She wondered what Linda was doing right now. Linda was probably in some safe place in Seattle, cheerfully reporting to her superiors that Clover Park was now ready for refugees loyal to the legitimate authorities. Linda had succeeded.

Used. That word kept ringing in Nancy's mind. She had been used. Linda got all the credit; Nancy had all the things underfoot to haunt her for the rest of her life.

In a rush of emotion, Nancy started to realize how all her "success" was just her being used by her superiors. She made all the sacrifices, she got people mad at her, and she made enemies, just to 'get the job done'. Their job, the superiors' job. She was at the end of her life with no friends, no real marriage to speak of, and no kids. Until a few days ago, she only had that thrill when she could tell people what to do or could get favors done because of her connections. That wasn't a life. That was a power trip masquerading as a life.

Empty. That word replaced "used" as the one running through her mind. An empty life, completely wasted by enjoying being the bitch. "You're the one who enjoyed it," she said to herself. "No one made you be this way." She started to relive the thrill of calling the Governor's chief of staff on her cell phone and getting a cousin a job, or placing a call and then someone she couldn't stand magically lost his job at a state agency.

But it didn't seem fun now; it didn't seem like a thrill. She felt horrified at the things she'd done. She now realized how ... awful she'd been.

"Time to do something about this," she said aloud again. She looked at the pistol box she was holding. Her hands and arms started to go wobbly. She had to set down the box. She spent the next minute or so staring at the pistol box and imagining that she was picking it up and getting the gun out. After several mental rehearsals, she thought

2

she was finally ready to actually do it.

She slowly bent down to pick up the box and hold it in her hands, just like she'd mentally rehearsed. She felt it. She paused. Then she suddenly picked it up.

"Might as well get this over with," she said. She recalled a root canal that she had postponed a few years ago and how relieved she had been when she finally got it done. Putting things off can often be worse than actually doing them.

She remembered the pain of the root canal and recalled the dental instruments and how frightening they looked when she saw them at the onset of the procedure. Then she started to wonder if the teabaggers had dental instruments. They would use them to torture her. They probably had things far worse than dental instruments. They would use them, too, because they were haters.

There was only one thing to do. It was in that box.

She opened the box and there it was: a gun. She stared at it. She'd never held a gun before. They were so dangerous. Guns were what rednecks and criminals used. People like her, good people, never touched them.

She closed her eyes. She couldn't look at the gun. It was too terrifying. Not what she would do with the gun – that part she was fine with – but guns were so evil. It was like looking at a poisonous snake; ugly and evil and painful if you touched it.

She remembered how, just a few moments ago, she had mentally rehearsed picking up the pistol box and then finally doing it for real. She could psych herself into touching the gun. Probably.

She imagined touching the gun with her index finger. She wanted to touch it and see if anything happened. She wondered if it would just go off if she touched it.

She stared at it more and pointed her index finger at it, slowly bringing it down to the handle part of the gun. She got about an inch away from it and jabbed her finger down onto the handle.

Nothing. It didn't go off. It was just a piece of hard plastic. She thought she'd try touching the metal part now. She psyched herself up again and slowly brought her pointed index finger down and touched the top of the gun.

Nothing. Now that she knew that it wouldn't go off just by touching it, she slowly touched other parts of the gun, except the trigger. She was very careful not to touch *that*.

She then decided to take it in her hand, doing so very slowly and carefully. It felt strange in her hand, like nothing she'd ever felt

3

before. "Makes sense," she said to herself, because she had never had a gun in her hand. *Of course* it felt like nothing she'd ever held before.

She slowly lifted the gun. It wasn't as heavy as she'd thought it would be. In the movies, guns always seemed heavy.

Now that she was holding it, she started pointing it at various parts of the empty football field, still very afraid it would go off.

"And, what?" she asked herself, "Hurt someone?" Like the things under the dirt? She wanted to laugh at her thought, but it seemed too dark.

She was moving the gun around, but still wasn't comfortable with it. She wanted to put it back in the box. She felt dirty holding it.

She put it back in the box and then wondered if it was loaded. She remembered from a movie that you could see the bullets in the little wheel thing on this kind of gun, the cowboy kind, not the fully automatic assault pistols with the high-capacity clips, like the Glock. This was the kind of gun the police used when she was growing up. A revolver, she seemed to remember them being called.

She slowly and carefully looked at the holes in the wheel thing and didn't see any bullets in them. She remembered from the movies that pushing a button somewhere made the wheel thing flop out so bullets could be put in it. There was only one button on the gun. She was afraid pushing the button would make it go off. She pointed it at the ground with the gun in her right hand and slowly pushed the button with her left hand.

Nothing. The gun didn't go off, but the wheel thing didn't flop out either. Finally, she pushed harder on the button and the wheel thing started to flop out.

She looked in the wheel thing and saw there were no bullets in it. She set the gun down, with the wheel thing open, and looked at the bullets in the pistol box. There was a box of bullets. She opened the box and carefully pulled a bullet out. She was careful because those things could just go off. They were miniature bombs, after all.

She tried putting the bullet in the wheel thing but the big end of the bullet wouldn't fit, so she turned it around and put the small end in the hole; the big end kept the bullet from falling through. That must be how to load it, she thought. She put in five more bullets. She only needed one, but realized that when the wheel turned, it might not have a bullet. She didn't want to put this up to her head, decide to do it, and then just hear a click.

Now the gun was loaded. She stared at it in the box, starting to psych herself up again. She began to imagine what it would look like if

4

she put the gun in her hand and put it up to her head.

She couldn't. She couldn't touch that thing. It was a loaded gun and was very dangerous. Touching it a little had been one thing, but this was different. This was final.

She started to think about the dental instruments and stared at the gun.

She decided to touch it again, recalling the root canal and how it was better to just do it than keep worrying about it.

She put the gun in her hand and put it up to her head.

"Boom!"

She swung around toward the sound of the explosion and dropped the gun.

"Boom!" There was a second explosion followed by the sound of a truck ramming something. It was coming from the direction of the back entrance to the campus.

It took a moment for her mind to switch from being a second away from killing herself to realizing that soldiers were coming to Clover Park.

It was Linda! Linda had sent soldiers to come and rescue her! All this would be over – right before she killed herself! She was the luckiest person on the planet. She was elated and on top of the world.

But why were they blowing up the gate and ramming it? If they were the legitimate authorities, wouldn't they have a key or something? Suddenly, Nancy's thrill of being rescued was turning to the terror of being captured. The dental instruments flashed through her mind.

She started to run, but soon fell down because her legs were so wobbly. She was terrified and still drunk. She got up, ran some more, and fell again. In the minute or two it took to run, fall, get up and slowly hobble her way back to the main building, the soldiers at the gate had made it onto the campus. She saw several regular pickup trucks, not military vehicles, racing on the beautifully landscaped campus grounds and tearing up the lawn and flowerbeds.

The legitimate authorities wouldn't have pickup trucks, she realized. She fell again when the thought of being captured by the teabaggers swept over her. As she was getting up, a man raced up to her with a gun and pointed at her.

"You're under arrest!" he yelled.

Chapter 292

Brewery Tour

(January 1)

It was weird. As they rolled down Highway 101 on the outskirts of Olympia, Grant realized that there was no one shooting at them. They approached each overpass carefully –very carefully. It took them all afternoon to go the few miles from Delphi Road to the Olympia city limits. They knew that the Limas would be concentrated in the city and would have more sophisticated defenses closer to town.

They did. Kind of. There were log obstacle booby traps on each of the overpasses after the Delphi exit, but no one there to pull the rope. Not a single person.

In fact, it was getting dark and they hadn't seen one enemy fighter all day. They'd seen scared civilians running away. Women and children. It was raining, so the women and children looked miserable and pathetic scurrying away.

Dark, Grant thought. It was getting dark. They needed to have a plan for the darkness. He looked at the next exit, knowing the area well because it was the exit he used to take when he came home from the cabin. It had the perfect hiding place.

"You guys ever taken the Olympia brewery tour?" Grant asked the Team and Donnie, seemingly out of the blue. The tour was famous because they let the visitors sample all kinds of beer. The Olympia brewery was a huge beer-making plant right off the exit. It had been shut down a few years earlier because new environmental regulations made it economically impossible to brew anymore. Before that, the brewery had operated for over a hundred years making the formerly famous Olympia Beer. Hundreds of jobs were lost when it closed. The brewery was now boarded up, just like most other businesses.

The guys, who were concentrating on spotting people trying to kill them, wondered why Grant was distracting them. They didn't answer. Each of them expected someone else to respond, but no one did.

"The reason I ask," Grant finally said, "is that the brewery would be a great place to bed down tonight. Lots of windows, up high with a commanding view. All those gates protecting the place. It's a nice defensible place. And it's abandoned, so no one would think anyone was there."

Still more silence. It was getting dark and harder to see threats.

"Scotty," Grant said, "call in to Ted and see if he thinks the brewery would be a good place to be tonight." Scotty obliged.

Ted, who had lived in the Olympia area for several years, was familiar with the brewery and, given its proximity to their current location as well as the capitol campus, he thought it would be a good place to be, at least for the night.

"Okay," Grant said, referring to the Team and Donnie, "we will clear out one of the buildings for ourselves and set up shop."

Grant had Scotty radio to Ted that the main convoy should park on the side of the highway as the Team exited and checked out the brewery.

The Team went off the exit very slowly. They were nervous. They were now at the Olympia city limits. If the reports were right, and they seemed to be so far, then the Limas would be concentrated in the city. They could easily set up ambushes at places like the exits coming into the city.

Then again, as Grant thought about how slowly they needed to proceed, he realized it was steadily getting darker. They didn't have much time. They couldn't have the convoy sitting on the side of Highway 101 all night. The Team needed to find a suitable place for the 17th Irregulars to park and set up a defense. Maybe even sleep a little. Eating would be nice, too.

So far, the exit to the brewery was clear, to the extent they could see in the partial darkness. There was a bridge over I-5—this exit was where Highway 101 fed into I-5—that would be very strategic. Grant would have blown it up if he were defending this city. Surely the Limas thought of that same thing.

But there was the bridge, amazingly intact. Grant figured it had to be rigged to blow up when a vehicle went across it.

"Want us to check the bridge?" Pow asked him, knowing the answer.

"Yep," Grant said, "this is an all-hands-on-deck thing. We need all the people possible. It's dark, so Donnie's scope won't be too useful. Donnie, you grabbed Anderson's AR, right?"

Donnie nodded. He was using a dead man's rifle. It was not exactly a good luck sign.

"Shouldn't Bobby stay behind in the truck?" Scotty asked. "We might need to take off and we can't be waiting for him to show up with

7

the keys."

He had made a good point. "You lucked out, Bobby," Grant said.

"I'll go in with you guys," Bobby said. He'd been missing out on all the fun so far by being the driver. "What about Donnie staying and driving, if necessary?"

His suggestion made a lot of sense. Donnie could drive and his sniper rifle was nearly useless in the dark. Bobby was also much better trained than Donnie for things like this.

"Donnie will drive," Grant said, trying to be as lieutenant-like as possible. It was his nature, especially around the Team, just to say, "Right on, bro." But Grant needed to practice being a military officer. He knew he would be giving orders in the city, so he needed to start acting like it now.

Bobby parked the truck in a reasonably safe place, far from the street light on the side of the exit. They got out and got ready to go. Ryan and Wes got out of the back. Donnie, in the driver's seat, had one of the intra-unit radios and Scotty had the other.

"Let's go take a brewery tour," Grant said.

It was hard to ignore all the gunfire in the distance and the occasional explosions. There were no fireballs or tracers like on TV during Desert Storm. This wasn't that kind of war. What was happening was more like evicting a bunch of criminals from a city. The Team moved in pairs toward the bridge, providing cover for each other as they did. One man constantly covered the rear in case anything came at them from that direction. They leapfrogged to the bridge.

They all had flashlights mounted on their rifles. They were costly items, but no one considered them to be a "luxury." They had Surefire Scout lights, which were extremely durable and bright. The Team knew that almost all fighting happened in low-light and dark conditions. They had to be able to see their targets, so a weapon-mounted light was a necessity. Everyone except Ryan, who joined the Team late, had lights mounted on their pistols for the very same reason. They used the lights on their rifles to scan the area for wires and to look for targets. Those Surefires were amazingly bright, over one hundred lumens, which was several times the brightness of even huge D-cell flashlights.

Of course, there was one huge downside to using their weapons' lights or any other flashlights. People could see them. They could see right where they were, shoot at the lights, and probably hit the person holding the rifle or pistol with the light. Oh well. There was no other way to do this, unless they wanted to sit there until morning, making them sitting ducks for hours. This would prevent them from advancing. Not acceptable. Surprisingly, walking up to a possibly booby-trapped bridge potentially with snipers all around was a better plan.

As they were searching the bridge and slowly moving across it in pairs, Grant was glad they had frequently practiced night operations at Marion Farm. For some reason, they had not done much night training before he came out to Pierce Point. The Team had done one night shoot with Ted back before the Collapse. They had done some training at night at the meth house back at Pierce Point, but that was it.

If Grant could have done it over again, he would have done at least half of their training in the dark. Regardless, they were doing a decent job tonight and were still much better than any civilians and most law enforcement. They were better than almost any unmotivated National Guard unit, though they would get beaten badly by a regular military unit. Hopefully there weren't any of those around.

After several minutes of very careful movements and plenty of time to scan for threats, they were across the bridge. This was the most dangerous time. Any halfway intelligent attackers would wait for them to get across the bridge and then attack, probably with attackers back at the entrance to the bridge too, cutting off their escape.

The brewery had several large buildings, each of which was surrounded by a very high chain-link fence. There were gates in front of each building. The Team fanned out from the bridge toward the first gate. Bolt cutters! Grant forgot to bring bolt cutters. What an idiot.

The gate was locked. They went to their right toward the next gate, which was already cut open. Good news.

Or was it? They quickly realized that this meant others could easily go into that building. Maybe lots of them. They huddled together.

"Ideas?" Grant asked.

"Let's go see who's in there," Pow said. "We'll sneak up on them. If they didn't get us on that bridge, they suck and will continue to suck. We can sneak up on them in that building."

"No lights on in there," Bobby said. "It's probably abandoned."

Grant doubted that. With the Second Great Depression going on, he knew these sorts of places would have to be full of squatters, and those squatters would fight like hell to protect their "home."

"We look for all the doors, see if they're open, and go in simultaneously from as many directions as possible?" Grant asked.

"I guess so," Pow said after a brief silence. No one had a better idea.

"Everyone got fresh batteries in their lights?" Grant asked, pointing at his weapon light. Everyone nodded. They would be relying on their lights right now, so this would be a terrible time for one to go out. Not only did they have fresh batteries in their lights, but they all had at least two sets of backup batteries in their kit. Batteries were second only to ammunition in importance in their kit.

"Okay," Grant said, "I'll go around the building and try all the doors." He pulled out a permanent marker from his kit. "I'll mark each door that's open with an 'X'. I'll put a 'No' on closed doors. You guys can stay here in a defensive perimeter. No use splitting all of us up to go check the doors. If there's shooting, it might as well be at one of us instead of all of us."

They nodded. They had all taken turns on point. Grant felt like it was his turn. Besides, he was in a hurry and wanted to get into this building and get it cleared for the rest of the convoy. He was getting nervous about that convoy just sitting there in what was now darkness.

Grant paused for about a minute as he and the Team quietly listened for any sound, any sign of life in that building or from anywhere else.

Nothing. There was a lot of gunfire in the distance, and the hum of the big street lights, but nothing from the brewery. There were no people talking, no barking dogs, no vehicles. In fact, there were no cars—zero—out on the streets.

That didn't seem right. Something was up. He readied himself for whatever was about to happen. He had the raid on the meth house under his belt, but the brewery felt different. Ten times harder than the meth house.

Grant looked at the building he was about to check on. It was four stories and there were no lights on. The windows on the first floor were boarded up, but the windows on the upper floors weren't. Most of the upper-floor windows were broken.

There was trash everywhere. It blew around in the street. Garbage pick-up had ended months ago when the city ran out of money. Besides, it was extremely dangerous to travel around town, so who in their right mind would go out and pick up garbage? The place looked like Detroit.

But then again, most of the country looked like Detroit now. Grant remembered arguing with his liberal friends before the Collapse that the big-government polices they loved so much would lead to the

"Detroit-ification" of America. They had laughed at him. Now he was looking at a boarded up brewery that once employed hundreds, surrounded by trash blowing through the streets.

As Grant took off toward the first door, he thought that this would be an okay way to die. It's gonna happen anyway, he thought. Heaven will be way better than what's down here. And he'd be with his guys when he died. Doing something for the unit. Trying to fix things. He actually smiled. This would be an okay way to die, he repeated to himself.

Grant used his weapon light to see his way. He came up to the first door, which was locked. He marked it with a big "No." He went to the next door. Same thing. Locked. He went to the third door and gently pushed on it. It was open! He marked it with a big "X." Okay, there's at least one open door which made it even more likely that squatters—or Limas—were in there.

Grant wanted to open that door and see, but he knew that would be stupid. If people were inside and heard that, they'd be ready for an attack. No, Grant needed to have the whole Team—and preferably the Team from several directions—open those doors and go in ready to shoot. Curiosity killed the cat and might kill Grant if he didn't hold back his curiosity. So he forced himself to move on to the next door.

The fourth door was open, too. He marked it with an "X." Two doors to enter from. Good. That was far better than just one.

Without opening the door, Grant looked around for any signs of life in the building. None, just the trash blowing around. He was trying to see if any of the trash indicated people living in there, like food wrappers or even freshly soiled baby diapers. He didn't see any trash indicating current occupants, but it was dark and he was trying not to lose his concentration on threats that might pop out when he was staring at the garbage.

Grant went around the last side of the building to see if there was another door, which there wasn't. Just four doors on three sides. It was dangerous moving on this last side of the building because it faced the street and there was a street light. He would be silhouetted. Oh well, he said again to himself. Nothing was perfect out here. He had no choice but to play the hand he was dealt. Grant had to check this last remaining side of the building. He couldn't have his guys running through that area only to find out a bunch of Limas were sitting there. He had to be able to go back and tell his guys that there was no one on the outside perimeter of the building.

Grant carefully advanced along the last side of the building. He was moving from behind cover each time. He turned his weapon light off since the street light illuminated the area well. The only purpose his weapon light would serve right now would be as a big "shoot here" target.

Grant looked at the street lights. They illuminated the rain coming down. It had turned from a steady rain to a light drizzle. Grant was soaking wet. He was glad he had that black knit hat to keep his head warm. HQ had even given him a little patch with a second lieutenant's bars. Grant had stapled that onto his knit cap. That's how low-tech they were: lieutenant's bars stapled onto a hat.

In the drizzle, Grant was glad he had Mechanix shooting gloves to maintain his grip on his rifle. The Team always trained with gloves on. Good shooting gloves, which weren't too expensive, protected hands from sharp edges, hot barrels, and accidental cuts from all the knives they used in the field. Any one of those things could injure a hand and put a guy out of action. Grant realized that he was hardly noticing something else: that he was wet and cold but didn't care. All he cared about was clearing that building and getting the 17th in there safely.

Grant stopped when he got to the last corner. He didn't want to run around that corner and have the Team shoot him, so he used one of the most low-tech communication devices they had. He had learned it from his Indian grandfather, although Grandpa never envisioned it being used that way.

He moistened his lips and let out a bird call. It wasn't a fancy one, or one that was particularly good. It was just a whistle loosely based on the sound birds in the area made.

The guys recognized that a person was doing a bird call and, given how much time Grant had been out, figured it was about time he would be coming around that corner. They gave him the same "bird call" back from around the corner. Good. The guys now knew that it was him and not an enemy. Grant realized that in training and planning they should have come up with a standardized and recognizable fake bird call.

As Grant rounded the corner with his weapon pointed around it but with his safety on, he saw the Team in a defensive perimeter. Grant joined up with them.

"Four doors, on three sides of the building," he said. "Doors one and two," Grant pointed to them, "are locked and have a 'No' on them. Doors three and four are on the second and third sides, unlocked, and have an 'X' on them."

"Did you look inside them?" Scotty asked. He was hoping that Grant had done so and found that no one was in that building. He really didn't want anyone to be in that building.

"Nope," Grant said. "I wanted all of us there when we announce our presence."

Pow split the Team into two groups of three men. He was the tactical commander and did a magnificent job at such things. Grant was glad to take a back seat on the building entry. He wanted it to be successful far more than he wanted to be the one in charge. Besides, Grant tried to be "lieutenant-like" in front of the rest of the unit; he didn't need to be that way in front of the Team.

Pow said that both groups would go the long way, which was the way Grant had originally gone, so they wouldn't have to go along the fourth side of the building with the street light; they could approach the final door, in the darkness.

There was risk to this. What if some Limas who were not on that side when Grant went by it had now located there? That was less of a risk than having half the Team spotted from a big street light.

They took off. The first group—Grant, Ryan, and Wes—stayed by the third door and waited.

Grant thought about body armor. He wished they all had it, but Pow was the only one with it. Body armor had been widely sold in the run up to the Collapse, but with all the other things they needed—guns, ammo, gear—it was always a second-tier luxury. But, man, Grant wished they'd secured some when they could.

The second group—Pow, Scotty, and Bobby—got to the fourth door. They would go in first and signal to the first group to do the same. They didn't have radios to coordinate this. They were a low-budget, low-tech, semi-amateur SWAT team, free styling.

Grant could feel, and actually hear, his heart pounding. He wondered if others could hear it.

He heard the second group entering the building, which was their signal. In a split second, Grant threw the door open. Ryan was the first in the door, weapon light on. Wes followed right behind him, with his hand on Ryan's shoulder so they wouldn't get separated. Grant took one last look around to his rear to make sure no one was coming after them. It was clear so he ran into the building.

It was pitch black except for the crisscross light beams from the weapon lights. It looked like a giant light saber fight from Star Wars.

Then Grant heard exactly what he didn't want to hear.

Chapter 293

"We're Here to Put the Bad People in Jail"

(January 1)

The sound of screaming children filled the building. They sounded terrified and were screaming their lungs out.

Grant had no idea what to do, and it was clear that the Team was also at a loss. They kept doing what they'd trained to do: sweep the whole area with light and be ready to shoot any threat that appeared. That was it. It wasn't much of a plan.

Someone was yelling for the kids to be quiet and to get to the "hiding place." From the little patches of light that Grant could see in front of his rifle, and from all the sweeps in various directions he had made, it looked like this building didn't have any interior walls. There were kids running everywhere, several dozen of them. They ranged from about five years old to teenagers, but most were younger kids. Screaming.

The Team fanned out as best they could with the kids running in their way. It looked and sounded like they were gathering in one place, and then the Team heard them running upstairs. Oh great. There were more floors to clear, which meant they were now exposed to potential Limas or armed, scared kids waiting for them at the top of the stairs. Pow yelled out for the two who were closest to him to stay down on the first floor while the remaining four went up the stairs. The two staying on the first floor turned out to be Bobby and Scotty.

Pow, Grant, Ryan, and Wes ran toward the staircase. They could see they were chasing lots of kids and a few teenagers toward the stairs. The kids were still screaming and crying. Grant thought it was unfortunate that they had to terrify these children even more than they already were, but they had to see if there were any armed threats in the building.

Grant looked around as they were running toward the stairs. He was so proud. Ryan and Wes were running behind him and sweeping the area with their rifles. The lights showed the sweeping. These two were protecting Grant and Pow as they went forward. It was automatic, instinctual. It looked smooth and choreographed, in sharp contrast to all the kids running around and screaming.

As they got to the staircase, Grant realized that they'd never actually practiced this. Going up a staircase with guns was tricky, and the Team had never had a two-story place to practice such a maneuver. No shooting range had this, and the meth house was only one story.

Grant found himself just doing what he'd seen in the movies – hugging every bit of cover and sweeping his rifle up the stairs. It was terrifying because there were so many places up that staircase for someone to hide and shoot them, or even drop things on them. They didn't have helmets. Like body armor, helmets were one of those "it'd be great to have" items that they never got around to acquiring.

But, somehow, they managed to get up the dark staircase to the second floor. By now, the screaming had stopped. The kids seemed to be hiding. It was quiet except for faint footsteps of running kids above them and the familiar voices of the Team shouting instructions to each other.

Pow tried the door to the second floor room, but it was locked. There was no noise from this floor. Maybe people were inside and had locked it to keep them out.

"I really want to clear this room," Ryan whispered to Pow, referring to the second floor, "before we go up to the third floor." Ryan looked around to make sure he was whispering softly enough so that no one other than Pow could hear him. "That way, anyone in the second floor room can't come out and cut us off from Bobby and Scotty on the first floor."

Pow nodded. "That'll have to wait, bro," he said, "'till we've assessed the whole building." Ryan nodded. They had to find where the kids went and whether there were any threats in the building.

They went to the third floor and also found it locked with no noises coming from inside it. They carefully moved up the staircase to the fourth floor.

The door to the room on the fourth and final floor was unlocked. Pow opened it and Grant went bursting through, sweeping the room with his weapon light.

He saw a sea of little faces. Dirty, frightened, crying little faces. Most had their hands up and then they started screaming. It was obvious that they thought Grant was going to shoot them.

Good, Grant thought. As evil as that sounded, he wanted everyone in that building to be scared of the Team so they would do cooperate and no one would get hurt. Then, if there was no threat in there and things calmed down, the Team could assure the kids that they were good army men, not bad ones.

A weapon light came through the door. It was Pow, who was followed quickly by Ryan and Wes. All four of them were sweeping the room and it looked like it was full of kids.

"Shut up!" Pow yelled. In broad daylight, he was an imposing enough figure, but in the dark, with kit and a rifle, he was positively terrifying. A round of startled screams went up.

"All of you, shut up!" Wes yelled, with an authoritative edge to his voice. "Now! Hands up!"

Most of the screaming died down and hands started to go up. Some kids, the very smallest ones who seemed about five years old, were still crying and not putting their hands up. "Who's in charge?" Grant yelled out. "Now! Tell me now!"

A skinny college-aged adult waved his hands. "I am," he responded, timidly. He wasn't going to move until someone told him to.

"Come here," Pow yelled. "Slowly," he said in a normal tone of voice.

The skinny man nervously walked over to Pow. "I'm Tom," he said.

"Why are all these kids in here?" Grant demanded.

"It's where we live," Tom said.

"The second and third floors are locked," Pow yelled at Tom. "Why?"

"Our stuff is in there. And our kitchen," Tom answered. "Up here on the fourth floor is where we hide. We would have locked it, too, but you guys got in here too fast."

Grant hoped that was true about the second and third floors, although the more he looked at these pathetic kids, the more he realized that this was not exactly a Lima commando base.

"Tell these kids to shut up!" Ryan yelled. "We don't need people to hear us."

"Everyone, be quiet," Tom said, very casually and calmly. Slowly, the crying and sniffling trailed off.

"Sorry we had to yell," Grant said, "We didn't know who you were. Hey, kids, we won't be yelling anymore."

"Who's got the keys to the second and third floors?" Pow asked Tom, in a calmer voice.

"Me," Tom said.

"Let's go," Pow said. "You're going to open the doors down there. Is there anyone in here with a gun?"

Tom didn't answer.

Wes brought his AR up from the low ready position and pointed it at Tom's head. "Any guns?" he asked. Wes, one of the nicest guys on the planet and a gentleman, was not interested in politeness when it came to something that could get him and his Team killed.

"Yes," Tom said. "I have one. Two others do, also. They're back there."

The air instantly felt tense.

"Tell them to drop their guns and kick them over toward us," Pow commanded.

"Do what he says," Tom instructed the kids.

They heard two metallic objects hit the ground and slide across the floor.

"Now yours," Pow said to Tom, who slowly drew his revolver from his belt and set it on the ground. He softly kicked it toward Pow.

"Any more guns?" Ryan yelled. "Last chance."

Tom said, "No. We only have three."

Pow motioned for Tom to go out the door. "Come on. Let's unlock those doors."

He went out the door with Pow, shining his weapon light right on the back of Tom's head. The safety was on.

"Moving! Staircase," Pow yelled down the stairwell to Scotty and Bobby downstairs.

Tom took Pow down the staircase to the third floor and pointed to his pocket. "Here's the key. Can I take it out?"

Pow nodded and Tom slowly took out a key ring. He needed some of the light from Pow's weapon light to find the correct one.

Tom put the key in the door, appearing very calm, which Pow took note of. If Tom acted like a hail of bullets would be coming through that door, Pow would have … well, Pow didn't have a plan for that.

Tom opened the door and motioned for Pow to look inside. Pow shined his light in there. Sure enough, it appeared to be essentially empty. It contained clothes and sleeping bags and even a crude kitchen. Otherwise, it was empty.

"Lights don't work," Tom said, motioning toward the light switch. The power had probably been cut off long ago when the plant closed.

"Second floor," Pow said. Tom closed the door and started to lock it.

"No," Pow said. "It stays unlocked." This would allow the Team to properly and thoroughly clear the room later.

17

"Moving! Staircase," Pow yelled down the staircase. He motioned for Tom to go down.

They walked down another floor. The whole time, Pow swept in every direction to see any threats. So far, there were none.

Tom opened the second floor door just as calmly as the third floor one. Pow looked in and saw another sleeping floor. There was no one in there.

Pow motioned for Tom to go back up to the fourth floor and followed him. He continued to sweep the staircase. It was a habit.

They got up to almost the fourth floor. "Moving!" Pow yelled to Ryan and Wes.

"Move!" Ryan yelled out, signaling that he heard Pow and Pow had permission to move.

Pow followed behind Tom up the stairs. They entered the fourth floor again.

"Okay," Pow said, struggling to remember Tom's name. "What the hell was your name?"

"Tom," Tom said. "Tom VanDykstra."

"Okay, Tom," Pow said. "Get all the kids downstairs to the first floor. We need them in one place where we can watch them. We need to clear this building and we don't need any kids running around."

"Are you the police?" a little girl asked from the corner of the room.

"Kind of," Grant said. "We're good police. We're here to put the bad people in jail." Grant started to tear up as he remembered Cole saying that Grant's "army men" were going to put the bad people in jail.

"Okay," the little girl said. "My daddy was a police officer." Grant wanted to talk to her, but this was no place for a conversation.

"Great," Grant said, a little abruptly. "Now listen to Tom and do what we say. We need to make sure you're all safe, so listen to us. We don't know if there are any bad people in here and we need to find out, okay?"

Many of the kids nodded their heads slowly, understanding the gravity of the situation.

Chapter 294

Tom's Kids

(January 1)

"Moving!" Pow yelled down the staircase. A faint "Move!" from Scotty could be heard from down on the first floor.

Tom and two older teenagers started to lead the kids down the stairs and back to the first floor.

"You expectin' anybody?" Wes asked.

"What do you mean?" Tom asked.

"Are any of your people outside and coming back here?" Wes asked. "If they come into the first floor, our men down there will be…" Wes realized kids were listening, so instead of saying "killing" he said, "encountering them."

"Oh," Tom said. "No, we're all here. Trying to wait out the…" Tom didn't want to say "shooting" in front of the kids, so he said "activity out there."

Tom still wasn't sure who these armed men were. They seemed nice. Rough, but nice.

Wes couldn't help but ask, "Who are all these kids?"

"Orphans," Tom said. "Not all of their parents are dead. Most of the kids have been separated from their parents. Some were refugees and got split up, others had their parents taken to jail, and a few of them were just abandoned." As food started to disappear, some parents – the really crappy ones that mistreated their kids before the Collapse – were doing the unthinkable and just leaving their kids to fend on their own.

Wes was trying to fathom how these kids could survive on the streets, during a war, on their own. But he didn't want to get in a long conversation with Tom, who might be trying to kill him.

"Who are *you* guys?" Tom asked Wes. The Team didn't remind Tom of the cops and soldiers in town, who were decent to the kids in the beginning, but, as things became harsh and mean, they started treating the kids like a problem. "Get those damned kids out of here," was usually what they said instead of, "how can we help?" By now, several months into the Collapse, the authorities didn't treat the kids like human beings, but like rats or some other nuisance.

As it became more obvious that there was no law of any kind, Tom saw that a few of the cops and soldiers started to prey on the kids. They'd beat, or do worse things to the stray kids they found out on the street. The FCorps were the worst. They had some serious psychos wearing those yellow helmets. The pretty girls would be "sampled" and then sold to the gangs. Tom could see, in his mind's eye, the faces of some of the girls he'd tried to help, only to see them disappear. Maybe they were okay now, maybe they weren't.

Tom thought about what he would say to Wes when they could talk and he could explain why he was there and how the kids got there. He would tell Wes that he was a youth pastor at a local church. He was twenty-five and loved working with troubled youths. He understood them and could talk to them. He protected them. He even got a few of them to believe in God, which was his ultimate goal, but theology took a backseat to survival nowadays.

He started taking kids into his church before the Collapse. The economy was in shambles and people who used to live comfortably were suddenly poor, which destroyed a lot of families.

One of the most common reasons kids came to the church was that their families needed to move to live with extended family in one house. The older kids didn't want to go because all their friends were in Olympia, so their parents would let them live at the church "until things got back to normal." Or some kids ran away and stayed in Olympia.

There were plenty of orphans, too. The number of deaths from crimes and from people going to jail, usually for political reasons or because the police and prosecutors were so corrupt, went way up.

Once Tom had a bunch of kids at the church, the word went out that he would take in kids. The kids who arrived started getting younger and younger. Tom remembered one crying mother who came to the church, handed him a baby and then turned around and drove away in her car stuffed full of all of her possessions.

Pretty soon, the kids were taking up too much space in the church. Tom gave a mini sermon one Sunday about how the government was supposed to be caring for people but wasn't doing a thing for all these kids. The sermon was met with scowls from the majority of the church members who, by and large, worked for government and didn't appreciate hearing that. Tom was asked to leave and take his kids with him.

"Not very Christian," was all Tom could say to the church elders when he was told to leave. "We just want our normal church back," one of them replied. "No kids running around and no political speeches. Things are hard enough without all that," he said to Tom. At that point, they wanted normalcy more than to help people.

So Tom found another place to go. The kids were starting to feel like his family by that point. He had a few older teens to help him as they traveled place to place. They were in regular homes and occasionally businesses during the spring and summer. Sympathetic adults would take in some street kids. As cruel and selfish as life had become during the Collapse, there remained surprising pockets of decency everywhere. It was still possible, early in the Collapse, to be charitable. Food was in short supply, but no one was starving in Olympia, which often had first dibs on supplies because of all the important government people in that city.

In the fall, when things started getting really bad in Olympia, Tom and his kids had to go to their first abandoned building. Luckily for them, there were plenty of abandoned buildings. Then the gangs moved them out. To his amazement, the first gang didn't try to steal any of the girls. The gangbangers were Mexicans and some of them – the reluctant ones, who were new to the gangs - even prayed the Rosary for the kids, but told them they had to leave.

The second gang to evict them was a Russian group and they were not nearly as nice. Tom managed to get the kids out of that place and they ran for their lives. That was when Tom and two of the teenagers secured some guns. One of the younger kids had them; they never asked her how she got them.

"Tom's kids," as they became known, would support themselves in various ways. They scavenged. They did odd jobs. Even though the economy was essentially non-existent, there were still little jobs to be done, like moving things, unloading things, and sweeping a parking lot.

They also stole things. Tom didn't like that since he was supposed to be setting a good example, but the first time one of the kids came back with a handful of stolen FCards, the decision was easy. They were hungry. Not "snack" hungry, but "haven't eaten for three days" hungry. And if they returned the FCards, they would never get back to their rightful owners. Tom viewed the FCards as gifts from God, not stolen merchandise.

By now, there were fifteen kids. The youngest was six and the oldest was seventeen. Completing the group was Tom and the two older teenagers, for a total of eighteen people.

Tom asked Pow who they were.

Before replying, Pow put his hand up. He had more important things to get done. "None of these kids leaves this place," Pow said firmly and quietly. "Got it?" He looked around to make sure no kids were listening.

Pow looked Tom right in the eyes and said, "If one of them tries to leave, we'll shoot all of you. Okay? No one can know we're here." Pow hated to be a dick and really didn't want to hurt any of the kids, but he couldn't have them running away and telling some Limas that they were at the brewery.

Tom nodded. "There are eighteen of us," he said.

Pow said, "Oh, I know, I counted. But thanks. You are responsible if one of them leaves." Pow gripped his rifle and said, "You understand what I'm sayin'?" He wouldn't really shoot a kid or Tom, but he needed them to think that he would.

"Understood," Tom said, believing Pow's every word. He believed Pow would shoot them because that's what everyone else in Olympia seemed to be capable of.

"So, who are you guys?" Tom asked again.

Pow put his hand up again and walked away. He had no time for that question. Pow went over to Grant and they huddled together with Scotty, who was talking to the convoy. They were working on getting one of the Team back to the truck where Donnie was waiting and then guiding the whole convoy in. They were trying to figure out where to park the semi. Chitchat about who they were would have to wait. Besides, they didn't want to tell these kids anything too important, just in case one of these kids decided to go tell the authorities.

Tom went back and told all the kids that they could not leave the building for any reason whatsoever. If they did, the soldiers would hurt all the remaining kids, Tom said.

"Who are these guys?" Carrie, one of the teenagers, asked Tom.

"Dunno," he said. "If they were a gang, we'd have known it by now."

"They look like military contractors," she said. Her dad had been at Ft. Lewis and was now a contractor, though she had no idea where he was.

That's what Tom had been thinking, too, and it made him wonder if the Team was somehow involved in what was going on outside the brewery with all the explosions and gunfire since New Year's Eve. That was more likely than them being FCorps or something else.

Tom started to work on getting the kids settled down, making sure they were warm, and keeping their spirits up. If these guys were Patriots, the police and soldiers would want to attack them, which meant his kids would be in the line of fire.

He heard a truck drive up and a few new soldiers arrived. Soon after, Tom heard a semi-truck idling. They pointed their headlights into the building so there was actually some light in there for a change.

More soldiers poured in and everyone instantly became busy getting things in order.

Pow came over to Tom. "I need you to get everyone up to the second and third floors and stay there. We'll assign a soldier to you so you can communicate with us. We'll be on the first and fourth floors."

Tom nodded. Pow pulled something out from under his shirt. It was on a chain around his neck and he kept his hand over it.

Pow motioned for Tom to follow him over to the kids. Once Pow had the kids assembled before him, he said to them, "Okay, you guys wondered who we are." He lifted his hand and there was his "badge." It was the concealed weapon permit badge he used when the Collapse started so he could avoid getting shot by the police when he had to pull a gun on someone.

"We're the good police, kids," Pow said with a big, warm smile and pointed toward his "badge." He was a softie and was feeling bad that he had to be so gruff with them. He was trying to make up for it. "I told you earlier that we are the good police and, here, I have a badge to prove it." The kids were in awe.

"We are here to take the bad people to jail," Pow said. "But we need your help. You can't leave here. The bad people might take you and make you tell them where we are and who we are. So no one leaves. Got it?" They all nodded.

With some decent light for the first time, Pow could see the kids' faces. They were filthy, and looked hungry, cold and scared. No kid should have to go through this. And no more will if we win, Pow thought.

Chapter 295

Bedtime Story

(January 1)

"I don't want to run a fucking daycare," Ted said after he assessed the brewery situation and found Grant. "Not to be a dick, but we're not here to be a daycare."

"I disagree, Sergeant," Grant said, asserting his authority, but doing so away from the hearing of the other troops. Ted had never heard Grant call him "Sergeant" like that.

"You're totally right that we can't let these kids put us in danger," Grant said, "but we're here to take care of them. And all the others in Olympia who aren't trying to kill us. We're here to be a daycare, and a kitchen, and a hospital. After we kill and capture all the Limas."

Grant paused for a moment and said firmly, "Our civil affairs mission starts right now. With these kids."

"Yeah," Ted said, realizing Grant was right, "but how are we supposed to take care of them when…"

Just then, Ted and Grant saw Franny walking up to the kids with a case of MREs.

"Hey," Franny said to the kids with a big smile. "Some of these even have Skittles and M&Ms. Who is going to find them first?" The kids started grabbing the MREs. It sounded like Christmas with ripping open presents. Or looking for the toy prize in a box of cereal.

Tom and the teenagers were opening up the MREs with pocket knives and dumping the contents on the floor. The kids were scrambling on the floor to get all the food.

"I got the Skittles!" a little girl yelled out.

"You have to share," Tom said. "We share everything."

"I got the M&Ms!" a twelve or thirteen year-old boy yelled out. With the semi idling, there was no danger that someone outside would hear the kids.

After dividing up the candy, the kids starting sharing the rest of the meals. Even the cold clam chowder was devoured. The finicky palate of a kid becomes less finicky when he or she hasn't eaten in days.

"Thank you, good police," a five or six year-old said to Franny, who swelled up with pride. This was exactly why he was doing this.

"We'll keep them locked up on the second and third floors," Grant said to Ted. "We'll stage from the first floor and use the fourth floor for observations. We'll go out now and clear all the other surrounding buildings. The kids' leader tells us that the other buildings are locked and empty."

"Fine," Ted said. "But the kids aren't coming with us, right?" Ted felt like a heartless bastard saying that, but he didn't want Grant to take in the stray kids and get them all killed.

"Oh, hell no," Grant answered. "That would be crazy."

Grant thought about it. "You know, we might stay here for a while. It's too hard to move a semi around the city streets. We're right here on a key off ramp. We're about a mile and a half from the capitol," he continued, pointing north. "It's right down this street, a nice wide street. There is plenty of cover the whole way down that thing."

Ted thought about it. "Hmm ... it's not a bad idea. They'll never suspect this old abandoned factory is our base. Brewery. I guess it's a brewery, not a factory."

Grant nodded. "What else do we need to be doing now?"

"Securing the buildings, setting up defenses," Ted said. "Coms are up and running. We've called in to HQ to tell them we're here and that any friendlies in the area are welcome to assemble here."

"When all that's done," Grant said quietly, "I need to take a nap. Is that okay?" He didn't know if taking a nap in combat was uncool, especially for a commanding officer.

"Sure," Ted said. "How long you been up? Thirty-six hours?"

Something like that," Grant said, suddenly noticing how tired he actually felt.

Over the next couple of hours, Grant was all over the place coordinating things, and working out problems. Details were starting to get blurry to him and he began having a hard time talking.

There were plenty of sounds to keep him awake. The sound of gunfire would go up and then down. There were some pitched battles taking place. HQ told them that the Limas were falling back quickly to the capitol campus, which was the beautiful park-like grounds where the domed legislative building and Governor's mansion was. The place was heavily defended; mortars, according to HQ. A couple of tanks, even.

According to HQ, the main Lima threat was roving bands of gangs sometimes mixed in with renegade cops and National Guard.

They were desperate and killing everyone they could. They knew they'd be killed by the Patriots so they were going to go out with a bang.

Grant decided that he could no longer function without a nap. He wanted a smile on his face before he napped, so he slowly went up the stairs to the second floor where the kids were. He wished he could tuck in Cole, but saying goodnight to some runaways would have to do.

He walked onto the second floor and saw something amazing. With the light of a lantern, one of the female soldiers, Corporal Sherryton, the former air defense computer tech, was reading the kids a bedtime story. Grant felt tears fill his eyes. He made sure no one saw him, while he stood there watching, taking it all in. He knew he was seeing something that would stay with him the rest of his life.

The story was over quickly and the kids were begging for Sherryton to read another one. At that point, Grant trudged—his feet felt like they weighed a hundred pounds each—up to the fourth floor to the observation point.

There were about a half dozen soldiers up there. They were illuminated by a big lantern and many of them were wearing headlamps. It was quiet there and the whole scene was surreal to Grant. He sat down on the concrete floor of the empty shop floor and closed his eyes.

Lisa was there. She was crying. She was asking him why he left a second time. She said no one was there to tuck in Cole. She started to push him.

Grant opened his eyes. A soldier was waking him up.

"Sorry, sir," he said. "Sgt. Malloy said I needed to wake you up."

Grant looked at his watch. It was 11:06 p.m. He'd been out for about three hours. He simultaneously felt great and horrible. The rest felt amazingly good, but he wanted, and needed, more. The thought of getting up was awful. He wondered if he could stand up, but he acted like it was no big deal. If the commanding officer was asleep … well, that set a bad example. He jumped up like he was wide awake, just like he wanted all his soldiers to be.

"Thanks," Grant said to the soldier. "I'm up now."

There were more soldiers than before up on the fourth floor. Something was going on.

The unit had one set of night vision binoculars. They were a civilian model which was available before the Collapse. HQ managed to snag a bunch of them and got one to Marion Farm about a month before. They were a Godsend. Grant wished that either he or someone on the Team would have not bought yet another cool knife or holster and instead bought at least one set of night vision binos. Grant wished he'd had them for the scouting work they ended up doing, but in all the confusion of them taking over the scouting duties, they didn't get the one pair the unit had. There were lots of little mistakes like this. It was inevitable. There were too many details, things moved too quickly, and everyone was sleep deprived.

One of the infantrymen, Kenny Barlow, was looking through the Nibs, as they called the night vision binoculars.

"Yep," Barlow said. "One, two, three … seven armed men are coming down that street. About 350 yards."

"ID?" Sap asked him, meaning could they be identified as good guys or bad guys.

"Negative," Barlow said. "But they have various weapons. Looks like AKs and ARs." Everyone was quiet so Barlow could concentrate.

"Whoa," Barlow said. "They're passing a container around." He looked some more. "Nope. It's actually a bottle. They're passing a bottle around."

Good, Grant thought. The unit's first kills would be easy ones. Hopefully.

Chapter 296

Coyote Bait

(January 1)

Jim Q. was up on the fourth floor since the radio reception was better and it was the hub of activity.

"Make sure HQ doesn't know of any friendlies around here," Sap said to him. Jim Q. started talking into his radio in his weird language. One word of English slipped out: "brewery." Apparently there was no word in their language for a brewery, which made sense, given what part of the world his people were from.

"Still walking down the street," Barlow said. "Right in the middle of the street, not even trying to take cover. Just strolling down the street and getting ripped."

"No known friendlies in the area," Jim Q. said. "But, then again, HQ doesn't claim to know where everyone is."

"They're kicking a garbage can," Barlow said. "There's no way they're ours."

By now Ted had raced up the stairs. Sap told him what Barlow was seeing.

"Pretty obvious, isn't it?" Ted said. "We got people out there. Squad 4, right?" Ted asked Sap. Sap nodded.

"They got a radio?" Ted asked. Sap nodded again.

"Tell them to take these jackasses out if, but only if, they come towards us," Ted said matter-of-factly. "Tell everyone else to be on alert. Once the bang bang starts, we'll attract a lot of attention, which is what I'm trying to avoid."

Well, then, Grant thought. This was it. A hot engagement. They got lucky in Frederickson and didn't have to start shooting. But now, with these drunken jackasses strolling toward them, they were on the edge of their first real combat. Months of training were about to be tested. At least they were taking on a handful of drunken thugs. "Always avoid a fair fight," Ted used to tell the Team before the Collapse. This certainly would not be a fair fight. Good.

"Two hundred yards," Barlow said. "They're at the intersection." Grant knew exactly where the drunken Limas were. During peacetime, he had gone through that intersection – Capitol

Boulevard and North Street – a thousand times on his way home. It was near the Baskin Robbins where he used to take the kids. That felt like a lifetime ago.

"They're turning left and going down that street," Barlow said with great relief. That meant they were going down Capitol Boulevard, the big main street that went straight to the capitol campus, which made sense. HQ said that was where the Limas were concentrating. Those clowns must be reinforcements, drunken reinforcements. The Limas were really hurting.

"They're getting away!" Corporal Sherryton exclaimed. She had come up to the fourth floor observation point after reading the kids bedtime stories.

"Avoiding a fight is a good thing," Ted replied. In the Special Forces world, where they are usually operating covertly behind enemy lines, avoiding a fight – and thereby remaining undetected – was the goal.

"Sgt. Malloy, could I see you over here?" Grant asked. Once they were out of earshot of the others, Grant said, "I disagree, Ted."

Grant looked out the window of the fourth floor and could see the drunken idiot Limas at the intersection. "Those guys are going to hurt people," he told Ted. "They're a walking time bomb. They're going to the capitol to reinforce the Limas. We need to take them out. What if they end up killing some of us or other Patriots or civilians? Especially civilians who are unlucky enough to run into them. These thugs might just knock on someone's door and start killing and raping. We need to take them out. That's my strategic call. Whether it's possible and how to do it is your tactical call. So, to be clear, it is ultimately your call. But I want to take them out."

Ted thought about it and knew that Grant was right. Ted's years of training and experience of avoiding fights when a unit is trapped in a jungle or desert didn't apply here. Sure, avoiding a fight was always best, but not if it meant letting those violent bastards walk down the street to kill people.

"Yep," Ted said, after very little hesitation. "This'll be easy. A nice little training mission for our green unit," he said in a whisper.

"Yeah," Grant said. He knew it sounded sick to be glad they had some easy kills so they could get some blood on their hands, but these Lima gangbangers deserved to die. And the 17th needed the experience.

Grant shrugged. "So what if the Limas know we're in this brewery? They're pinned down at the capitol. They can't do much about us. This isn't like the kind of war you've been trained for where the bad guys can call in an airstrike on your position if it gets known. Besides," Grant said, "killing douchebags like this is why we came here." He wasn't being macho, just telling the truth. Killing shitbags like this was, indeed, exactly why they'd come here.

"Roger that," Ted said with a nod. "We're the 'good police'," Ted said, referring to the story he heard about Pow's talk to the kids a few hours before.

Grant and Ted went back over to the group of observers on the fourth floor.

"Okay, we're going to take them out, despite their best efforts to avoid us," Ted said.

"How?" Barlow asked. "They're walking away from us."

"Coyote bait," Grant said. Everyone looked at him like he was insane.

"When I hunted coyotes," Grant quickly explained, "we'd use bait to bring them toward us." Grant and Ted had worked up this idea about a month ago. Using "bait" to get bad guys to come to them.

"What bait?" Barlow asked.

Grant and Ted looked at Corporal Sherryton, a very attractive twenty-something woman. She was in civilian clothes so she didn't look like a soldier.

"Sherryton," Grant said, "you wanna be the bait?"

"Yes, sir!" she said without a pause. She had been eager to get even with thugs after what they had done to her family back in Chicago. It was a different gang, but all part of the same thing. They were the bloodthirsty bastards that the "legitimate government" allowed and even encouraged. She wanted some payback. "Go out there and act like you're drunk and horny," Ted said. "They'll come over to you. Run back toward Squad 4 and they'll chase you. Once you get them within fifty yards or so of the squad, find some cover and plug your ears."

"Yes!" Sherryton yelled as she jumped up. She got her coat and looked around for instruction.

Sap said to her, "Follow me." The two of them ran down the stairs and out to Squad 4 and quickly told them of the plan.

Sap pointed to a big utility box on the street that the Limas would be running down toward them. "That's your cover." Sherryton nodded.

"Put your rifle over there behind it," Sap said. "Go!"

Sherryton took off her AK-47 and hid it in the bushes by the utility box. It was one of the sweet Century Arms C-39s they got from HQ. She made sure the safety was off. She didn't want to mess with that in a critical time.

She looked up at the intersection and felt a surge of adrenaline. This was it. It was what she'd been working so hard for the last few months. Payback time.

Chapter 297

Anne's Revenge

(January 1)

"Wahoo! Hey! Over here boys!" Sherryton was yelling, in a drawn out slur. She was doing a magnificent acting job.

She started to run toward six or seven heavily armed men, who were drunk and above the law. She was a very brave soldier.

She quickly arrived at the intersection and was in the street lights, yelling down the street to the men. She yelled, "Come and get some, boys!"

The Limas turned around. They couldn't believe their eyes. She was hot, and drunk or high. They looked at each other, smiled, turned around and ran straight toward her. Some crazy drugged out chick wanted them, and they were happy to oblige.

This was semi common for them. Women who wanted protection or food would let them have their way with them. It was partying; it was business. It was both nowadays.

She let them get closer. When they were close enough for her to see them, she became terrified. They were civilian gangbangers. They all had rifles and looked sinister. She could sense the pure evil in them. They looked just like the gangbangers who came after her family. She was having flashbacks to Chicago.

In an instant, she snapped out of it. She turned and ran. She couldn't even feel her legs under her. All she knew was that she was running faster than she'd ever run.

She got to the intersection, turned right and headed down the street and toward Squad 4. She looked right at where the squad was and couldn't see them. Had they left? Was she all alone with them chasing her?

She looked behind her and saw the gangbangers a hundred yards behind her. They were also running as fast as they could.

She saw the utility box coming up and tried to slow down. It was hard to slow down, but she did. She grabbed her AK and took cover behind the utility box.

This is it, she thought. This is payback. She put her sights on the closest one.

"Boom! Boom! Boom!" Gunfire everywhere – a thunderous wall of gunfire came from behind her. She could feel the explosions in her chest. It was extremely loud. She had always trained while wearing hearing protection, so the loudness of the gunfire surprised her.

She saw some of them in her sights and felt the recoil and muzzle blast from her AK. She was firing at their shapes, not really aiming. She was pretty sure she hit one. Everything was happening in slow motion.

In a second, all the shapes were gone, but she kept her rifle pointed on target anyway.

It was silent except for the ringing in her ears. She started to shake, but it wasn't fear. It was like there was a drug in her. There was. Adrenaline. She felt stronger than she'd ever felt, like a super human.

There was no movement where the gangbangers had been.

"Cease fire!" Sap yelled. More silence. Nothing was moving.

"Check 'em out," Sap yelled as he walked toward the bodies. He had his rifle pointed at them and all of Squad 4 was covering him. He had a weapon light on his AR so he could see them.

Sherryton felt another surge of adrenaline. She jumped up and went toward where she'd been shooting. She kept her AK aimed at the bodies of the men strewn in the street. Her training kicked in. She remembered "search and assess." She started scanning all around with her rifle for anyone who might be sneaking up on them. Slowly, the members of Squad 4 started getting up and doing the same. They were a few yards behind her.

Sherryton got up to the first body which was torn to pieces and looked like it had been blown up. He must have been shot several times. She came up on the other bodies. Same thing. The crimson red blood looked purple in the streetlights, and it was slowly flowing down the street. It was amazing how much blood six or seven men had in them.

"Still alive!" Sap yelled. "One of them is still alive!" Sap had his rifle aimed right at him.

Sherryton ran up to the wounded man Sap was yelling about. She could see him moving slowly on the concrete. She clicked the safety on her AK and slung it over her shoulder. She walked up to the wounded man and got down on her knees over his chest so his face was right under her. She didn't even realize what she was doing, but she took out her knife, an old M7 bayonet.

That face. She hated that face down there. That gangbanger's face that smirked while he was raping helpless women and girls. And shooting their fathers in front of them, like back in Chicago.

She knew what to do. She gripped the knife, which felt cold in her hand. In one quick movement, she plunged it in his face. He winced and tried to scream, but he had too much blood in his windpipe to make any sound.

It felt magnificent. She kept stabbing him, faster and faster. She couldn't stop.

"That's for Ashley!" she yelled. "Lydia! Mom! Especially Mom! And Dad, too!" She kept stabbing until she heard the tip of knife hitting the pavement. She realized she'd stabbed right through his whole head.

She looked at that ugly face. Or, at least, what was left of that ugly, ground up, bloody, former face. She stood up and looked down at him. She had her knife out and was standing there like she'd take on anyone else.

Sap just stood there and watched her. He had nothing to say. He couldn't stop her and he didn't want to. She would be better now that she got that out of her system. Or she'd have nightmares of that mangled face for the rest of her life.

Sherryton looked at her knife that was covered in blood. A tremendous amount of blood had splattered on her. It was all over her sleeves and her face. She wiped off her knife and tried to remove the blood from her hands. It was useless. She was just making a mess.

Sap came over and said to her, "Go back to the squad." He wasn't sure if she'd snap on him, too. She seemed to be slowly processing everything that had happened.

Sherryton stumbled in a daze down the street back toward the squad and walked right past them and to the brewery building. She wanted to wash all the blood off of her. The blood was from that man, and she didn't want any of him on her. She also didn't want the kids to see that. That's all she could think about: the kids can't see this.

Anne Sherryton collapsed. She could no longer stand. As soon as her knees hit the pavement, she started throwing up. Great, she thought. Puke and blood all over her clothes.

Sap was busy having Squad 4 move the bodies out of the street, which they threw into the bushes near the utility box. They needed to get those out of the way in case some Limas came by. Ted was getting all the other squads out along an even bigger and more reinforced defensive perimeter. Grant was up on the observation floor making sure no Limas were coming and listening to Jim Q.'s radio.

Nick stayed with Sherryton to make sure she was okay.

"Did the kids hear this?" she asked him.

"No," Nick said, lying. He wanted to reassure her so she could focus on recovering. "We told them to cover their ears right before everything happened."

Sherryton smiled and felt relieved. She didn't want the kids to hear such violence. They'd already lost so much innocence.

After a minute lying on the ground, she wanted to get back up. She felt embarrassed for having this reaction and knew, as a woman, she had to be extra-tough to prove her worth. She didn't want to get ripped off and only get the easy work just because she was a woman and couldn't hack it. Although she knew that she had proven herself by volunteering to be the coyote bait. And what she did with the knife.

"Still no Limas," Barlow said up on the fourth floor. "For now." He questioned the wisdom of baiting the gangbangers. He would have let them go and focused on remaining undetected.

"What's next?" Grant asked Ted.

"A counterattack," Ted said matter-of-factly. "If they can possibly muster it. Which, I'm starting to think, they can't. But we need to be ready for it anyway." Ted told Grant about the various squads on the perimeter. They even came up with a quick evacuation plan, which included grabbing the kids in case a bunch of Limas or some armor came at them.

Grant hoped no Lima reinforcements came because he wanted to be right about his idea to attack them. He couldn't contain his concern about his decision, so he looked for confirmation from Ted.

"Still think it was the right decision to attack them?"

"So far, yes," Ted said. "If we get attacked, then no. But," Ted pulled Grant close so no one else could hear and whispered to Grant, "never second guess past decisions. It'll get you killed. Make a decision and go with it. Don't look back. Don't let the men know you're having second thoughts. Got it?"

Grant whispered back, "Sure. Thanks."

In his normal speaking voice, Ted answered Grant loud enough for the men to hear. "Yes, sir, that was the right decision. Those bastards had it coming. And now the 17th has shown the world that our training paid off. I'm proud of this unit."

Killing those guys was a big morale boost. Not that people enjoyed killing. In fact, they hated it, but they had worked so hard for months. Many of them were raw civilians. They didn't know if they could pull off such a feat. They'd been keyed up for about thirty-six hours now. Two of their friends had been killed and a third injured.

And now they had worked together and killed some bad guys. They'd put all their training together and done some nice work. They knew that their training had turned them into fighters.

They spent the rest of the night on the perimeter, rotating people in for an MRE and a nap. Everything was quiet except for the sound of gunfire and occasional explosions in the distance.

Grant felt way better after eating an MRE. He couldn't remember what meal it was; he just knew that it tasted good. He had been getting woozy before he gobbled it down. After eating, he grabbed a twenty-minute nap which made all the difference in the world.

Chapter 298

Regular Military

(January 2)

"We have visitors," Barlow said as he looked through his binoculars.

Sap called in an alert to all the squads with radios. Runners from the "Chairborne" squad went from the squads with radios to the squads without them.

"How many?" Sap asked Barlow.

"Uh oh," Barlow said. "Uh oh," he repeated.

Grant sat up from the floor he was resting on and looked at his watch. It was 3:23 a.m. and silent on the fourth floor. The only sound was the gunfire and explosions from somewhere outside.

This might be it, Grant thought. They had gotten lucky with a half dozen drunken thugs. All eyes and ears were trained on Barlow and his NVBs. Barlow was concentrating.

"At least thirty of them," Barlow said. "Oh wait." He started counting under his breath. "Correction: more like fifty."

Everyone on the fourth floor was terrified, including Grant. Especially Grant. He instantly thought his decision to kill the gangbangers was about to get his guys killed.

"Actually, make that eighty-five," Barlow said. "Military uniforms. Standardized weapons. M4s," he said referring to the military designation for ARs. "Some big tubes. Looks like anti-armor weapons. Could be Javelins," which was the military name for a shoulder launched anti-tank rocket.

This was very bad news. Whoever these guys were, they would be able to kick the 17th's asses. While the 17th had the advantage of being in a defensive position at the brewery, the trained soldiers had gear like Javelins. It wasn't much of a match.

"They're moving like they know what they're doing," Barlow said. "Definitely regular military."

Grant shuddered. "Regular military." That scared him. He realized that they had thought they were pretty badass slaughtering some drunken idiots, which was child's play compared to a real military unit.

Irregular, Grant said to himself. The 17th was only an irregular unit. They were tough and could fight, they just didn't have as much training, or especially the gear like rocket launchers, radios, night vision, and machine guns, like a regular unit.

And the kids. Grant thought about all the innocent little souls on the second and third floors. One of those Javelins could kill all of them.

"They are stopping at the intersection," Barlow said. That was the same intersection by the Baskin Robbins that the gangbangers had stopped at. "Setting up a defensive perimeter while they call in on the radio."

The radio. Duh. Grant and Sap simultaneously told Jim Q. to ask HQ if any friendlies were in their area. Jim Q. did so, talking in that weird, incomprehensible language.

After a moment, more of that weird language squawked on the radio. Jim Q. smiled.

"We have friendlies in our area," Jim Q. said in English. "HQ is making contact now with who they think is at that intersection."

Another pause followed by more squawking in that weird language.

Jim Q. said to Barlow, "The friendlies have been told to have three men hold their rifles up in both hands as a signal to us."

Barlow was looking through the NVBs. Nothing.

Grant looked at Sap. He mouthed "Go time" to Sap. As in, it's time to fight this regular unit. Sap closed his eyes as if to say, "Oh God."

This was it, Grant thought to himself. We'll see if you really don't mind dying, he thought. He waited for his brain to say something to him. All it said was "Don't fail your men." Not "be afraid of dying."

Sap walked over to Grant. They had some planning to do. Sap told a soldier to go find Ted and get him up to the fourth floor.

"The signal!" Barlow yelled out. "There's the signal. Three men with rifles over their heads!"

Jim Q. said something excitedly in his language into the radio. A moment later, something came back over the radio in that language.

"We are supposed to link up with them and temporarily house them here," Jim Q. said.

Sap got on the intra-unit radios and told the squad leaders what was happening. A welcoming team of three soldiers from the 17th went up to the regular unit and brought them into the brewery building.

Grant went down to the first floor to greet their guests. Thank God they weren't Limas, he kept thinking. He had a whole new appreciation for how much danger they were in. Up until this moment, Grant and the Team had always been the best armed and trained in any fight. The looters in Olympia, the meth house in Pierce Point, the Blue Ribbon Boys that the scouts took out and, of course, the gangbangers.

Grant was curious to see who this regular unit was. As its members came into the first floor, he looked for any insignia on their uniforms. They had the standard "Wash. State Guard" name tapes.

Soon, a man in his 30s came in and asked to see the commanding officer.

"That's me," Grant said as he saluted the man who returned the salute. It was battlefield conditions and they were in a building—two reasons not to salute—but this was a momentous occasion. Both of them saluted without even thinking.

"Captain Edwards, Bravo Company, Third Battalion," said the man.

Awesome, Grant thought. A regular military unit. A company commander. That meant a company of about a hundred men.

"Lieutenant Matson, 17th Irregulars." Grant said.

"Pleased to meet you, Lieutenant," Capt. Edwards said. He looked around and was very impressed with this irregular unit, which appeared squared away. They had decent weapons and were organized.

"What can I do to assist you?" Grant asked. He needed to remember that Edwards was a Captain and therefore Grant wasn't the head honcho anymore. That was fine with Grant. But, he had to admit, it was weird taking orders from a guy ten years younger than him. Oh well. That's how it was. And Grant was happy to take orders from a regular military officer, which meant they were now paired with a well-trained and well-equipped unit, and thereby had a better chance of successfully completing their mission and making it back home alive.

"Is this place secure?" Edwards asked, as he was looking around.

"Yes, sir," Grant said. He and Ted explained the perimeter defenses.

Edwards was not overly impressed with the defenses. They were okay and, for a lightly armed irregular unit, pretty decent, but Edwards was an FUSA Army officer. He was used to having plenty of

39

equipment. Helicopters, radios, battlefield computers, mortars, anti-armor rockets. He worked with soldiers who had several years of structured training, not a few months of training in some remote camp.

"We'll augment your defenses here, Lieutenant," Edwards said.

"Excellent," Grant responded.

"I'll rotate my men and feed and rest them," Edwards said. "You have food here, right?"

"Yes, sir," Grant said. "Not a lot. MREs." There went the rest of the 17th's MREs. But Bravo Company was on the same team. Sharing was an unspoken expectation. Those MREs didn't belong to the 17th. They belonged to the mission.

Grant and Ted briefed Edwards on all the aspects of the brewery, including their guests on the second and third floor.

"Kids?" Edwards asked, appearing slightly puzzled and annoyed.

"They came with the brewery," Grant answered.

"I understand the situation you're in," Edwards said, "you'll get them out of here as soon as it's safe, right?"

"Yes, sir," Grant promised.

"What are your orders?" Edwards asked Grant, now that the immediate issues were resolved and they could focus on the bigger picture.

"To enter Olympia from Highway 101 from Frederickson, where we were based, and to assist regular forces. Occupy. Stabilize. And do civil affairs. That's kind of my specialty."

Edwards's eyes lit up. "Civil affairs?" he asked. He hadn't expected a specialized mission from an irregular unit. "That's great," he said to Grant. "That's what we need on an urban battlefield. Especially when the civilians are our own Americans. What was your civil affairs unit? The 84th Brigade at JBLM?"

"No, sir," Grant answered, sheepishly. He looked around to see if others could hear him and softly said, "No prior military training. I sort of took a small community outside of Frederickson and turned it into a thriving and functioning place. I had help, though," referring to Rich, Dan, and the others at Pierce Point.

Edwards nodded. Oh great, he thought. The commander of this irregular unit is some civilian ... politician. Some small town mayor or something. Fabulous.

"What did you do in civilian life?" Edwards asked Grant.

Grant hesitantly said, "Lawyer."

"Great," Edwards said sarcastically. He quickly realized his tone would undermine his men's, and Grant's, respect for Grant's authority. He decided to fix that. "Actually, that *is* good," Edwards said. "We'll probably be detaining and hanging a bunch of these bastards." Edwards decided to give Grant even more esteem in the eyes of the soldiers. "Hey, we're citizen soldiers so we welcome everyone from every background. Welcome to the battlefield, Counselor."

Edwards turned to Ted and asked, "What's your background?"

"1st Group, sir," Ted said, referring to his former Special Forces unit at JBLM, knowing that Edwards would know who 1st Group was. "Me and a former ODA team member of mine," Ted said pointing to Sap, "trained these guys." ODA referred to an "operational detachment alpha" or A-team, which was the twelve-man Green Beret team that went out into the field and trained guerillas. "I'm proud of this unit, sir." Ted said, making sure all the soldiers could hear it. It was true, and the 17th needed a little credibility boost with the regular military.

Edwards was relieved. At least these irregulars had some good training. Ted introduced Sap. Better yet, thought Edwards. This irregular unit had two SF trainers.

They talked about the 17th's capabilities. Edwards acknowledged that, despite the irregular nature of the unit, there were some good soldiers in the group. Edwards met the Team and was fascinated by them. It was very unusual to come across a group of civilians who had that kind of gear and carried themselves that way. Edwards was trying to figure out Grant. It was also so unusual for a regular Army guy like Edwards to work with an irregular commander, especially one with no prior military experience. Not to mention he was also a lawyer.

Ted told Edwards the story about how the Team had done the scouting work. Grant told the story about how they had found the spy at Delphi Road and administered just the right amount of force.

Finally, after they were done swapping stories, Edwards asked Grant the big question.

Chapter 299

Volunteers

(January 2)

"Any of your guys want to volunteer to join Bravo Company in the assault on the capitol?"

They were off to the side where no one could hear them. Edwards didn't want rumors to fly around. The commanders had to control the flow of information on things like this.

"Of course," Grant said. He wasn't thrilled about his unit being handed over to another commander, but "his" men weren't really his. They belonged to the mission.

"How many do you need here?" Edwards asked. The question reminded Grant of a used car salesman asking a customer "what kind of payments can you make?"

"I'd need at least half," Grant said. "Five squads. I need my Quadra radio man. I need my medic. I need my Chairborne unit." Grant explained that term to Edwards. The Chairborne people wouldn't be much help in active combat, but would make the civil affairs mission go much smoother.

"I need my cook," Grant said. "Oh, and I need my RED HORSE and his guys," he said, referring to Don, the Air Force guy who was a whiz at setting up and maintaining bases, and all the guys Don had helping him on wiring, plumbing, base defense, and everything else. Everything they needed to have that brewery running as an HQ, and everything they'd need to get Olympia back up and running as they did their civil affairs mission.

"What about the Team?" Edwards asked. He wanted them.

"They are free to volunteer," Grant said reluctantly. He wanted his guys to stay with him. He wanted to go through this adventure with them. He wanted them to protect him, but he knew he couldn't pry them away from a mission like taking the capitol.

"Okay," Edwards said. "I'd like five of your squads. I'd like one of your SF guys to lead them."

"Sap," Grant said. "He can do it. I need Ted here to tell me what to do."

"Roger that," Edwards said, appreciating Grant's candor.

Bullshit had no place in a serious situation like this. The absolute truth was required. The truth that people could bet their lives and their buddies' lives on.

They made plans for half of the 17th to join with Bravo Company. They would leave in two hours. It was 4:04 a.m. now. It would still be dark in two hours. They would be able to leave fed and a little rested, which was a huge advantage.

The next two hours were a whirlwind. Grant, Ted, and Sap coordinated who would leave, what gear they would need, and what people and gear needed to stay behind.

Edwards assumed this would be an organizational nightmare—a "cluster fuck," as they called it in the military.

It wasn't. The 17th's squads were so well integrated with each other that people knew what to do. They formed into new squads, which were very similar to their old squads.

The next thing was for the 17th squad leaders to integrate with the Bravo Company squad leaders. The semi-trained irregulars of the 17th would be taking orders from Bravo Company leaders. This should be interesting, Edwards thought. But, then again, the military organized itself in a way that made it much easier for new people to plop into a unit and work as a team. It was designed that way.

It was almost 6:00 a.m. and time to ship out. Grant went down to the first floor where all the coordinating was going on. He saw Pow, who came over and gave Grant a bro hug.

"We're doin' it, man," Pow said with a smile. "We're goin' in."

"You'll do great," Grant said. "Show these regular Army guys what some UCGs can do," referring to their joking designation of "Untrained Civilian Goofballs." "Oh," Grant said, "and take care of the boys for me," referring to the rest of the Team. "Bring 'em back, brother."

"Roger that, brother," Pow said. "Roger that," he repeated as he straightened up his posture. Pow paused and then threw out his hand as if to say, "It's nothing."

"We've done lots of shit that we weren't supposed to know how to do," Pow said with a grin.

"I'd go with you," Grant said, "but..."

Pow cut him off. "Don't give me this. You're not wimping out, dude. You have some shit to do here. That's been the big plan all along. You do your thing; we'll do ours."

Pow looked Grant right in the eye and said in a serious tone, "You have skills, Grant. The Man Upstairs wants you to do some things here. Do them."

That was the most serious thing Pow had ever said to Grant. Normally, Pow talked like a surfer dude, but not now. He was serious about this.

"Will do," Grant said. "And, if you come back from the capitol and I'm not here because I cut myself on some paperwork and bled to death," they both laughed, "well, thanks for getting my family out of Olympia. 'Gonna eat that pickle?' Classic, dude. Classic. You guys risking it for my family meant everything. Thanks."

"What?" Pow asked with a questioning expression. "This isn't some goodbye, dude. Don't even talk that way. We'll be back in a couple hours. Couple days, tops." Pow smiled his beaming smile of confidence.

By now, Scotty, Bobby, Ryan, and Wes had assembled around Pow. It was time to go. They all bro hugged Grant. The Bravo Company guys thought it was weird for some contractor-looking guys to be bro hugging a commanding officer, but whatever. They *were* an irregular unit.

"Let's go!" yelled one of the Bravo Company squad leaders, and off they went. No one from the 17th looked back. They wanted to, but didn't want to look like wusses.

As they started walking off toward combat, none of them could possibly imagine what was going to happen in the next two hours. None of them saw it coming.

Chapter 300

"Kah-mah-la-malik!"

(January 2)

It was strangely quiet at the brewery after Bravo Company and half of the 17th left. It was noisy in one sense — radio traffic, people running around coordinating things, everyone asking Ted and Grant to make decisions — but it was quiet in another sense. Not seeing half the unit around was weird.

Grant had thought of a lot of scenarios over the past few months for combat in Olympia, but half his unit getting poached by a regular unit wasn't one of them. He felt nervous. He always had a plan for everything. Everything. But not for this. He used plans like a crutch in stressful situations, and he didn't have his crutch now. Everything seemed chaotic. And he was tired, which amplified his emotions.

Grant motioned for Jim Q. to come over. "Tell HQ that civil affairs is up and running in the brewery." Jim Q. started talking in his code, but Grant heard "brewery" in English as he had before.

A reply came back on the radio. Jim Q. said, "Boston Harbor says they'll start sending civil affairs assets and problems here. We're the official civil affairs operation." Jim Q. smiled. He was very proud of the people he was with.

More weird language on the radio. "We should be getting some MREs here on a couple of trucks. One white pick-up and one black one."

Ted was way ahead of Grant. "Let the perimeter know," he told a runner.

"Tell HQ that I could use a field kitchen and some more food here, too," Grant said. "We can feed our forces and civilians." Jim Q. started relaying those messages.

There were trucks and troops, friendlies, arriving now. There were so many of them that they stopped trying to identify the good guys. Everyone was a good guy. Grant was starting to get the feeling that there weren't any bad guys around.

Grant looked at his watch. It was 7:58 a.m. and the sun was finally up.

"Boom!" The explosion was so loud and deep that it shook

everything in the brewery. It was far off, but still. Very powerful. Gunfire erupted in the distance, right in the direction of the capitol. It was a full-on pitched battle with what sounded like hundreds of shooters, not the random pops they'd been hearing all night. It sounded like a major assault. Bravo Company was probably in on it. Grant prayed for his guys. He prayed for all the Patriots, but especially for his guys.

Grant tried to keep acting normal. He didn't want his people to get alarmed.

"What the hell was that?" someone on the fourth floor asked. Everyone was quiet so Jim Q. could hear the radio and tell them.

Jim Q. shrugged. There were no reports yet.

The noise of the activity kept going, like the delivery of MREs, but people weren't talking much. They were listening.

A few more minutes passed. Everyone was pretending to concentrate on their work but most were really straining their ears for word of what had happened. And what might be happening.

"Kah-mah-la-malik!" a jubilant voice came on the radio speaking in Jim Q.'s language. He was bursting with joy. "Kah-mah-la-malik!" he kept repeating.

Grant had no idea what "kah-mah-la-malik" meant, but it must be really good news.

"Victory!" Jim Q. yelled. "The Limas in the capitol buildings surrendered!"

Everyone started jumping and yelling. It was the happiest moment of Grant's life. He felt guilty admitting that. The happiest moment of his life was supposed to be the birth of his children, but this was better. The horror was over. Things would be fixed. Finally. Finally.

"That quick?" Grant asked Ted. "How the…"

"Weird shit happens," Ted answered with a huge smile on his face. "We knew the Limas were weak here, but twenty-four hours? That's all it took? Wow."

"The Limas detonated their ammo storage," Jim Q. said breathlessly, relaying the reports he was getting from HQ. "That's what the big explosion was."

Grant looked out the windows facing the capitol buildings. There was a big black mushroom cloud rising in the early morning sky. He'd never seen a mushroom cloud. He always had associated them with nuclear explosions, but a large conventional explosion apparently could cause one, too.

Grant just watched the mushroom cloud. He'd waited years to see that. He'd worked and worried for years. He'd risked his job, then his marriage, then his life for this. And it just happened. A giant cloud of smoke slowly climbing into the air.

The gunfire was starting to die down. It sounded like some desperate people fired everything they had, some confident people returned fire, and then the desperate people dropped their guns. At least that's how Grant hoped it was going.

Suddenly, the lights came on. Whoa. Grant looked at the other brewery buildings, the ones that were supposedly locked. The lights were on in those, too.

"What the hell?" Grant yelled.

Just then Don, the RED HORSE airman, came running into the fourth floor observation point.

"Ta da!" Don said. He took a bow. "You can thank me later."

"How did..." Ted started to ask.

Don shrugged and then smiled. "I got skills. My guys got skills."

Don looked at Grant, "I took the liberty of breaking into all the surrounding buildings and getting the electricity going. Water's up and running, too. I thought we could use the facilities for all that will be coming our way." He smiled and said to Grant, "I assume that was okay with you, Lieutenant?"

"Fuck yes, it was okay!" Grant yelled. "Oh – fucking - kay, indeed." Grant wanted to hug Don, but that wouldn't be appropriate. Oh, what the hell. He ran over and bro hugged Don. Not a full hug, just a bro hug. Hey, they were an irregular unit. They could do things like that.

Another coincidence, Grant thought. Right now, when wounded prisoners and civilians would be streaming to the only functioning civil affairs operation in the city, they suddenly had electricity and water.

You have a lot of people to help in the next few hours and days. I am helping you help them. Grant felt that instant calm come over him. He felt the goose bumps on his arms. He soaked in the feeling of hearing from the outside thought, and knowing he was doing what he was supposed to be doing. He realized he needed to get back to work, so he turned to Jim Q.

"Tell HQ," he said to Jim Q., "that we have full electricity and water at all the buildings at the brewery. We can accommodate a field hospital, prisoner processing, and even civilians here." Grant was so proud. The 17th, just a hillbilly irregular unit, was able to call in that piece of great news.

"Roger that, 17th," a voice said in English over the radio. That was the first time Grant had heard English.

Another voice came on in English. "Please be advised that Quadras are no longer needed for routine traffic. We have too much radio traffic. Using Quadras for everything is slowing things down. Sensitive tactical communications should still go through Quadras, but routine traffic, such as the coordination of relief can be conducted in English."

Jim Q. smiled. His job was done. He had accomplished what he wanted to: Olympia was in the hands of the Patriots and there was no longer a need for him to be using his language on the radio. That meant victory. His family would be honored for this. They would be proud of this for generations. Jim Q. took a deep breath and soaked in the feeling. Honor for generations. That, and avenging his cousin's imprisonment, was why they did this.

About an hour later, the first wounded started to arrive, followed by a medical unit and then more wounded and medical units. They were feverishly setting up a field hospital in one of the brewery buildings and Don and his guys were helping them. Random members of the 17th split themselves off into work details to help. It was amazing to watch. They were just helping their buddies like they'd done for months at Marion Farm.

"Get the kids out of here and somewhere else," Grant said. They needed the space for the wounded. Someone ran down the stairs to the second and third floors. Pretty soon, the kids were gone.

Anne Sherryton went with them. She would protect them. Actually, being with them was more for her recovery than their safety. She knew she wouldn't do an awful thing like she'd done a few hours ago if those kids were around. Besides, she promised the kids that she'd read them bedtime stories. And she was going to keep that promise. That was what normal, good people do.

The next few hours were a blur. Grant hadn't had any real sleep in ... he actually had no idea. There was so much to do. He needed to make sure the 17th personnel got all the incoming soldiers and civilians to where they needed to be, and ensure HQ knew what they were doing at the brewery. He needed to make sure the area was still secure and that the civilians could be controlled so they didn't swarm the place. He also needed to make sure there were no Limas hiding among the civilians and trying to detonate a suicide bomb.

"Put up signs for the hospital, prisoner processing, and kitchen," Grant remembered telling someone who ran off and, presumably, followed his instructions. Franny asked Grant if the brewery had any refrigerators or freezers. "Try the Baskin Robbins up the street," Grant suggested.

The radio was full of urgent messages. Everyone in the Patriots' Olympia forces seemed to have something to say to the civil affairs hub or ask the hub for. And, though Grant was technically in charge, most of the time he had no idea what he was doing. He was just doing. Occasionally he would hear himself talking and was amazed at how authoritative and knowledgeable he sounded.

After a while, Grant's voice was getting hoarse. He had to stop and … just not talk. He was getting woozy again so he tried to eat an MRE, but he couldn't. He tried to lie down and get a quick nap. He couldn't. He had to continue doing all the stuff he was doing.

Keep going. This is no time to stop.

He jumped back up, full of energy and ran at full speed until dark.

He saw some of the Bravo Company squad leaders coming up to the fourth floor, which had become the command post.

"Any casualties?" Grant asked the squad leaders.

They nodded. "Two," a sergeant answered.

"Who?" Grant asked. He was praying it wasn't any of his.

"A couple of ours, Lieutenant," the sergeant said. "Your guys are all fine."

Grant tried not to act happy. Two Bravo Company men were casualties and that wasn't good news.

"How bad?" Grant asked.

"One KIA," the sergeant said, meaning killed in action, "and one with some shrapnel to the legs. He'll be okay."

"My condolences," Grant said to the sergeant who nodded slightly at Grant.

That reminded Grant that they needed a place to put bodies. He had a runner find Don to see if any place in the brewery had a functioning refrigeration system. Nope. Don and the commander of the medical unit came up with a temporary solution and Grant didn't want to know what it was.

Pastor Pete and a couple other chaplains had set up a makeshift chapel in one of the brewery's office buildings. They were counseling soldiers one on one. Lots of grieving over lost comrades. Lots of people who had never seen or done what they had just seen or done, like killing people. Or watching people kill and be killed. Or seeing horrific injuries. There were lots of Anne Sherrytons. Nice people doing horrible things and trying to figure out what just happened.

Grant saw the Team coming up to the fourth floor. They looked tired.

"Welcome back," Grant said. "How'd it go?"

"Shitty," Pow said. "We didn't see any action."

The Team went on to tell Grant about how they slowly made their way down the main street to the capitol only to hear of the surrender right before they got into position. There were Limas running away from the capitol and straight toward their general position.

"Bravo Company got a bunch of them who wouldn't drop their weapons," Wes said. "We were holding an intersection and the bad guys went the other way." Wes was a little disappointed.

Capt. Edwards came up and said to the Team, "Get something to eat and maybe a nap. We're going back out in an hour. Night patrol." The Team nodded slowly. They wanted to go back out and kill some bad guys, but … they were so tired.

Grant pulled Edwards aside. "Can I ask a favor?" he asked Edwards after a bright idea jumped into his mind. "I need to motivate some of my guys."

"What do you have in mind?" Edwards asked.

"Could my Team do a motorized patrol with you guys?" Grant asked.

"Sure," Edwards said. "As long as you supply the motor." He looked at Grant, "Why a motorized patrol?"

"Kind of an inside joke," Grant said. "But it'll motivate them."

"Okay," Edwards said. He didn't care about some joke. If Grant wanted his guys to ride, and if he provided the ride, whatever.

Grant went to find the Team as they were just finishing their pancakes. He got an eerie feeling as he watched Wes eat his pancakes. He couldn't put his finger on it, but he sensed something bad.

They got their gear and slowly went outside to Mark's truck. Grant handed the keys to Bobby. "Get in."

The Team got into the truck, wondering what was up. Once they were in, Grant said, "This never gets old."

"Beats the shit out of selling insurance," Pow said with a smile. It was a tired smile, but a smile nonetheless.

They all laughed. Then teared up. It was exactly what they needed to hear. They needed to be reminded that they were part of a team, something special. They had come a long way. They'd been doing this for months now — years, counting all the pre-Collapse training they had done together. They could do this. They were tired and cold and heading out into pockets of fierce Lima resistance, about to face urban combat which was the most dangerous kind. But they could do it. Because this was what they were made to do, and who they were made to do it with.

This never gets old, Grant thought to himself as he watched them drive away.

Chapter 301

The Blur II

(January 2)

Grant wanted to join the Team and Bravo Company, but he had work to do.

The brewery was now the field headquarters of the Olympia operation. Grant was totally overwhelmed. He thought he was organized and good at things like this, but he was in over his head. Way over.

The wounded kept flowing in. It was hard to tell if they were friendlies or enemy, but it didn't matter. They all got treated. Grant had never understood that. Why waste precious medical supplies on the people who had been trying to kill you just a little while ago? But doctors and nurses took an oath to treat the wounded. It was also part of the Geneva Convention. As if the Limas followed that. But the Patriots did, to the best of their ability. Luckily for Grant, the medical units took over those operations. All he was doing for them was giving them a building with electricity and water and providing security for the area. Well, several other units were augmenting the 17th on security. At this point, things were very blurry for Grant. He didn't know what he and the 17th were doing exactly; he just knew that stuff was getting done somehow.

At some point in the middle of the night, prisoners started trickling in. Some came from the field hospital after being treated. Others walked in under their own power to surrender. Most came with their hands already zip tied by Patriot units. But some just walked up to the brewery with their hands up. They were mostly young National Guard kids who were glad this whole stupid thing was over. They'd been told the Patriots would torture and kill them, but everything else their Lima officers had told them was a lie so, they figured this must be, too.

The amount of prisoners was becoming a problem. The brewery building they were using was quickly filling up. And it wasn't too secure. They needed to figure out where to set up a makeshift detention facility.

"The high school is about a mile that way," Grant explained to a major who said he was the head of the MPs, or military police. Grant was pointed up the street toward the Baskin Robbins. "Lots of lockable rooms and a big kitchen. High schools are kind of like prisons anyway," Grant said with a laugh.

"Good idea, Lieutenant," the major said. He started yelling to get a team together to go check out the high school. He found a local civilian who would show them where the high school was.

There were lots of civilians pouring in to the brewery—the word got out that this was the place where the Patriots were—to offer help. There were two kinds of civilians at the brewery. The first were hungry civilians, or those with untreated medical needs. They had no political ideals; they viewed the Patriots as just another provider of food or medical treatment. They didn't care. There were way too many hungry kids. They got first priority in the kitchen, right after soldiers going back out to fight.

The second category of civilians streaming in to the brewery was the closet Patriots and gray men and women who wanted to offer their help. People like Ron Spencer.

Earlier, a neighbor of Ron's, an Undecided, had come running to Ron's house to tell him the Patriots had taken the capitol campus and had set up a headquarters at the brewery. Ron wanted to race to the brewery and offer his help but, after thinking about it, decided to stay in his neighborhood. Ron had his shotgun and was ready. He was going to protect his family. The three members of the "Carlos Cabal," as they called the neighborhood Lima leaders, could try to come after Ron and his family. Protecting his family was his first priority. Killing Limas was a distant second. Besides, Ron had done his duty by tagging the three Carlos Cabal houses with that big black "L" on the front door, which would help the Patriots when they finally got to the Cedars.

The fourth floor observation point was becoming a communications center. Radio after radio was carried up those stairs and being set up.

The fourth floor com center was a family reunion of Quadras. They were reunited after being in separate units for months and not seeing each other. They hugged and did a short dance that looked like a Greek wedding dance. They talked a thousand miles an hour in their language, laughed, and threw up their arms in joy. Then they went back to work relaying the very sensitive communications with huge smiles on their faces.

No one was working on political affairs, Grant realized. Everyone at the brewery was a military person working on military issues, like a field hospital, communications, field kitchen, and holding prisoners. Grant realized this was a critical time for politics.

Grant was very respectful of others' rank and position, but he needed to assert himself on the political affairs. If someone wanted to tell him to stand down, he'd be happy to let them handle it while he took a nap. He was getting delirious at this point, but the outside thought had told him to press on so that was what he was going to do.

Grant found the major who was in charge of intelligence. "Major," Grant said as he re-introduced himself, "I'm in charge of civil affairs." That was kind of true. No one had told him he wasn't in charge of civil affairs.

"Great," the major said, assuming Grant had actual training and experience at civil affairs. "Go do it. What's your plan?"

That was a great question. "We'll start off," Grant said authoritatively, "with some political messages. We'll brief the troops on what to tell people they encounter. That message will basically be that we're here to help, not carry out revenge killings."

Grant held up two fingers and said, "There are two messages, one to enemy military and one to the civilians. To the enemy military, the message is that we accept Lima—or, pardon me "legitimate authority"—surrenders and will treat them well. Feed them, that kind of thing."

Grant put up his second finger and continued as if he knew what he was talking about, "The message to the civilians is that we are here to feed them and treat their medical needs. We will establish order and protect them from the gangs. Enemy military and law enforcement will get fair treatment; gangs won't. They're criminals and the civilians need to see that we're not a gang and won't tolerate it."

The major nodded. In his mind, Lima military and police got fair treatment because they were uniformed enemy. Gangs weren't. They were just criminals.

Grant continued, "So we get those two messages out to the troops and then we start to get the messages out to the civilians who are coming here. Every soldier should have the spiel down. The civilians will take the messages they receive back to their neighbors. The good news that we're treating people fairly will spread like wildfire. Then we try to get a radio station and broadcast. I'd love to print up pamphlets but, let me guess, we don't have printing capabilities."

"There was a copy center on the way in here," the major said. Of course. Grant had forgotten about the copy center two blocks away.

If their copy machines hadn't been stolen and they had paper and electricity, then they were in business. It was pamphlet time.

"Great," Grant said. "I'll put one of my men on making pamphlets." By "one of my men," Grant meant … he'd hand write them himself.

"Go at it … what's your name again?" the major asked.

"Lt. Matson," Grant said. "I'm in command of the 17th Irregulars." He knew his credibility would go down with his lowly rank of lieutenant and the fact that he was in a mere irregular unit. So he smiled and added, "We're the guys who brought this fine brewery to you."

"An irregular unit did this?" the major asked and looked around at the humming observation center up on the fourth floor.

"Solid," the major said. "Very solid, Lieutenant." Then he thought about it: a good chunk of the Patriot forces were irregular units. He shouldn't have been that surprised.

Grant started on the pamphlet. He got a runner to go to the copy center, break in, and check out the equipment. He asked him to return with a ream of paper and any pens they could find. The runner saluted and took off.

Some new people came up to the fourth floor. One of them was a lieutenant colonel.

"Who's in command here?" the Lieutenant Colonel asked.

"I am, sir," Grant said and walked up to him. "Lt. Matson, 17th Irregulars."

"I'm Lt. Col. Brussels, 3rd Battalion CO," he said. "I'm in command now."

"Yes, sir," Grant said. Okay, that was that. Grant could now focus on civil affairs and taking care of his people in the 17th. What a relief.

"What's the status here?" Brussels asked.

Grant briefed Brussels on everything.

"How did you end up in command of this?" Brussels asked.

"We took the brewery," Grant said. "Everything just flowed from that. This is the perfect facility in the perfect location. Everyone just started using it as a headquarters, and I was running things until someone came to relieve me."

Brussels nodded. "Thank you, Lt. Matson. Go back to your unit and have them support the mop up."

"Yes, sir," Grant said.

Mop up. That meant this wasn't over yet. Grant had mentally

considered the Limas' surrender to be the end of hostilities. Wishful thinking. The remaining Limas out there were diehards. "Diehard" as in they will die … hard. These Limas, and especially gangs, had committed so many crimes and hurt so many people that they knew no one could just forgive and forget. If the Patriots didn't kill them, they figured the civilians would. They had nowhere to go, so they might as well go down with a fight. Better to die than be captured by the teabaggers.

Twenty four hours of euphoria over what seemed like a quick victory came crashing down. For the first time since he arrived at the brewery, Grant realized that this was going to be a long, hard slog.

Chapter 302

Watershed Park

(January 2)

Grant looked around as he walked out of the fourth floor observation point to go back to his unit. He remembered walking into this room just a few hours ago. It was dark, cold, dangerous, and empty, totally empty. Now, just a few hours later, it was packed full of people and radio equipment. Grant looked at all the hustle and bustle on the empty brewery floor and smiled. He was proud of what he'd got up and going. It was kind of like when he left Pierce Point.

Now Grant got to do what he really wanted: get the civil affairs mission going. More importantly, he could be back with his guys, the 17th Irregulars.

It was 4:15 a.m. and pitch black. The lights were on now so Grant could see the place outside where he had watched the Team leave in Mark's truck just a few hours earlier. There they were, without him, sitting in the back of the truck with their kit and ARs, grinning for the whole world. They were in heaven, doing what they loved. Going out to hunt some Limas and gangbangers.

"You guys are locals, right?" Capt. Edwards asked the Team as they were waiting to head out.

"Yes, sir," Pow said, pointing at Scotty, Bobby, and Wes.

"So you guys know the area then?" Capt. Edwards asked.

"Yes, sir," Pow said. "Very well. We drive these streets all the time."

"If you were retreating, desperate Limas, where would you go?" Capt. Edwards asked. Might as well get the thoughts of the people who knew the area.

"I'd get away from the capitol," Pow answered, pointing north, "where all the Patriot forces are. I'd go south and try to rally at the airport," he said, pointing in the opposite direction. Edwards recalled from the briefings that Olympia had a small regional airport about five miles to the south.

"I hear we are holding I-5," Pow continued, "so they can't get back up to Seattle, their stronghold, and I guess we landed some people at the port so they can't leave by sea, so the airport is it."

"Well, too bad," Edwards said, despite thinking that Pow had a great idea. "That's where I would go to, but we have orders to go straight toward the capitol, to a place called 'Watershed Park.' You guys know where that is?"

Pow had the strongest urge to tell the Captain that they needed to go to the airport. He started to speak up but hesitated. He didn't want to sound like he, an UCG, knew better than battalion or whoever had decided to send Bravo Company to Watershed Park.

He had this overwhelming urge to say something, but he just couldn't.

"Over there," Scotty said, pointing roughly north. "It's a huge park over the area around the waterfalls. That's where the city gets its water."

"I can get you there," said Bobby, who was in the driver's seat of Mark's truck.

"Watershed Park?" Wes said. "Are you sure, Captain? That place is hairy."

"Whatcha mean?" Capt. Edwards asked.

"It's thick woods in there," Wes said in his southern accent. "I mean thick, sir. Thicker than the North Carolina pines I come from. It's dark, too. There are acres of steep terrain and extremely thick foliage, right in the middle of the city, if you can believe that. It's basically Ambush City, sir."

"Yeah," Bobby said, "it's not a 'park' like with swing sets. It's more like a big nature preserve in the middle of the city. Super steep terrain, too."

Edwards pulled out a map that he'd received from gray men inside the city right before the invasion. He spotted Watershed Park on the map.

Crap. It was a huge wooded area about a mile from the capitol. It would be a natural Lima magnet. Anyone with an ounce of sense trying to get away from the Patriot forces would go there, and could set up ambushes there and kill Patriots for days or even weeks. Edwards hoped other Patriot units had sealed off the route from the capitol to that park.

Pow had another urge to suggest they go to the airport, but he didn't want to look like a coward, so he didn't say anything.

"Orders are to go Watershed Park and clean it out," Edwards said. "Anyone got a problem with that?" Edwards asked. He wasn't being a dick. He wanted to see if these irregulars, who weren't used to military discipline, would participate in the operation. If they wouldn't, Edwards could get some regular troops who would.

"No, sir!" Ryan said. He was a Marine and knew how to take an order.

"No, sir," Bobby and Scotty said more slowly.

Wes shook his head and said, "No problem, sir."

Pow was silent.

"Okay, show me on the map how you're going to get us there," Edwards said. "Remember, we're walking behind you so you'll need to just idle it."

"You got any scouts?" Ryan asked.

"Nope," Edwards said. "You guys, my locals, are my scouts." Edwards pointed to the map again. He didn't want a conversation to start with these irregulars about how dangerous the mission was or how they didn't have any scouts. It was time to get going. He wouldn't even be wasting his time with the contractor-looking guys if they weren't the locals he needed to get the company to the objective.

The Team showed Capt. Edwards where the park was and how to get there.

"Only about two miles," Capt. Edwards said. "A short walk for my men." He was proud of the fact that his company was a regular unit used to walking several miles in full gear.

"Okay, let's go," Edwards said. The Team did a press check and checked their magazines. Just like the last time they did that, they had a round in the chamber and a full load out of topped off magazines.

The sun wouldn't come up for almost four hours. It was still drizzling and cold. Darkness and nasty weather for the dark and nasty things that lay ahead.

The Team got into Mark's truck. Everyone expected Pow to say, "This never gets old." But he didn't. They didn't feel like they were kings of the world like when they patrolled around Pierce Point. Things felt different.

No one talked much during the slow drive to Watershed Park. They kept their eyes peeled for threats. Ryan and Wes stood in the back of the truck without the tarp. They could be out in the open now. No use hiding it. In fact, they wanted the civilians to see them. Help had arrived.

As they traveled down the Olympia streets toward Watershed Park, they were struck by how downhill the city had gone. They hadn't really been noticing it when they went with Bravo Company toward the capitol right before the surrender. They had been expecting a full-on fight with regular forces, so they weren't noticing little things.

Now they were. There was garbage blowing everywhere. Most businesses were boarded up. Graffiti was everywhere; mostly gang graffiti, but an occasional Patriot message in yellow paint. "I miss America" was everywhere.

There were a few civilians out. Ryan and Wes would cover them from the back of the truck, using the top of the cab as a platform to hold their rifles steady. The civilians were harmless, especially when they saw about a hundred regular troops behind the pickup. Regular troops with uniforms and high-tech weapons.

At one point, some civilians came up to the truck at an intersection. They were not afraid of Ryan and Wes pointing rifles at them.

"Do you have food?" a middle aged woman desperately asked. She looked like hell, so thin. "Please. Food. For my children."

"Stand back, ma'am," Ryan said.

"There is a limited amount of food at the brewery," Wes said. "Do not bring any weapons. You will be searched."

"Thank you!" she said. "Thank you," she repeated as she started to walk toward the brewery and Bravo Company.

"Whoa!" Ryan yelled. "Don't move, ma'am. Wait here with your hands up until the troops behind us get past you. Okay?"

She nodded and put her hands up. She kept looking toward the brewery like it contained the solutions to all her problems. Because it did. They had food there.

Scotty radioed to the troops behind him that the woman there was going to the brewery for food and would keep her hands up while they passed by.

"Roger that," the Bravo radioman replied.

Mark's black truck crept down the streets for another twenty minutes. The idling of the diesel engine was loud, but soothing. It meant they had transportation when no one else seemed to have any.

The Team and Bravo Company came to the intersection where they needed to turn left. Scotty called into the company what direction they'd be taking.

"Trouble!" Ryan yelled. Wes swung around to the direction Ryan was pointing. There were four men with what looked like hunting rifles or shotguns. They started to run.

"Can't identify," Wes yelled. Scotty was calling it in.

"Don't shoot unless you can identify as enemy," the radio said after the men had disappeared.

Not shooting unless you could identify the enemy made sense. It wouldn't have made sense if they were invading a foreign country and everyone with a gun was a bad guy, but they were in America. As reassuring as it would have been to shoot anything with a gun, this was a city full of Americans. Who knew if they were civilians protecting their neighborhood from the gangs, were gray men out to whack Lima neighbors, or were plainclothes Limas. There was no way to tell. The Team didn't mind rules of engagement that spared unnecessary civilian deaths when the civilians were their neighbors. Rules of engagement to make politicians happy or to prevent bad footage on CNN were another thing entirely.

Seeing those armed men, whoever they were, put the Team on edge. This wasn't at all like their previous cakewalks. This was the real deal.

They crept along for another half hour or so. Even at idling speed, they had to stop periodically to let Bravo, on foot, catch up. They were in good shape but had tons of equipment and had been up for a few days. They were tired.

"Heading into the wooded area," Scotty said into the radio. "Be ready for ambushes from the right or left flanks." Or from the front, he thought, right at our truck.

"Should we kill the headlights?" Scotty asked Bobby and Pow.

"Nah," Pow said, "we need them to see anyone ahead of us."

"Plus, we're cleaning the place out," Bobby said. "So if they see our lights, they might go further into the forest. Concentrate themselves." Made sense.

They spent the next half hour barely moving along. The high beams on so the headlights were lighting up their path. Nothing.

Edwards got on the radio and said they would stop here, dismount, and go into the woods. Ryan and Wes relaxed. They had been careful to stand up in the back of the truck while staying ready for a sudden lurch if Bobby had to take off. It was exhausting, but now they could relax.

"Dismount, dude," Wes said and stood in the back of the truck.

"Boom! Boom!" Bursts of fire.

Fire was coming from everywhere. And tracers! They had a machine gun! Green tracers were like laser beams from a science fiction movie.

Bobby punched the gas and the truck flew forward. He swerved and slammed on the brakes. The truck was now sideways in the road, providing plenty of cover, just like they'd practiced.

A burst of machine gun fire blew out the windshield just as they got out of the truck. Scotty was about two feet away when he got sprayed with glass. He didn't even feel the glass. He was moving away from the truck in slow motion.

Bravo Company, now behind the truck, lit up the right and left flanks. They, too, had machine guns. Red tracers spit out from behind the truck and into the sides of the road and bounced all around the forest.

The Team was shooting into the woods. They couldn't see what they were shooting at, but it felt so good to shoot back, which was better than just sitting there feeling helpless.

Pretty soon, Pow yelled, "Save your ammo!" It was impossible to see what they were shooting at. Now that they'd got a half magazine out and didn't feel helpless anymore, they could start thinking this through, which was what Ted had told them before the Collapse. He warned them to resist the urge to shoot just so they could feel like they were doing something. They'd want those rounds back if they start to run out and they *will* run out. That being said, Ted admitted to them that he emptied a mag the first time he got ambushed.

"Moving!"

"Move!"

"Moving rear!"

"Covering!" The Team was doing what they'd practiced, moving to the best cover behind the truck and covering each other's movements. With live rounds coming at them this time. They felt remarkably calm, now that the initial shock was over. They could feel their training kicking in and getting them through this. And the wild volleys of green tracer fire showed them what Ted had always said, "Your enemy is probably a shitty shot." Whoever was spraying at them wasn't hitting crap.

After a minute or two, the fire started to die down. It was pretty obvious that neither side was hitting what they were aiming at. The Team could hear yelling and rustling bushes. The Limas were completely disorganized. It was starting to become obvious that the Limas had just started spraying poorly aimed machine gun fire, and now were getting the hell out of there.

Edwards realized the same thing. He and a SAW gunner—a soldier with a light machine gun—ran up to the Team, who were behind the truck.

"You guys give us cover fire left, right, and front," Edwards yelled, because he couldn't hear with all the gunfire. "And my guys will move into the woods left and right. You hold the point. Got it?"

The Team nodded or gave a thumbs up.

Except Wes.

Pow wondered where Wes had gone, and assumed he was hiding behind some cover.

"Give me cover fire in thirty seconds," Edwards said, as he ran back to his company. They were still taking pot shots into the woods to keep the bad guys' heads down.

The SAW gunner counted off the thirty seconds. The Team was counting. The SAW gunner got a good position on the ground.

"Twenty-nine ... thirty," Pow counted to himself. All of the sudden, the SAW and the Team opened up on the left, right, and front.

"Loading!" Ryan yelled, meaning he was changing a magazine.

"Check!" Scotty yelled and threw out cover fire so Ryan could load.

"Loaded!" Ryan yelled when he was done.

"Loading!" Scotty yelled.

"Check!" Ryan yelled. And so they did this for a minute or two as they coated the woods with bullets.

They had done this so many times that they could keep track of who had reloaded and who would need to reload soon.

They didn't hear Wes call for a reload.

Bravo Company moved into the woods on both sides. Pretty soon, they could hear scattered shots in the woods. Hopefully it was Bravo shooting escaping Limas, rather than the Limas ambushing Bravo.

"Wait!" Pow yelled out to the Team. They hadn't received any fire from the woods so they stopped shooting. There was no need to, unless someone took a shot at them. Besides, their guns were getting hot from a couple magazines of firing.

"Pop! Pop!" The shooting in the woods continued, but was dying down. Pretty soon, it was over. The Team sat there scanning the left, right, and front. Nothing. Each of them kept imagining a Lima running toward them out of nowhere and them shooting him. They kept imagining it to keep sharp, and to make it easy to do when it happened.

The bushes around the Team started to move. They swung their rifles around to the movement. It was Bravo, or some military unit with the same kind of uniforms. It could be a FUSA Lima unit, but given how calmly they were walking up to them, it probably wasn't.

The Team quickly started recognizing individual members of

63

Bravo coming back from the woods. Edwards was one of them.

"We ain't running into their trap," Edwards said to Pow. "The map says there are two points in and out, where this road goes into and out of the park. Do you know of any other points?"

"No, sir," Pow said. "The steep hills go down into the watershed. It would be hard to cross that water and get out of here."

"Good," Edwards said. "We'll seal up the two exit points and wait for the sun to come up. We can go in there in the light, but not in the dark. I only have a handful of NVGs," he said, referring to night vision goggles. If all his guys had them, and especially if he knew the enemy did not have them, then he would have gladly walked into the woods in the dark.

"We'll split the company up and put them on each exit point," Edwards said. "We'll take this first exit point and have you drive up to the next one, using your headlights the way you were."

To get shot at, Pow thought. Oh well. There were pluses and minuses that came with riding in the truck.

"We'll be ready to go in a minute," Pow said. "Let me know when the half of the company following us is ready, sir."

Edwards nodded and ran off to get his company split into two.

The Team left their cover and gathered around the truck.

"Where's Wes?" Ryan asked.

Chapter 303

A Missing Friendly

(January 2)

Everyone looked around. Wes wasn't there.

"Hey! Wes!" Ryan yelled. "Let's go."

Silence.

Pow figured Wes was back with Bravo, so he said, "These Lima dickheads really suck. Did you see all that spray and pray machine gun fire? What a bunch of jackasses. These guys can't fight worth a shit. We so outclass them."

Ryan got out his flashlight and started looking around the truck. Wes wasn't there.

Oh, God. Ryan remembered that Wes had been standing in the back of the truck and not bracing himself when Bobby hit the gas. He ran back to the point where the truck had accelerated. Everyone followed him, as they were now realizing the same thing.

Ryan looked around with this flashlight.

"Shit!" Ryan yelled out. "Come here, guys!"

The Team approached and saw Wes' rifle on the ground. It had been dropped, but Wes was nowhere to be found.

They stood there stunned and silent. Finally, Scotty got on the radio and grimly announced, "We have a missing friendly."

"We have to go find him!" Pow yelled as Edwards came up.

"What?" Edwards asked. The Team filled him in.

"We can't go look for him," Edwards exclaimed. "We can't be walking around those woods at night! Not without NVGs."

"How many do you have?" Ryan asked.

"I dunno," Edwards said. "Seven, I guess."

"We need them. Where are they?"

"Whoa, soldier," Edwards said, using his captain's voice. "We're not going into those woods until sun up."

"But we are," Pow said pointing to the Team. "Captain, we're volunteering. Give us the NVGs and we'll go get Wes. We won't ask for any support."

"No way," Edwards said. "Negative. Understand me?"

The Team was silent. They were going into those woods to go

get Wes one way or another. He was a member of the Team. They had agreed long ago that they wouldn't leave a teammate behind. It just wasn't going to happen. They didn't need some captain's permission to do so.

"No, sir," Ryan said. "We are going into those woods, NVGs or not. Your choice, Captain. We go in with NVGs or we go in without them. Your choice, sir."

"You don't talk to me that way," Edwards yelled to Ryan. No one ever challenged his authority this way. No one, especially not these irregulars. What a pain in the ass it had been even letting them come out with a real unit.

"We're irregulars, sir," Scotty spoke up and said. "We consider ourselves under the command of Lt. Matson and he would let us do this."

"That's the stupidest fucking thing I've ever heard," Edwards yelled. "First Sergeant, get over here. We have a discipline problem."

The First Sergeant and two others came over. "What's up, sir?"

"These irregulars want to go off into the woods and find their friend," Edwards said. "I told them no. They say they'll disobey my direct order."

"Do as the good Captain says," said the tough-as-nails First Sergeant.

"We're done," Pow said. "We're resigning our commissions or whatever."

"You don't have commissions and you couldn't resign them on a battlefield anyway," Edwards said. These irregulars had no idea what they were talking about. Who were these fucking goofballs? Edwards wondered, his frustration level rising.

"Let's go, guys," Pow said as he walked toward the woods. He walked right past the First Sergeant and the Team followed.

They got a few yards away and Edwards yelled, "Halt!" The Team thought they might get shot by Edwards and his men. What a way to die, shot by your own side for not obeying an order.

Wes. Wes was in those woods and time was wasting. That was all they could think about.

Edwards had been briefed in advance of this mission that regular military units could not expect irregular units to obey orders like professional soldiers did. If the choice came down to trying to arrest irregulars for insubordination, Edwards' commanders told him to let the irregulars go ahead and do whatever it was they were going to do – as long as it didn't get other Patriot forces hurt. The Team guys going out into the woods with no support wouldn't get any other Patriot forces hurt, Edwards realized, and they were irregulars who were just volunteering. They could go get killed if they wanted.

Edwards turned to the First Sergeant and spoke loud enough for the Team to hear.

"Sergeant, you are my witness. "These men—irregulars who assert I have no command over them—are going into the woods against my orders. They have acknowledged that they're on their own. I wash my hands of them."

"Yes, sir," the First Sergeant said.

Pow turned on his weapon light. It lit up an amazing swath with its 110 lumen Surefire. The rest of the Team did the same. It suddenly became easy to see.

And easy for the enemy to see them. The Team knew it.

"We made a pact," Bobby said to the Team. "We don't leave anyone behind and we take care of each other's families." The Team started to think about Kellie and the baby she and Wes were expecting.

"I couldn't look Kellie in the eye," Scotty said, "and tell her I didn't go out to get Wes."

The Team started to move out into the woods.

Not very well. It was pitch dark and their weapon light almost over-illuminated the woods. They were getting blinded by their lights. And their weapons lights couldn't light up the foliage at their feet unless they constantly swept their rifles up and down. Their arms were going to get tired from all the sweeping of their rifles to see their way.

They had no idea where they were going or how to get back to the road. They knew that, in general, they needed to go downhill to find Wes, and they needed to go uphill to get back to the road.

Bobby thought about how he had punched the gas when they got ambushed. A heavy sense of remorse came over him. He shouldn't have done that, or he at least should have realized Wes might not be braced back there. But when all those machine gun rounds came at them, Bobby just punched the gas. There was no time to think, only act. He knew it was crazy, but he felt like this was his fault.

Ryan was also feeling a sense of guilt. He should have been ready to catch Wes. If he'd caught him, Wes would be here right now. If something bad had happened to Wes, he'd have no one to blame but himself.

By now, it had been almost a half hour since the firefight and when Wes must have fallen out of the truck. They wanted to get into those woods and find him.

Bobby checked his dump pouch, the pouch on his kit where he put empty magazines. He had two in there which meant he was two mags down out of a total of seven.

"Could we grab a couple of mags from you?" Bobby yelled back to Edwards.

"Why the fuck not?" Edwards said, bitterly. "You disobey my orders and now you want stuff from me. First Sergeant, get them replacement magazines. Anything else you ladies want? A pedicure?"

Despite being pissed at these guys for disobeying his orders, Edwards understood why they were doing what they were doing. He had a moral obligation to provide them with the magazines. At the very least, he knew that the Team would be flushing out Limas and not interfering with Bravo's mission of sealing off the two entry and exit points into Watershed Park. Edwards hated to admit it, but the Team had been useful getting Bravo Company to Watershed Park. He didn't need them anymore. They could go do stupid shit on their own.

The First Sergeant came up to the Team and gave two magazines to each man. The Team changed their partially used magazines out and inserted new ones.

They finally started out into the woods. No one said anything as they got a few yards off the road into the woods. It was almost impossible to move because it was pitch black and the brush was so thick. They had a point man illuminate the woods with his weapon light while everyone else behind him used their weapons lights to light up the ground in front of them and navigate through the brush and trees. It was hard work to move a few yards.

Chapter 304

"Every New Year's Day from Here on Out"

(January 2)

Ryan put Wes' rifle over his shoulder as he walked through the woods so he could give it to Wes when they found him. He couldn't wait to give it to him.

"Take point, dude," Pow said to Ryan, who was much better at moving through the woods with people trying to kill him since he'd done it before as a Marine. The rest of the Team was pretty good at urban stuff, but not this. It was new to them, and it showed.

They moved slowly. The streams of light looked like the Star Wars light sabers when they went into the brewery for the first time. The trees and bushes threw off ghoulish and frightening shadows, like a scene from a movie.

They occasionally heard bushes move or twigs snap. Twice they saw glimpses of moving shapes that looked like people. There were definitely people in the woods, and they were trying to kill the Team.

This was the most afraid they'd ever been, except for Ryan. This was as frightening for him as a couple of times in Afghanistan.

Ryan stopped suddenly. He gave the signal, a clenched fist, to stop. Ryan stared ahead, trying to see, but the weapons' lights had destroyed his night vision. There was definitely something up ahead, something strangely bright.

Finally, Ryan turned around and whispered, "Lights up ahead." He peered at them some more. "Stationary lights."

Ryan signaled that he'd go ahead and look some more and that the rest of the Team should sit tight. He quietly moved ahead, but only got about twenty-five yards until he turned and motioned for the Team to come up to him. "Looks like an outbuilding or something," Ryan whispered.

"The rest area," Bobby said. He had been in this park before, a couple of years ago and remembered a rest area on the trail.

"Yeah," Ryan whispered, "That's what it looks like it could be."

"Let's go check it out," Pow whispered. They started toward it with Ryan still on point and a few yards ahead of them.

They got about fifty yards when Ryan suddenly gasped. "Oh God!" he said loudly. "No!"

The Team rushed up to him. Then they saw it.

Wes was hanging from the light post at the rest area, dangling and swaying in the wind. He was hanging from a rope like a criminal, like Frankie, the meth head, they hung at Pierce Point. Wes' body was absolutely still. His life had been taken out of him; it was just his body swaying on that rope. It was strangely silent, the rustling wind being the only sound.

They heard some bushes moving very close by and quickly clicked their safeties off. A person suddenly flew out of the bushes and started running away. Pow was scanning the area by looking through his Aim point red-dot sight. He saw the movement and put the red dot on the shape of the person running away.

"Boom! Boom!" Pow put a quick double-tap into the person running away. The others swung around and got some rounds off in the general direction of the movements.

Pow ran toward the person he'd shot, with Scotty and Bobby following him. Ryan headed straight for Wes.

When he got up to him, Ryan looked up and could see that Wes had been beaten. His face looked purple in the sodium lights of the rest area. He was just hanging there, limp, vacant. With a smile on his face. A smile.

Ryan grabbed a garbage can from the rest area to use to climb up to Wes. Once he got up to him, he unsuccessfully tried to find a pulse. Wes was still warm. Ryan tried again, but could not find a pulse in him. He must have been hanged just a little while ago. Wes was dead. Ryan held him.

"I should have braced you, man," Ryan cried. "I should have braced you." Ryan remembered how Wes was just standing in the back of the truck; Ryan could have done something. Ryan realized how easy it would have been to hold onto Wes, but Ryan was busy ducking the machine gun tracers. Ryan looked at Wes and remembered all they'd done together. He remembered the first time he met Wes, his rich North Carolina drawl, his overpowering love for Kelli, their plans for a baby. Ryan could see all things in life Wes would never experience – a baby, training wheels on a bike with his child, high school graduation, his child getting married, and then growing old with Kelli. Ryan was overcome with the feeling that just a few minutes ago, Wes was alive and had his whole life ahead of him. Now he was a beaten corpse swinging on a rope. His life had been taken. Taken. Stolen.

Ryan heard people coming. He turned around and pointed his rifle at the movement. It was Pow, dragging someone who was kicking and gasping but not screaming. Pow had amazing upper body strength and was dragging the person like he was a ragdoll.

Pow had a look on his face that Ryan had never seen. It was rage. Supreme rage. Calm rage, at this point, but it was going to explode any minute. The look on Pow's face was even more terrifying in the yellowish sodium light of the rest area.

Pow looked at the person he was dragging, who was a typical looking high school boy in civilian clothes. Pow said softly, "Look what I found. A piece of shit." Pow's voice was terrifyingly calm. Even the Team was afraid of what he would do next.

He threw the teenage boy onto the pavement of the rest area. The kid was bleeding from the upper left shoulder. It looked like a bullet had exited out through his throat, which explained why he wasn't screaming. .

Ryan pointed over to Wes' body. "They hung him. Fucking animals."

Ryan took out his pistol, jammed it in the teenager's mouth, which was covered in blood from the exit wound in the throat. He pointed at Wes' body and whispered, "You do this?"

Before the kid could respond, Scotty came up and said, "Don't shoot him, man. He's a prisoner. We need to take him back."

The kid was in too much pain to answer, and seemed only semi-conscious. Pow got down on the ground and searched him. He pulled something out of the kid's jacket pocket and started shaking his head.

"This better not be what I think it is," Pow said to the kid and then revealed a small video camera. Pow replayed the recording which showed a group beating, and then hanging, Wes.

"You're an independent filmmaker, huh?" Pow asked the kid, in that same terrifyingly calm voice, like they were in a casual conversation. "You think it's cool to film this kind of shit?" Pow asked with his voice rising. "So you can put it on fucking You Tube?"

"No, Pow," Scotty said. "We gotta get this prisoner out of here. Now."

Pow put the camera in his pocket. He couldn't stand to witness the footage, but the others in the unit needed to see this to see what kind of people they were up against. He was going to bring it back to base.

Pow continued to search the kid who was starting to come to

and become more lucid. He pulled out a Zero Tolerance folding knife out of the kid's pocket. It was Wes'.

"Oh, a knife collector?" Pow asked, in his casual and conversational tone. "You stole my friend's knife, dude. Now that wasn't very nice."

Scotty stood up and grabbed the unopened knife from a surprised Pow.

"Click!" The Zero Tolerance knife made its distinctive opening sound. Scotty displayed the blade to the kid to show him the knife he had stolen and then he smiled a ghoulish smile no one had ever seen from him. He had lost control of himself.

In an instant, calm and decent Scotty started thrusting and slashing with the knife, which caused a slight popping noise as it broke the skin. It was like a muffled pop of bubble wrap.

Scotty slashed every square inch of the kid. His torso, his arms, his legs. Scotty was cutting the kid to ribbons. Blood was flying everywhere. The rest of the Team stood by and watched, stunned by Scotty's savagery and the quarts of blood spurting everywhere. They couldn't believe that Scotty had gone from his usual calm self to a butcher in such short order. It was seeing Wes' Zero Tolerance – the knife that was the Team "membership card" – in the hands of that kid that put Scotty over the edge.

A few seconds into the slaughter, the kid tried to scream, but he couldn't because of the damage to his throat. The only sound he could make was a soft and raspy wail, coupled with the gurgle from the blood in his throat. It was the horrific sound of a wounded animal dying.

After the burst of slashing, Scotty momentarily regained control of himself. He stepped back and looked at the bloody mess who was a crumpled heap on the ground. The blood was purple in the sodium light, and it was everywhere. Scotty stepped back, looked at his handiwork, and picked the kid up with his left hand. With his free hand, Scotty slashed the kid's throat for good measure. Blood gushed everywhere.

He threw the motionless kid back on the cement. "You took his knife," Scotty screamed. "You shouldn't have taken his knife." Scotty just stared at the bloody shell of a former human being on the cement of the rest area. Without a move or a sound, he towered over the body, blankly staring down at what he'd just done.

Everyone was in shock. Bobby wanted in on the destruction of the fucker who had killed his friend.

"Let's hang this little bitch so his buddies can see," he said.

It was a fine idea. They took the rope off Wes' neck and gently put him on the ground. Ryan made sure to position his body so Wes could see what was happening in his honor.

They hoisted the mutilated and blood-soaked teenager up and put the noose around his neck. When they let go, the pressure of the noose caused most of the kid's remaining blood to squirt out everywhere.

"Fucking animals!" Scotty screamed. There was shrillness to his voice that no one had ever heard from him. Scotty wished he could kill the kid over and over again. He could kill him ten times over and it wouldn't feel like enough revenge.

Pow had filmed everything on the video camera. "Part two of the story," Pow said on camera as the teenager was hanging. "Part one was killing our brother, Wes. This is how the story ended, you Lima fucks. We ended it."

They all looked at Wes, who looked so peaceful. That smile. Why was he smiling?

They took turns carrying Wes out of the woods. It took forever. One guy took point, two swept every direction, and the fourth carried Wes. It took a half hour to get back to the road which was only a few hundred yards. They were beyond exhausted, physically and emotionally.

They all felt like they'd lost a brother. They would never be the same. A part of them was gone. They could all feel it: a part of them was gone, taken by these animals. Why? What good had it done to that teenage kid to hang Wes? To put it up on the internet? Why? Was it worth getting shot, stabbed, and hung? Why were people doing all this?

In between wondering why all this useless killing had happened, the Team was concentrating on getting out of the woods alive. Their weapons' lights were painting a huge "shoot me" target for a hundred yards around them. There were plenty of Limas in those woods. The Team fully expected to have to shoot their way out of the woods, and maybe lose another brother or two.

Finally, Ryan, who was on point, saw the road. He had never been so glad to see a road. The Team waited for a while and caught their breath.

"I'll go back to Bravo and get the truck down here," Ryan said. He needed to get Wes out of there so those animals wouldn't try to hurt him again. It made no sense, but it was what was driving Ryan:

get out of here.

Ryan walked down the road for … who knows how long. He used his weapon light to see and to be seen by the Bravo sentries.

"Halt!" Ryan heard a soldier say. He was hoping it wasn't a Lima, but he knew that was highly unlikely.

"I'm Ryan McDonald of the 17th Irregulars," Ryan said.

"Who's your commander?" the sentry asked.

"A guy named Grant, but you wouldn't know him," Ryan said. "Your commander is a Captain Edwards or Edmonds or some shit." Ryan was spent. He had no time for military courtesies. "Hey, quit fucking around and get the truck down here. We got a KIA and need to get the body out."

The soldier ran off to tell someone what had happened. In a minute, Ryan heard the truck approaching. The headlights lit up the area. Ryan looked at his kit and arms. Both were covered in blood.

"That fucking kid messed up my kit," Ryan said out loud even though no one was around. "Now I need to get it dry cleaned. I don't have time for that shit."

Ryan started crying at the absurdity of what he'd just said. At the absurdity of killing a teenager. At the absurdity that Wes, a bad-ass gun fighter, died in basically an accident, falling out of a truck and getting hauled away. The absurdity that Ryan was actually talking about dry cleaning a tactical vest. Everything was so absurd. This war, this Collapse, this life.

The truck came up to Ryan and he pointed down the road toward the rest of the Team. "Go get them and bring them back here," he said to the driver.

"Hop in," the driver said.

The truck returned with the Team. They had silently and solemnly put Wes in the back of the truck. The Bravo Company soldiers saluted Wes. The Team appreciated the respect.

They slowly drove the truck back to the brewery. It was the longest, quietest ride in their lives. Everyone was silently reflecting and thinking about Wes, what he'd meant to them, what all they'd done together. His southern drawl, which was so unique up in Washington State, would be irreplaceable to the group. His father, who insisted that he become a Ranger, would be proud. Wes died a hero's death, fighting bad guys and protecting the innocent.

And Kellie. Poor Kellie and their baby. He or she would never meet his or her father.

"Every New Year's Day from here on out," Ryan yelled all of a sudden to the guys in the cab, "one of us is going to spend it with Kellie and tell Wes' child what a great man he was. Is that a promise?"

No one had to even answer.

Chapter 305

"What Else Could Go Wrong?"

(January 2)

At the brewery, before word about Wes had come back, Grant was glad that he got to be the commanding officer of the 17th again now that Lieutenant Colonel Brussels had taken over command of the brewery. That was a lot less to worry about than trying to hold everything together at the brewery. Grant looked for Ted because he really couldn't do much with the 17th without Ted.

Grant found him napping. It was about 5:30 a.m. on whatever day it was. Grant had lost track of the dates, and days of the week. At this point, he only knew daytime and nighttime, and even that was getting blurry.

The 17th had taken over the third floor where the kids had stayed. There were several members of the 17th there, the ones who hadn't been put on a detail with another unit. Grant couldn't resist. For just a second, he was going to let himself lie peacefully on the cement floor and rest his eyes.

He woke up when he heard Ted saying, "Wakey, wakey, Lieutenant."

"How long was I out?" Grant asked, rubbing the sleep from his eyes.

"Two and a half hours," Ted answered. "Let's get some food." Good idea, Grant thought. He was beyond hungry, although he was so used the feeling of hunger by now that it didn't really bother him.

The sun was coming up. They went to the field kitchen and got some pancakes. Nice. Pancakes never tasted so good. Grant popped a caffeine pill and got ready for a day's worth of work. Or a night's worth. Or whatever it would end up being.

The runner came back from the copy center where the copy machines were actually working. The runner gave Grant a ream of paper and several pens. Grant neatly handwrote a small leaflet—four to one page and double-sided—that made four simple points. First, the Patriots had liberated the city. It was over. Second, civilians should stay indoors unless they had an emergency, in which case they could come to the brewery. Third, military and law enforcement of the "former authorities" could turn themselves in for consideration of a full pardon. Finally, gang members would be treated like the criminals they were. The pamphlet also said that anyone who reported a former regime member would be rewarded for assisting the Patriots. Grant had no idea if they had anything to reward informants with. He just wanted the Limas to see that they couldn't trust anyone, especially the general population.

Grant had the runner and a newly formed work detail make as many copies as possible and then cut them up into quarters for distribution.

He then spent the next half hour or so talking to his troops, making sure they'd had some sleep and some food. But, he just generally wanted to perk them up and tried to do so by telling them how important their job was, and how the 17th had made the whole brewery HQ possible Grant also told his troops how he thought they might have Olympia wrapped up in a couple weeks and maybe they could get back to Pierce Point, or maybe they'd go up to Seattle. But Grant let his irregulars know that he wouldn't volunteer the unit for any missions that weren't absolutely necessary. Individual members could volunteer for missions, but Grant wasn't going to obligate the whole unit just so he could please his superiors.

A runner came up to Grant and said, "Battalion Commander wants to see you right now!" Grant ran with the runner up to the fourth floor.

"Yes, sir," Grant said, breathlessly when he saw Brussels. "What can I do for you?"

Brussels had a pamphlet in his hand. He screamed, "Is this yours?"

"Yes, sir," Grant said, a little timidly. This wasn't going well.

"Did you clear this with me?" Brussels screamed. Everyone on the floor became quiet.

"No, sir," Grant said, getting mad. Who the fuck was this guy to question Grant's civil affairs work?

"This headquarters is under my command and you are in my headquarters," Brussels seethed. "You are under my command."

"Not really," Grant blurted out. Oh great. That wasn't very diplomatic.

"What did you say?" Brussels asked in a calm voice that showed he had the power.

"Well, sir, I'm not really under your command," Grant said. "I was ordered by Lt. Col. Hammond, Special Operations Commander, to take care of civil affairs here. I am doing that."

"What's this about pardons?" Brussels asked. That must be what was pissing him off. Either that or he needed to yell at someone just to show he was in charge. Or he was tired. Or all of these things.

"We want to get the Limas to turn themselves in," Grant said, stating the obvious.

"We?" Brussels yelled. "We do? No, Lieutenant Irregular, *you* want the Limas to turn themselves in. *I* want to kill them."

Oh, so that was it – a difference in viewpoint about reconciliation after the victory. It was the old American Revolution versus French Revolution thing.

Might as well go for broke, Grant thought. He knew he'd have to win this argument with Brussels, or all he'd been working for would be lost.

"That would not be the most effective strategy from a civil affairs perspective," Grant said.

Brussels exploded. "Oh, Mr. Civil Affairs, tell me again what civil affairs unit you were in? What training you've had for this?"

"None, sir," Grant said with a little edge in his voice, feeling himself getting pissed. He wasn't used to being screamed at and his exhaustion lowered his inhibitions. People were usually pretty happy to have him around. "But I have been put in charge of this, of civil affairs, and I'm doing my job, sir."

Now Brussels was being challenged in front of his men. Grant wished he hadn't done that, but it was too late now.

"Get me Hammond at Boston Harbor," Brussels screamed to a radio operator.

About thirty silent and tense seconds later Lt. Col. Hammond was on the radio.

"Yes, what is it?" he asked.

"Did you tell some lieutenant in some irregular unit to do all the civil affairs here?" Brussels asked.

"Yes, Myron," Hammond said, not knowing that other soldiers were listening. Since they were of the same rank, Hammond could call Brussels by his first name, "Matson knows his shit. He's done some great stuff since this all started."

"This Matson guy has put out a pamphlet saying Limas will be considered for pardons," Brussels hissed. "Did you know anything about that?"

It was silent for a moment.

"No," Hammond said. Grant's heart sank.

"But it makes a hell of a lot of sense to me, Myron," Hammond added, speaking peer-to-peer to Brussels. "Let him do his thing. Besides, I know for a fact that the Interim Governor is a big fan of pardons. It's how the General wants to do it, too. Mercy, not a bloodbath. Copy?"

"I don't appreciate your irregular people fucking with my operations here," Brussels said. That's about all he had.

Hammond was used to his special operations activities making regular units mad. It happened all the time.

"Want me to get the General on the horn?" Hammond asked without any emotion. Hammond knew that the man who didn't get emotional was perceived to be the one in control.

"Not necessary," Brussels said abruptly. "I have a city to pacify." That was the end of that.

Brussels looked at Grant and said, "Watch yourself, Lieutenant. Now go pass out your little pamphlets while we fight a real war."

Fuck you, Grant thought. You idiot regular units will be fighting insurgents in this town for months unless the Limas have an incentive to give up. Dumbass.

"Yes, sir," Grant said and then stood there waiting to be dismissed.

"Dismissed," Brussels snarled.

When they were out of earshot of everyone, Ted pulled Grant aside and whispered, "You know he's going to try to motherfuck you at every turn, right? You do know that?"

"I do now," Grant said. He knew that he'd have numerous challenges to his reconciliation mission. He just never thought it would be someone on his own side, and so early in the process.

"What else could go wrong?" Grant asked. Then he saw Mark's truck pull up. And he looked in the back.

Chapter 306

Ringleader

(January 2)

"On your knees! Hands to your sides!" screamed the man in military contractor clothes and gear.

Nancy Ringman wondered who he was talking to. She looked around. There was no one there.

"Me?" she asked in bewilderment.

"On your knees!" the man screamed. "Yes, you!"

Nancy fell to her knees. The man's rifle, one of those assault weapons, looked terrifying to her. She started to cover her face with her hands.

"Hands to your sides – now!" he screamed.

She froze. She could not move to save her life.

She heard a click and, without knowing anything about guns, realized it must be a safety to the gun. She'd seen that in movies. This man was about to shoot her. Suddenly, she realized she needed to put her hands to her sides, which she quickly did. Her hands were shaking uncontrollably.

"Spud Six, Oscar Romeo, got a prisoner here by the football field," he said without pushing a button on a radio mic. He had a voice activated Quietpro headset for his radio.

"Roger, Oscar Romeo," a voice said into the man's earpiece. "On the way."

"How many of you are here?" the man yelled to Nancy.

She couldn't talk. She was so scared that her mouth wouldn't move. The man gave her one more second to talk before he would seriously consider her to be a decoy or ambush bait.

"Spud Six, Oscar Romeo," he said into his voice-activated radio, "Prisoner won't say how many more are here. Expect lots of bad guys. Smoke 'em if you gotta."

Hearing that made Nancy realize these soldiers or contractors or whatever were deadly serious – and that they considered her a threat. She felt herself losing bowel control. She felt so embarrassed and helpless as she realized she has just shit her pants.

"No more," she said meekly to the man.

"What?" he yelled at her, as he was moving with his gun trained on her head. He wanted to be mobile so he'd be harder to shoot.

"No more people here," she said a little louder. "I'm the only one."

"Right," he said dismissively.

"Prisoner says she's the only one," he said into the radio. "Whatever. Expect bad guys."

"If there is anyone else here," he said to Nancy, "You'll hear a loud noise and a tremendous burning sensation as I shoot you." He let that sink in. "It'll hurt. A lot."

Nancy started crying.

"So," he said, "I'll ask again: how many others are here?"

"I'm it," Nancy said between sobs. "Everyone else left."

"Where did they go?" the man asked.

"I dunno," she said. "They just left. This place isn't safe."

"Like the football field?" he screamed. "Yeah, it's pretty dangerous out there. We know what you guys did." He wasn't going to tell her that the Patriots had captured several of the Clover Park guards who confessed to the massacre at the football field. He was one of the Patriot special operations troops behind the JBLM line who conducted raids and executed other impromptu missions, like liberating prison camps. He'd seen some awful things, but a mass killing like this was the worst he'd heard of.

"We had to make room for refugees," Nancy blurted out, realizing that she was incriminating herself. While she suspected this man was a teabagger, she still couldn't fully believe they were operating behind the JBLM line. That wasn't supposed to happen.

"So then, you were part of the football field incident?" the man asked, thanking his lucky stars that he seemed to be getting a confession from this prisoner.

"I didn't do any of it," she said. "Others did."

"Why are you here?" the man asked. He turned when he heard people running up to his position. They were his teammates.

"I," she started to say and then the other contractors started talking to the man about other threats and where to search next.

"You what?" the man finally said, after talking to his teammates.

"I told them to do it," she said. She realized she shouldn't have said that, but she wanted to get it off her chest. She immediately felt better.

"Spud Six, Oscar Romeo," the man said, "I got the ringleader."

Chapter 307

"Let's Go Fix This State"

(January 2)

Patriot EPU agent Mike Turner heard what he'd been waiting for ... for years.

"Carrot cake."

That's what the radio operator at the Think Farm said.

Mike felt a surge of adrenaline when he heard those two magical words.

"Cream cheese frosting," Mike responded into the radio, which was the encoded reply showing that he received the code phrase and would carry out the mission.

This was it. Mike's years of watching the government slowly imploding. The corruption. The outright theft. Putting innocent people in jail. Letting guilty ones go. Maintaining a secret membership in Oath Keepers and worrying about getting caught, then defecting from the State Patrol's Executive Protection Unit, or EPU, a few months ago and becoming a guerilla behind enemy lines. All of it. It all came down to "carrot cake" which was the code phrase for the order to bring the Interim Governor and his staff in to Olympia. It meant the Patriots had taken the city and were holding it. That they would start governing and fixing things. Everything Mike had risked his life for during the past several years was finally here.

It was 11:32 p.m. Time to get going while it was still dark. Mike alerted his fellow former EPU members that it was time to go. They woke the families, who had been expecting this.

They'd heard the faint gunfire and explosions in Olympia for the past two days. In fact, they were getting nervous that the Patriots hadn't taken the city yet. They were relieved to get word that they had to get into cars and drive into a city where lots of people wanted to kill them. That was a relief compared to the thought that Olympia had not been taken, which would mean they would be hiding out on the Prosser Farm forever. Or worse.

The Interim Governor, Ben Trenton, and his chief of staff, Tom Foster, would go into Olympia with Ben's director of legislative affairs, Brian Jenkins. Also joining them would be Carly Johnson. She would be the assistant director of legislative affairs. She risked her life to get the EPU out to the Prosser Farm so all of this could happen.

Wives, and especially children, would stay behind at the Prosser Farm. They would be protected there. To everyone's knowledge, no one other than the immediate neighbors knew who was staying out there. That had been a miracle, but hiding on a farm where all the neighbors were relatives made that possible. The presence of the EPU agents and their sophisticated equipment, to the extent anyone even saw them, was explained with the story that Tom Foster had a rich relative who had paid for a private personal security detail. Rich people were hiring lots of former military and law enforcement people, and sometimes current ones, to protect them. That seemingly outlandish story made perfect sense in the insane world of post-Collapse America.

After everyone was awake, there were quick goodbyes. The wives, Karen Jenkins in particular, were scared. They knew their husbands were in amazingly good hands, but still it was hard to say, "Okay, go off into a war zone and become the enemy's biggest target for assassination. See you in a while. I won't worry."

The kids were taking it pretty well. They were mostly older, around middle school age and a few in high school. They had been told for quite a while that their dads would be leaving to go back to Olympia and do some important things—things that would allow the kids to go back to their normal lives. To live in their own homes, to go to school, to not have people with guns around. Well, that last one wouldn't change. These kids, given who their parents were, would have EPU agents around them for the rest of their lives. But, overall, the kids' lives would be back to normal when their dads could go back to Olympia and fix all the bad things that had happened.

Packing took no time at all because they had all their bags pre-loaded. Ben changed out of sweatpants and into jeans. Brad, the chief of the EPU unit, didn't want to waste any time with apparel changes.

"Governor, no one will see you arriving," Brad said. "We have suits your size coming from the Think Farm. You'll have a tailor there at the capitol to finish them off. You'll look fine." Brad was used to vain dignitaries that he had to guard. Ben wasn't vain—he was amazingly humble, in fact—but he *was* a politician.

Ben smiled. "I'm not getting into jeans for fashion," he said. "My sweats won't hold a holster belt." Ben showed Brad the Sig he was carrying and Brad smiled. A holster belt was an acceptable reason to make an apparel change, especially given what they would be doing in the next few hours.

The families gathered in the living room and just stood there silently. They didn't know what else they were supposed to do. They'd never had to watch their fathers and husbands leave with a personal security detail to a battlefield before. Not many people had.

The plan was for Brad and Jerry Schafer, the EPU agent who was a former Marine, to accompany the "principals," as protectees were called. Jerry would drive. They would travel light, with just two EPU agents, but it was just for a while and then they'd pick up an escort detail.

Two EPU agents, Mike Turner, the coms guy, and Chrissy Mendez would stay. They needed coms back at the farm and Chrissy, besides being a spectacular gun fighter, was very good at calming kids … and wives.

"Okay, let's go," Brad said. He looked at the families. "You'll be in extremely good hands with Mike and Chrissy." There was a tradition in the EPU that the protectees could call their agents by their first names instead of "Trooper Turner" or "Trooper Mendez."

"Bye," the kids and wives said one by one. Everyone got a final hug.

"Let's go," said Brad. He had radioed in to the first checkpoint that they'd be there in a few minutes and he didn't want to be late. Being late in a personal security detail was a big deal.

The protectees and agents got into one of the two EPU vehicles, a black armored Chevy Suburban. Very nice. Brad had stolen it during the chaos of the Collapse. Mike had stolen the com van, too. With all the budget cuts right at the end, Brad and Mike, and most of the other state employees who weren't politically connected, hadn't been paid in a few months, and what salaries they got were totally eaten up by the runaway inflation. So they decided to settle up with the state by taking a couple of vehicles. Fair trade, they thought.

Jerry started up the Suburban. A full tank of gas. Of course. Tires inflated to the correct pressure. A map of the route for the driver and navigator. Radios set to the correct frequencies, a notebook with backup frequencies, and plenty of charged spare radio batteries. Plenty of firearms and ammunition, and a bulletproof vest for each protectee. Of course.

They took off down the long driveway and looked at the Prosser Farm. For the last time?

Of course not, Ben reassured himself. The Prosser Farm would hopefully be a museum in a few years. Showing where the Governor had to hide out during the Collapse. Hopefully. If everything worked out. It had so far, Ben reassured himself.

Ben had never ridden in the Suburban before. It was a smooth ride. There was a strong vibe about being in the "war wagon," as they called that Suburban. It made them feel like they really were special, worthy of a personal security detail. It was really cool, Ben had to admit. He still couldn't fully believe he was the Interim Governor … but riding in the war wagon made it very believable.

Brad was working the radio. He looked at his watch, "ETA four minutes." Ben recognized the voice on the radio answering him as one of the Delphi guards.

The plan was that they would go from the farm to the Delphi guards. A Patriot escort would be waiting there who would take the Suburban into the capitol. The actual capitol campus was still a little hairy with some remaining holdouts barricaded in individual rooms. The Patriots were having to go room to room—and closet to closet, and heating duct to heating duct—to clear the buildings on the capitol campus and the buildings within sniping range of the campus, but the Patriots had a place for the new Governor and his staff to stay temporarily.

The Suburban pulled up to the Delphi guards, whose eyes popped wide at the sight of the war wagon. They had already been impressed with the Patriot escort that had arrived a few minutes before. An armored Humvee with a .50 caliber machine gun and three pickup trucks with serious-looking, very well-armed soldiers. They had kit and beards. Maybe they were contractors, but there was something about them that made the guards believe they were in a military unit of some kind, maybe Special Forces or something.

When the Suburban stopped, Brian asked, "Are we supposed to get out?"

"No," Brad said. "Please don't get out until we tell you to. Ever." He seemed very stern and serious.

Brian nodded. Of course. He'd never had a personal security detail before. He didn't know how it worked.

Brian noticed that one of the pick-ups was maneuvering to the left of the Suburban and another was on the right. The third one was behind the Suburban and the Hummer was in front. They started to move.

The trucks stayed alongside the Suburban until they got to the on ramp to Highway 101, which was only wide enough for one vehicle to safely travel. There, they peeled off and went to the rear. The

Suburban accelerated with the Hummer in front setting the pace. When they got onto the highway, the left and right pick-ups zoomed past them and resumed their positions on both sides of the Suburban. Brian felt very safe.

There were no other vehicles on the road. The lights were off in most homes and businesses. The power was on, and some homes and businesses had their lights on, but most were dark. They were probably hiding out and trying not to draw attention from the bands of Limas and Patriots roaming the streets. Not to mention the gangs. They could be out in full force, Brian thought. What he didn't know was that now the gangs were hiding. Last he knew, when he was still in Olympia, was that they were tough guys out strutting around and terrorizing unarmed citizens. There had been nothing for them to hide from. But now they were being hunted down and killed one by one by Patriots. They weren't so tough anymore and weren't showing themselves.

"Okay, Governor," Tom said, getting into his new role as Chief of Staff, "What's your first message when we get to your new offices?"

"I thank everyone for making this possible," Ben said. "The EPU, the troops, the civilians. I let everyone know that I'm only the Interim Governor, that fair elections are our first priority once order is restored."

"Excellent," Tom said. They had worked together for so long it was easy for them to go over things like this.

"Brad, correct me if I'm wrong," Ben said, "but we still don't have Seattle and the surrounding metropolitan areas, right?"

"Correct, Governor," Brad said, without taking his eyes off the road. "We have Olympia, all of rural Washington, and all of Eastern Washington. Seattle is a little patch of enemy territory. Once you get settled, one of your first meetings will be with your Commandant of the State Guard to get a briefing on the military situation. You are the commander in chief of the State Guard."

Ben let that sink in. "Who, by the way, is my Commandant?" Ben asked.

Brad told him the name of someone Ben had never heard of.

"Oh, okay," Ben said. "I guess he's doing a good job since we're going to Olympia." It seemed odd to him that someone as important as his Commandant would be a stranger, but then Ben realized he wasn't really in charge of the state. He had been picked to be the interim Governor but couldn't leave the Prosser Farm. He trusted that the Patriots, probably the Think Farm, would be picking good people. Ben, while he was a leader, was not a control freak. That being said, he was still a little surprised that he didn't know his Commandant. But they were putting the state back together on the fly, so he expected lots of seat-of-the-pants governing in the beginning.

The trip in to the capitol area went remarkably fast because they were speeding. The pick-ups on the sides were doing a great job keeping the Suburban perfectly shielded from attack although, with the highway empty, it wasn't hard to keep pace like that. There were no cars to get in the way.

"Boom! Boom! Crack! Crack!" A line of red tracers went up from their right and over into some buildings ahead of them.

"Blue!" Brad yelled into the radio. They sped up. Everyone in the Suburban was scared, except Brad and Jerry.

"Yellow two," a voice said on the radio. Brad relaxed.

"That was nothing," Brad reported to the protectees. "Just some fighting, not aimed at us."

In a minute or two, they were off the highway and onto the exit. They took the exit fast and raced through the red light at the intersection, knowing that being off the highway was a dangerous time because they would be moving more slowly and exposed to numerous buildings that made excellent cover for an ambush.

The street took them past the brewery which was blocked off.

"There's your military headquarters," Brad said to Ben, pointing to the brewery. There were vehicles and soldiers everywhere around it.

"We're going there?" Ben asked. "To have me, you know, talk to the troops?" Ben was still trying to feel comfortable in his new role as commander in chief.

"No, Governor," Brad said. "We want to keep your arrival under wraps for a while. We have this all planned out. We'll get you in front of the troops, soon and often." Brad's protectees were usually elected officials. He learned early on that politicians like them loved to talk to crowds, even when it was dangerous. It made his job of protecting them harder, but it was part of the deal.

They went on the side streets around the brewery and down towards the capitol. The lead driver gave the passwords at the military checkpoints and they went right through. It was extremely well planned and orchestrated.

The rain had stopped but everything was still wet. There were burned out pick-ups and a few military vehicles. There were boarded up buildings, covered in graffiti, surrounded by trash and debris. They hadn't been in Olympia for months. They had no idea how bad it had become.

"We're cleaning up this garbage, right?" Ben asked. "Can we get some Loyalist prisoners to do that?"

"Look at you, Governor," Tom said with a smile. "You're governing."

It hit all of them. They really were governing now, after all the bitching they'd done about the former government. Now it was up to them to get things done, to fix things. They finally got what they wanted: a chance to do things their way, the constitutional way. But now, any failures were on them. They couldn't blame the "powers that be" any longer. That was them now.

They had inherited problems almost too vast to imagine. It was a civil war, although they never used that term because it didn't fit very well. A "civil war," everyone thought, harkening back to history, was a large army of blue and gray troops fighting big battles. This wasn't. that. It was a breakdown with one side trying to hold onto power and another side trying to clean things up. There weren't large battles. Instead, it only took a slight nudge to topple a broken and battered government that could barely stand up. To call it a "civil war" was an exaggeration.

They also inherited a complete breakdown of the economy. Economy? What economy? Gangs stealing everything in sight wasn't an "economy." Handing out FCards, usually based on political loyalty, wasn't an "economy." Commandeering truckloads of food wasn't an "economy." The closest thing to an "economy" was people doing little tiny odd jobs to get paid in food or gasoline or ammunition.

But that would be the basis for restoring the economy. People, at least some of them, would still work. They would still trade things. That was how the American economy recovered after the devastating Revolutionary War. It would be the basis now for a complete rebuild. No more government-controlled economy. No more crushing taxes and regulation. The briefing binders in the Suburban were full of ways to make sure the government didn't resume its old ways of taxing and controlling. And destroying.

"Winter kill-off," Brian said looking at all the garbage, burned-out vehicles, and boarded up buildings. "You know, like a field at the end of winter. Everything, including the weeds, is killed off, which makes it possible to plant seeds that will grow in the spring and summer. It still takes constant work, making sure the weeds don't come back, but you start with a clean slate."

As they passed through more destruction of their formerly nice city, Brian said, "This is our clean slate."

Everyone sat and thought about that. The destruction, especially the destroyed vehicles and burned out buildings, got worse the closer they got to the capitol.

"This area looks familiar," Carly said as they went down Capitol Boulevard toward the old WAB building.

"It should," Brad said as they turned in front of the brick WAB building. The headlights from the Suburban and convoy showed that the WAB building had burn marks on the outside of its beautiful brick walls. The windows were smashed out. More garbage. It was caked up against the walls of the building like a snowdrift.

The parking lot was full of vehicles, some military and many pick-ups. There were dozens of soldiers and more of those contractor-looking guys, like the ones in the pick-ups accompanying them. The lights were on in the building.

"Here's your temporary headquarters, Governor," Brad said. "We still have some cleanup to do at the capitol, but we should have it ready for you in a few hours, maybe a day."

Ben, Tom, Brian, and Carly had forgotten just how destroyed the WAB building had been. It was scarred and ugly, and was a symbol to them of how destroyed the State of Washington itself had become. A formerly beautiful and functioning thing, like that historic building, was now a trashed shell of what it had been.

The WAB building had been intentionally selected as the temporary headquarters. The political people back at the Think Farm wanted to put the new Governor and his staff in the proper frame of mind when they returned to Olympia. They wanted the new leadership to realize how all the formerly good things had been destroyed. And nothing symbolized that more for the former WAB people than the trashing of their beautiful building. Besides, the WAB building was only a few blocks from the capitol and the security people said it would work as temporary headquarters.

As the Suburban stopped, the occupants now knew better than to get out without being given the okay, though it was weird to just sit in a car after it stopped.

Brad was checking things out and working on the radio. Finally he said, "Some people will be opening your doors. Let them. And then quickly follow them into the building. Let them be your shields. That's their jobs. They're all volunteers." He wanted to, but didn't, say, "They're your bullet catchers."

All the passenger doors opened at the same time. There were

military people and those same contractor-looking guys. Everyone got out of the Suburban and walked quickly into the building. Sure enough, the soldiers and others formed a shield around them as they went in.

The place was cleaned up and orderly, not like the last time Tom had been there. And it had a functioning office. There was even a receptionist who they didn't recognize at the reception desk. There were other obvious Think Farm staff members. Ben recognized some of them as the political people he used to hang out with socially. They were the "known conservatives" who had to go underground when the Collapse started.

When they walked in to the lobby, the receptionist said excitedly, "Welcome back, Governor." Ben looked around to see who she was talking to. Oh. It was him. He acted like he knew that she meant him, although it was pretty obvious he didn't.

Brad led them into Tom's old office. It had new office furniture—well, new to them, but obviously old furniture from somewhere else. It looked like an office someone could actually sit in and get some work done like things were normal again.

Ben, Tom, Brian, and Carly were blown away. They had been cooped up alone at the Prosser Farm for months and had no idea all the preparations that had been going on for them. Carly had told them that the Think Farm was buzzing day and night with planning for the eventual victory and then governing, but that was just vague generalities. Now they could see tangible proof that the Think Farm had planned everything and they were ready to govern.

Tom started to sit at the desk in his old office. It felt natural.

"Uh, Tom," Brad said, "I believe this is Gov. Trenton's office."

Everyone laughed. Tom was embarrassed. That would be one of the other changes he would need to get used to. Tom's former employee, Ben, was now his boss.

Tom extended his hand to Ben as if to say, "Here. Sit at your desk." So Ben did just that. He sat in the comfortable office chair and observed all the people in the room who were looking at him with joy on their face. He was their Governor. Him. He remembered the drunken conversation he'd had with Grant Matson while watching the Seahawks in the 2005 Super Bowl about the insanity of thinking Ben could ever be the governor.

Ben couldn't smile, though when he thought about Grant. He wondered if Grant was still alive since he was a "prepper" and had that awesome cabin and all those guns. But, he was also on the POI list.

Ben wondered if Grant had been picked up, maybe never making it to his cabin.

That was the bittersweet nature of all this, Ben thought. There was the sweetness of something wonderful, like being the governor and having a chance to fix the state. But it was at the cost of bitter things, like whatever happened to Grant and all the others.

Everyone in the room—staff from the Think Farm, Brad and Jerry the EPU agents, Tom, Brian, and Carly—was looking at Ben with a huge smile. Ben, sitting in that desk had been what they'd worked for, and risked their lives for, for months. Years, actually, counting the risks they were taking before the Collapse by being "known conservatives" or Oath Keepers.

Someone started clapping and soon, everyone joined in. Ben couldn't take it. They were clapping for him, but he didn't deserve it. They did, all those people who sacrificed for him to be able to sit in that chair. Ben stood up and started clapping. He started to tear up.

Ben couldn't stand it any longer. He was not worthy of applause. He walked from behind the desk and went up to Brad and Jerry and hugged them. Tom, Brian, and Carly joined in. Pretty soon, the Think Farm staff was in a big huddle, too. Everyone was crying.

After a while, Ben realized he needed to project the image of a calm decision maker, not a crying man. So he said, "Okay it's time to get to work." The huddle broke up and Ben thanked everyone before going to his desk.

"Let's go fix this state."

Chapter 308

Under Arrest

(January 2)

"What's your name?" the man asked Nancy Ringman, this time in a softer tone because she'd just admitted to being the ringleader. He already had what he needed on her. Besides, she was an overweight woman in her sixties. She wasn't exactly a tactical threat. But it was a little after midnight at a big school facility so there could be threats everywhere.

"Nancy," she said timidly, starting to realize what was happening. She was being captured by the teabaggers. This was the most terrifying thing that could happen to her. She had heard stories about what the so-called "Patriots" did to prisoners.

"Nancy what?" the man asked, in a kind, almost a sympathetic, tone.

She started to give her last name and then it hit her: she was guilty. She'd done horrible things. Sure, the people under the football field were teabaggers and they needed the room at Clover Park for the good people who needed a place to stay. But they were people and she ordered them to be ... she couldn't finish that thought.

"Ring..." she started to say.

"Ringleader?" the man asked.

Then she fully realized what she'd done. She was the ringleader. She had been a moment away from killing herself when the soldiers came. She might as well have the teabaggers do it for her at this point.

"Ringman," she said. "My name is Nancy Ringman and I ordered the killings." She felt a biggest sigh of relief of her entire life.

The man was silent. He was trained to let people confess without interruption.

"Thank you, Nancy," the man said. "My name is Chad. Stephenson. My friends call me 'Otter.'" He was giving her a tidbit of personal information as a goodwill offering. This helped build rapport with a suspect.

Nancy started crying again at the thought of whether she could call him "Otter." She didn't feel worthy of being his friend and calling him that because of what she'd done. Finally, she summoned up the strength to talk to him.

"What's going to happen to me, Mr. Stephenson?"

Otter noted that her use of his last name meant she didn't trust him as a friend. That's okay, he thought. Whatever works.

"You're under arrest, Nancy," he said. "We need to find out what happened here. Can you help me with that, Nancy?"

She was still on her knees with her hands at her sides. Her head was down, and she stared at the hard concrete below her.

She looked up meekly at Otter and said, "Sir, I need to stand up. My knees hurt. This concrete is killing me."

"A couple more minutes," Otter said. "Can you do that for me, Nancy?"

Still looking up at him, she nodded.

"Thanks, Nancy," he said. "We'll get you out of here soon, okay?"

She was relieved. These teabaggers weren't so bad after all. So far, at least. She had the oddest feeling that, even though he was pointing that terrifying gun at her, Otter wasn't going to shoot her. She started to realize that he was pointing it at her because he didn't know if she had a gun herself.

Nancy heard some people running up to her as Otter was saying "Over here" into his radio. She was looking up at him and swerved her head to the left where she heard people coming. They were more soldiers like Otter, dressed in military contractor clothing.

"Got her covered," one of the other soldiers said.

"Copy," Otter said.

Suddenly, Nancy was scared again. She had just started to feel like she could let her guard down, but now there were other people pointing guns at her. She felt like the safe minute or two she and Otter had together was over.

"This is Nancy Ringman," Otter announced to other soldiers. "She told me she ordered the..." he hesitated to say "killings" because that might spook her. "She ordered the events at the football field."

Nancy looked down at the ground in shame.

Seeing that her eyes were down, Otter allowed himself to smile to his teammates.

Chapter 309

"It Will Show Everyone the Legitimate Authorities Are Still in Charge"

(January 2)

Ron Spencer grabbed his shotgun. He was half asleep on the couch at almost midnight. He slept there when he thought someone could be trying to break in, which was always lately.

He heard it again. There was a knock at the door, a timid knock. A "sorry to wake you" knock. If this was a home invasion, it was by the most polite people.

"Who is it?" Ron yelled.

"Judy Kilmer," a woman's voice said. It sounded like her. She was the former administrative law judge who lived in the neighborhood. Everyone was a "former" whatever they were before the Collapse. Now, Judy held hearings for prisoners a few hours a week which got her a big, fat FCard.

"What do you want?" Ron yelled. He didn't like Judy. She was one of those typical government workers in this neighborhood, fully integrated into the system. She was one of its minions. For years before the Collapse, she had screwed people on a regular basis with the little administrative hearings she performed. She was part of the kangaroo courts that let the government take things from people, but gave them a "hearing" so they felt like it was somewhat fair process. No one could ever explain why the government won 99.5% of the "fair" administrative hearings.

"We need to talk," Judy said through the door, trying not to yell and wake people up.

"It's the middle of the night," Ron replied, but he was already awake, as was most of his family by now. It was hard enough to get any rest with a war going on all around you, and now this.

"We need to talk," Judy repeated. "I have important information for you."

Ron would open the door to get some important information, unless this was the Carlos Cabal and some ambush, which it very well could be. Ron had been expecting an ambush any time. It was so weird that the Carlos Cabal—Carlos the FCorps guy, Ron Maldonado his right hand man, and Scott Baker the Lima snitch—had all taken off when the shooting started. They must know something Ron didn't.

Ron gripped his shotgun. This might be the big fight he was expecting. He was actually relieved that it was happening. Living in constant fear of being attacked was brutal. It was no way to live. Might as well get this over with.

Ron had a plan for this. He had hours a day on his hands with nothing to do but think of things just like this.

"Just a minute," Ron said to the door. "I need to get dressed."

He was already fully dressed and even had his shoes on. Sherri hated it when he wore shoes in the house, but she understood that they might need to run out of the house with no warning, so now the whole family wore their shoes inside, even to bed. The floors were taking a beating, but it was worth it.

Ron ran upstairs and told Sherri to get her gun and be ready to get the kids out. "Just like the plan," he said as he ran out of their bedroom. He heard Sherri running to the kids' rooms.

Ron ran downstairs and out the back sliding glass door. He ran around the house toward the front door and stopped at the bushes at the front of the house. He saw Judy at the door, illuminated by the porch light. She appeared to be alone.

At first, he wanted to run back in the house and let Judy in because he didn't want to leave someone waiting at the door. Proper manners were that you didn't leave someone waiting at your door. You let them in. Ron started to run back into the house so as not leave his guest waiting.

Guest? This bitch? Who had sided with Nancy Kingman early on when the weenies were trying to take over the neighborhood? The same Judy who wanted to get rid of the guards and ridiculed Ron for having guns? The same Judy who seemed to have plenty on her family's FCard because she was a "judge"? A judge who made a living from signing the paperwork that let the government steal from people and put them in jail just to maintain their power? This person deserved courtesy from Ron? Courtesy that might cost him and his family their lives from an ambush?

He successfully fought the urge to let the waiting guest in the door and just stood there watching her. She was still alone and there were no movements of any kind around her. She wasn't looking back or whispering to anyone. She was either truly alone or was a magnificent actress and highly trained assassin. Ron laughed to himself. He knew which was more likely.

He started to move from the bush he was behind to one that was closer to the front door. He was moving out away from the house so he was more and more behind Judy. He couldn't believe she didn't hear him. But, then again, he had been out spray painting graffiti in the night and had become very good at moving slowly and using cover. It was slightly windy and that made it hard to hear tiny little sounds of bushes rustling.

Pretty soon, he was several yards behind Judy and had his shotgun pointed right at her back.

"Okay," Ron said out loud, causing Judy to jump, "what do you want to talk about?"

Judy was looking around for Ron, looking at the front door. She had no idea he was behind her. Ron enjoyed seeing her terrified.

"Over here," he said. After locating him, she nervously looked at the shotgun. She thought guns "just went off" and could explode at any given moment. They frightened her.

"What do you want?" Ron asked gruffly. She had woken him and his family up, and she was a Loyalist bitch.

"Carlos, Ron, and Scott are coming back at dawn to get you," Judy whispered.

This was simultaneously a surprise to Ron and perfectly expected. It was a surprise because no one had ever told him people were coming to attack his family; it was expected because he'd spent hours planning for this. But hearing it made it real.

"Why are you telling me this?" Ron asked. He didn't necessarily believe her, but was curious why she was telling him this.

"For you and your family," Judy said, stunned that anyone would ask why she was warning them.

"Judy," Ron said, "you're not exactly a friend of mine. You're a Loyalist. I'm not. You are part of the shitty system that caused all this." Hearing that the Patriots had taken the capitol earlier in the day gave Ron a sudden burst of confidence to speak his mind. He kept going, because he'd bottled it up for so long. "You have a fully stocked FCard while I have to scratch out food for my family. I'm not really interested in your pure motives."

Judy was stunned. She was a "judge." No one ever talked to her that way. But she was hurt that Ron was questioning her motives.

"Your kids," Judy said, still stunned, "your adorable kids. I don't want anything to happen to them."

Ron couldn't help himself with Judy. He had held back on the truth for so long it was like an avalanche now.

"It might be true, Judy, that you don't want anything to happen to my kids, but 'teabaggers' like me need to go to one of your TDF concentration camps. The camps run by your little friend, Nancy Ringman. Nope, Judy, I'm not buying that you care about me or my family."

Judy was absolutely floored. She had expected to be treated like a hero for risking arrest to warn the Spencers. If the legitimate authorities caught her out after curfew, she'd lose her FCard. This was the most courageous she'd ever been in her entire life. Her heroic moment wasn't turning out like she'd thought.

Judy just stood there in the cold on Ron's front porch, unable to speak, staring at a man with a gun, which was against the law to possess, her judge mind started to tell her.

Ron was starting to sense that Judy might actually be sincere. Or, again, she was a magnificent actress. He thought he'd test her.

"Why did you really come here, Judy?" Ron asked. He knew that the first thing people blurted out was often the truth.

"I was just trying to keep my job," flew out of her mouth. "I'm not really a Loyalist. I'm not. I have just been doing what I needed to do keep my job and my FCard. I didn't want any trouble. Things were changing so fast. Everything got crazy. I didn't know what to do. I just did what everyone else was doing." She started to cry.

"I'm sorry," Judy whimpered. "I'm sorry for what I've done." She had her face in her hands and was crying loudly.

Ron was a sucker for a crying woman. There was something genetic about it. Ron relaxed his grip on his shotgun.

Then he regained his senses. He swung around and swept the area with his shotgun. A hysterically crying woman would be a great trigger for an ambush. He swept some more as Judy had her face in her hands. There was no one. She really was alone.

He started walking up to her, with his shotgun lowered, but ready to point and aim instantly.

"Let's go inside," he said and she quietly followed him inside.

"I hope I didn't wake your family," she sobbed as they got inside.

"Too late," Sherri said from the living room, where she stood with a revolver in her hands.

The sight of the gun startled Judy. Those were strictly illegal. Judy wondered if her FCard would be taken away for even being the same house as a gun.

Ron offered Judy a seat on the couch. "Okay," he said, still not entirely convinced that this wasn't a scam or ambush of some kind, "what is it that you want to tell us?"

Judy had felt miserably guilty for weeks. It welled up in her and was pouring out right now. She started her confession by repeating how she was just doing her job. She spent several minutes rationalizing why she went along with the government.

"I was just trying to help people," Judy said. Yeah, Ron thought, trying not to roll his eyes. She was trying to "help" people by presiding over "fair" hearings that took everything away from them? By accepting all the benefits of system that took things from people? Ron wasn't persuaded by Judy's ramblings, but was letting her get it out of her system so he could find out about the supposed Carlos Cabal raid coming at dawn.

"I was just following the law," Judy stated. Ron almost asked if Judy ever thought to question the laws she was following, but he didn't want to get into a philosophical debate. He wanted information that could save his family's lives. He'd put up with the left-wing babble for a little longer if it meant getting that information.

"So that's when I decided I had to come over here and tell you," Judy finally said. That was Ron's cue to find out what really mattered.

"Tell me about what Carlos is planning," Ron said patiently, relieved that she finally was telling him something he cared about. He motioned for Sherri to take the kids back into their rooms. They didn't need to see one of their neighbors describing how some more of their neighbors were trying to kill them.

"Well," Judy said, defensively, "he and I talk," referring to Carlos. Ron let that go. Judy talked to Carlos, Ron wanted to say, because they were two Loyalist peas in a pod. A "Lima bean" Ron joked to himself. Humor was his coping mechanism these days

"Apparently," Judy said in a whisper, "the tea-bag..." she corrected herself, "the Patriots have taken the capitol." Ron grinned. Yes, we have, Ron wanted to say. And, Ron thought, that's why you're here, you sniveling little bitch. You're here so the "teabaggers" don't haul you out and shoot you. And stopping by my house is your desperate plan to stay alive.

"Carlos, Rex, and Scott got scared," Judy said.

"Why would they be scared?" Ron asked sarcastically. "They're the 'legitimate authorities.'" He was having too much fun.

Judy crinkled her face and scowled. She didn't appreciate the smartass comment. She was used to being the judge, where no one got to be sarcastic to her. "I'm trying," she said, "to help you. Can you just let me talk?" She was coming out of her crying and turning back into the bitch she was. Oh well, Ron thought. Who cares if she's a bitch? She might have useful information.

"They're scared," Judy continued, "because on Christmas morning they had black 'L's painted on their doors." She whispered, "I think that means 'Loyalist.'"

"That's what I've heard," Ron said, trying not to smile, though the tone of his voice did the smiling for him.

"When the attack started," she said, referring to the New Year's offensive, "they left to go to the capitol and help. They turned around when they saw all the tea…"

"Patriot?" Ron said sarcastically.

"Patriot soldiers," Judy said. "They came back here a few hours ago and then left. They said they're going to come and get you."

"How do you know all this?" Ron knew that Judy had talked with them, but wanted to test it anyway.

Judy looked down at the floor. She was ashamed. "They told me." She looked like she'd betrayed someone. She had.

"Told you when?" Ron asked.

"A few hours ago," Judy said, looking down at the floor again. "Right after it was dark."

"And you guys were just chatting," Ron said, dripping with sarcasm, "about the weather or whatever and they said, 'Oh, hey, we're going to kill Ron Spencer and his family.'"

Judy started to cry again. "You're making this hard on me."

There was that crying again. He couldn't be mean to a crying woman. He just couldn't.

"I'm sorry, Judy," Ron said. "But I need to know the circumstances of that conversation."

"Okay," Judy said, recovering from her crying for a moment. "They were over at my house because we often … talk." She looked down at the floor yet again.

"It's how I keep my FCard," she explained, her eyes still pointed downward. "I have to do this. I have to. I'm dependent on them. I don't have silver like you do."

Oh, the word was out about his silver. Great.

Ron chose not to react to her statement, which would just verify the rumors out there.

Dependent. Yep, Ron thought, you sure are, honey. That's why you were selling out your neighbors. Dependent. It's why Ron didn't have to sell out his neighbors. He wasn't dependent. That's what it all came down to.

Ron started to feel like a bully. He had been pretty hard on Judy. More than a couple of times, she had admitted that what she had been doing was wrong. And she was taking some risk by trying to warn him. Ron needed to be a decent person and quit batting her around like a cat with a mouse.

"Thanks for coming to us," Ron said very sincerely. "Thank you, Judy."

Judy cried some more. That was what she'd been waiting to hear from Ron. Finally he had said it. She was so relieved.

"Now tell me about their plan," Ron said.

"They will come here right before dawn," she said, once again looking down at the floor. "With guns. They have guns." She paused. This next part was hard for her to say.

"They're going to burn down your house," she said, with her face in her hands. She started crying again. This was a deep and shuddering cry. She was letting out a monstrous evil that she had been carrying with her.

Oh God, Ron thought. Burning down the house. Their house.

"Then Len's," she said, referring to Len Isaacson, the other Patriot in the neighborhood.

She cried some more and then said, "They said it will show everyone that the legitimate authorities are still in charge."

The "legitimate authorities" burned down houses and shot people trying to flee? That was "legitimate"?

Judy saying the "legitimate authorities" would burn down people's houses starkly illustrated just how illegitimate the authorities really were. The authorities Judy worked for. And now she was finally realizing how evil that system was. It took something like this to open her eyes.

"Thank you, Judy," Ron said and got up to hug her. "You are a hero for coming here and telling me this." Judy needed that hug. She deserved it.

Chapter 310

Picking the Wrong Side?

(January 2)

It had been just over twenty-four hours since Jeanie Thompson had learned of the Patriot attack. At first, it had seemed like they were attacking everywhere at once. It was a trick, she realized now. The Patriots were creating diversions to draw attention away from their real target: Olympia. In the early stages of the attack, they went after targets in Seattle and the suburbs. They hit Seattle-area political targets, police stations and FCorps facilities, mostly. They also assassinated several dozen government officials, including some high-ranking ones. Jeanie wondered if they got any of the people she had given tours to at Camp Murray.

The Patriots also raided the homes and mansions of some of the big government contractors. They killed the guards and the CEOs, but spared the spouses and children. They had very good intelligence and made pinpoint strikes. It looked like some of the guards were in on the raids. This sent most of the remaining elected officials and big government contractors into hiding. They couldn't trust anyone anymore. This had a devastating effect on the government's command and control; with so many officials in hiding, they couldn't direct a counterattack. All of this was possible as soon the Limas couldn't trust their own security guards.

The Patriots had also attacked throughout the state. They hit county seats, going after courthouses, county police stations, and any FCorps facilities in the rural areas. They hit some of the corporate food processors in the agricultural areas of eastern Washington. They stole truckloads of food and let the Mexicans, who were basically slaves on the farms, go free.

The Patriots' goal was to cause massive confusion and force the Loyalists to rush out in every direction in an attempt to reinforce all their forces. All the while, the main target was Olympia. The state capitol. The symbolic state capitol.

Olympia fell after only twenty-four hours. The political people had basically abandoned Olympia in the last few weeks. Everyone who was anybody had slowly and quietly moved from there to Seattle. The good troops and equipment were moved to JBLM and Seattle. All defensible resources were concentrated into one area, and it wasn't Olympia.

Of course, the National Guard and Lima police trying to defend Olympia would have liked knowing that they were a hollowed out outpost with no backup. They would have gone AWOL like everyone else, except for the hardcore Limas who knew they'd never be pardoned by the Patriots. Jeanie shook her head when she thought of all the poor National Guard kids who were sacrificed in Olympia.

Camp Murray was pretty much empty now that everyone important and even not-so-important was in Seattle. They left lowly people, like Jeanie, behind. Camp Murray was not yet in any danger of being taken by the Patriots because it was still in the JBLM ring and was heavily fortified. But the same thing that happened to Olympia could happen to them inside the JBLM ring: diverting forces from there to Seattle and then falling quickly to a Patriot attack.

People kept coming up to Jeanie and telling her how they never supported the "legitimate authorities." Many were more coy than that because they could never knew if the Patriots would lose and the legitimate authorities would be back in power, so they hedged their statements by saying things like, "Politics are so stupid. I just want things to get back to normal." That was odd because Jeanie knew some of them were actively involved in politics when their side was in power. It was funny how people feign a sudden disinterest in politics when it might cost them something.

Jeanie had no idea what would happen next. She was on the fence on whether she should just wait it out or make her way to Olympia. She told herself if she *did* go to Olympia, it would just be to see what was going on there. It's not like she was retreating from Camp Murray and going back to an area the Patriots controlled. It's not like she had picked the wrong side she kept telling herself.

Chapter 311

An Extra Day Off

(January 2)

In Seattle, it was almost midnight and Prof. Carol Matson was getting ready for work tomorrow after the New Year's Day holiday, which had been surprisingly extended. They were scheduled to return to work the day after New Year's Day, but they got an extra day off. Apparently there had been some logistical snafus on New Year's Day and all the employers in Seattle, which were almost all government and quasi-governmental agencies, let their workers stay home. An extra day off! Carol thought of it as just one example that showed how much better things were now that the progressives finally got to run things. The workers were now being treated much better than they were when the corporations ran everything.

Carol had been following the events of New Year's Day and the day after. She tuned into NPR, which always had good news on. NPR was broadcasting that some police stations were hit by the terrorists on New Year's Day. She rolled her eyes at the teabaggers – New Year's? Really? They were so unimaginative. "New year, new bosses," was probably their message. How juvenile.

NPR commentators discussed how the teabaggers were attacking police stations to steal guns. That made sense: the Neanderthal teabaggers loved their guns – and using guns to impose their narrow views on everyone else.

NPR was reporting that, in a weird set of coincidences, some government officials were killed in apparent home invasions by street criminals. The break-ins were probably just to get some food to eat, Carol thought. NPR explained that people who broke the laws, usually greedy people thwarting the Recovery, had their FCards revoked and probably were stealing to eat. Just follow the laws, Carol thought, and you'll be taken care of. Society was a compact where the people agreed on the laws and punishments for breaking them; break the laws and society doesn't need to take care of you. It was only fair. Revoking FCards from lawbreakers was how the authorities were helping people make sure to follow the laws.

Lastly, NPR mentioned that there had been some attacks in

Olympia, but the legitimate authorities put it down and were firmly in control. NPR said to expect some teabagger propaganda soon with altered photographs claiming to show they had taken Olympia. The police captured some documents in which the teabaggers detailed their plan to falsely claim that they took Olympia. That was just like the teabaggers, Carol thought. The only thing they have is lies. Who would believe those so-called "Patriots"?

Carol forced herself to turn off NPR so she could get to sleep and get to work well rested. She was careful to quietly go into her bedroom. Her little off-campus house was full of new houseguests. Her first set of guests in June, Maria and her two adorable little boys, Enrique and Fabiano, were refugees from Los Angeles after the riots. They were undocumented immigrants and the good people of southern California, unlike the rednecks in Texas, tried to accommodate as many of them as possible. But years of underspending on social services and public infrastructure in California meant there weren't enough resources for them down there. Seattle gladly took them in, and Carol volunteered to house them. They were issued FCards and lived with her until right before Thanksgiving. Then they were given jobs in eastern Washington at a potato processing plant. They were sad to leave but understood that everyone needed to do their part for the Recovery.

This freed up Carol's little house for more houseguests. Right before Christmas, she received word that she'd be getting a family from Olympia. She wasn't told much about her new family, a nice couple with two high-school aged sons, due to security concerns. Apparently, the mom in the family worked for some important state agency and the family was relocated to a safe place like Seattle. They didn't talk much about Olympia, but it sounded to Carol like things had been rough on government officials down in Olympia over the previous few weeks. Not everyone was pulling their weight for the Recovery, it seemed, and there were some greedy people jealous of officials who were working hard to help people. The mom still worked for the state agency in the offices they took over at the University, and the dad volunteered for the FCorps. The sons had joined the National Guard and were preparing to start training. They were a very nice family.

Carol appreciated the extra FCards the family brought to her house. As public employees, all four of them had a generous amount of credits, which was good because food and little luxuries were becoming harder to find in Seattle. They were still available, it just took

105

some searching. The mom, in particular, seemed to know which stores had things. The alternative was the black market, which seemed to be gaining strength every day. It was becoming common for people to openly buy and sell from the little stands that were popping up on street corners. Everyone knew the buying and selling, usually by barter and without all the necessary permits, was illegal. Yet no one seemed to shut them down, except occasional ones who were made into examples. Carol made her first illegal purchase at the end of December. She really, really needed some pretty wrapping paper for a winter solstice gift for her new houseguests. She traded a pound of coffee she purchased with her FCard for the wrapping paper, which was adorned with cute little reindeer. It was for a good cause: she was brightening up her houseguests' holiday after they had to relocate.

Carol tried to be as quiet as possible when she tiptoed from the living room into her bedroom. As she walked by the two sons sleeping on the couch and floor, she wondered why her family, mainly her brother, couldn't be like them. Nice. Helping in the Recovery.

Chapter 312

Life in Forks

(January 2)

It was almost midnight in Forks and Steve Briggs was getting ready for tomorrow. It would be January 3rd tomorrow and would be another day in Forks of … surviving. But, in reality, his day tomorrow would consist primarily of just visiting with people. There wasn't much to do this time of year in the near-constant rain and long periods of darkness; no gardens to tend, no decent hunting, and few fish in the rivers. There were things to repair, but usually no parts, and routine patrols to go on in town, but life in Forks meant doing a whole lot of nothing.

Surprisingly, this was just fine with Steve. The Collapse Christmas in Forks had been monumental. The whole town seemed to pull together. Carolers strolled through the streets singing Christmas carols. People gave each other meaningful, but simple, gifts. And there was that fabulous after-dinner moonshine sipping session after Christmas dinner at city hall. It was not a bad way to spend the winter.

People weren't eating as well now as they were in the fall or especially summer, but the majority of people stored food from the times of the year when it was plentiful. Not all of them did, and some who did didn't store as much as they should have. Everyone was losing weight, which wasn't such an awful thing. Steve had to admit that country living before the Collapse put on the pounds. Big country breakfasts made sense when people worked hard physically all day logging or doing something similarly as exerting, but before the Collapse, that wasn't exactly the way of life. People just ate like it was. When the Collapse hit, people became physically active in ways they had never been before, while no longer having access to a grocery store full of sausage, butter, and gravy mix. It became common for those XXXL shirts to start draping over men and women like an oversized blanket on their now-L frames.

Crime was still a sporadic issue, but there was no looting. Shooting people early on worked, as much as Steve wished it hadn't had to happen. Now, with a couple months of the Collapse behind him, Steve could see things differently. The pre-Collapse shitbags in town (and there were quite a few) could be shitbags when the living was easy, when the EBT cards had money on them and the store had plenty of Doritos. Now it was much harder to be a shitbag. They got over their lazy lifestyles pretty quickly now that they had to actually work and no one just handed them anything. Oh, sure, it took a period of adjustment and some of the shitbags never adjusted, but they were quickly shunned by the community or, in some cases, shot when they were caught stealing.

Steve was especially happy to see some of the young people change their shitbag ways and ... grow up and become productive. He had to admit it was hard to be a young person in pre-Collapse America and not give in to the shitbag lifestyle. They were told, starting in middle school, that it was okay to get "public assistance." In high school, the schools were one-stop social service centers preparing the kids for a life of public assistance if that's what they chose. And there were almost no jobs for them, so who could be surprised that so many got on the dole? He went from being mad at them to feeling sorry for them. It was so obvious that politicians created this. They got votes from people for "caring" and providing "public assistance," and they got votes from young people, the few who bothered to vote, to keep free stuff flowing. Those "caring" voters and young voters were often just enough for the side proposing even more spending to win. Now, after the Collapse, it was so obvious to Steve.

The perfect example of this was Steve's nephew, Phil McGuire. He drifted through high school without ever having a summer job or working after school, much to Steve's chagrin. But it was rare before the Collapse for teenagers to work; they needed time to play video games and text their friends. Phil fit into this category perfectly. After high school graduation, he couldn't find a job, but he didn't really try to find one. He lived with his mom, Steve's sister, and her boyfriend. When he turned eighteen, he was told about all the free stuff he could get, including the magical EBT card. It was free money and he didn't have to do anything to get it. He spent the next few years on the couch at his mom's house and having a carefree life.

When the Collapse hit, he was bewildered that he couldn't sit on the couch and get everything given to him. At first, he was mad. Steve told him that life had changed, but "Uncle Steve" was just being his hard ass self, Phil thought.

But slowly, Phil started volunteering for various jobs. Steve took him under his wing. He had to teach Phil how to work. He had to teach him to get up on time, to wear work clothes, and to actually get a job done. Phil would constantly want to take a break after working a few minutes. He had no concept of finishing a job; he was just putting time in and thought he got credit for just showing up. "We don't quit until the job is done," Steve would have to tell him.

Phil improved considerably in the fall. By Christmas, Steve could tell him to do a project and it got done, always slowly and sometimes poorly, but Phil was finally putting in true effort. His transformation was complete when, after Christmas, Steve told him to split and stack firewood for an elderly neighbor lady and, to Steve's pleasant surprise, the job was done before dark, with no supervision from Steve. Phil seemed much happier because, for the first time in his life, he was productive. He had finally grown up and was a man.

Like so many other things during the Collapse, the good, like Phil's transformation, came with the other side of the coin, the bad, like all the people dying of simple illnesses that winter.

The big concern in town was the all the deaths from pneumonia and the flu. People were so run down, especially the elderly, and were cold and weren't getting the nutrition they needed. All the stress from the Collapse also degraded their immune systems. Little colds were turning into full-on serious illnesses and there were no antibiotics. Steve was going to way too many funerals lately. Including that of Grant's mom.

The talk at the latest funeral Steve went to was about how the Patriots supposedly took Olympia on New Year's Day. Steve listened politely and was rooting for the Patriots, if the stories were true. But, Steve hated to admit, he didn't really care. Whoever sat in some capitol building 150 miles away in Olympia wouldn't affect whether people in Forks had enough to eat this winter or could treat a simple cold before it became pneumonia. Governments didn't really matter anymore in Forks.

Chapter 313

Dmitri's Rules for Gray Manning

(January 2)

In west Seattle, Ed Oleo had been staying under the radar all fall. He and Dmitri talked a lot about being a "gray man." Back in the fall, Dmitri gave Ed a lesson in "gray manning" – lessons Ed was putting into place just before midnight on the day after New Year's.

Dmitri was a gold mine of information about how to be a gray man, like he had been in the former Soviet Union. Dmitri's people had gray manning down to a science, which, in large part, was why the Soviet Union collapsed.

The first rule of gray manning, Dmitri explained, was to be and remain gray – that is, to blend in and not alert the authorities that you are resisting them. A gray man or woman can't do the resistance any good if he or she is in jail because he or she decided to spout off about politics or some other waste of time in a repressive regime. "There is no upside and much downside," Dmitri said, using his favorite American businessman's phrase, "to openly making political statements" during the Collapse. Several people in TDFs learned this the hard way. Anonymously making political statements, like the "I miss America" graffiti Dmitri and Ed were seeing in Seattle, was a different story, Dmitri explained. "Don't let the authorities know it is you making the statement," he would say. "Let them, and especially the general population, think it is everyone making the statement."

The second rule of gray manning, Dmitri explained to Ed, was to not try to do too much. "It is not up to you," Dmitri, "to take down the system. It cannot be done by one person." Instead, Dmitri explained, "the system was built by many people, and needs many people to sustain it." This meant, "It takes many people to bring it down." Dmitri would laugh and tell Ed, "You Americans care so much about the individual. You think individuals can do anything. That is true of some things, but you are wrong about an individual being able to take down the system. It takes many gray men to bring it down."

The third rule of gray manning, Dmitri said, was to use the system against itself. For example, if the system requires a person to submit an application to do something, like have a garage sale, then submit an application. The system will spend its resources processing the application. By spending a little time to submit an application, a gray man can cause the system to spend much more time and energy processing it. Don't complain out loud that you shouldn't have to have a permit to hold a garage sale, he would say, "Send in the application and let them work on it. Let all the problems they create for you become their problems."

The fourth rule was to do everything possible to strengthen alternatives to the system. The best example was the black market. It competed with the official system, so the stronger the black market was, the weaker the system was. This was one of the things about gray manning that directly benefited the gray man: the black market often had things the system could not provide.

The fifth rule was to notice things.

"Just keep your eyes open," Dmitri said, "and notice little things." Dmitri gave examples like when the police changed shifts, when your neighbors came and went, when the stores had food and when they didn't. "All of these things will help you make a plan to do things, like sabotage, and they are also useful pieces of information to tell allied forces when they arrive."

"Sabotage is the next rule," Dmitri said. "You know the phrase, 'throw a monkey wrench?'"

"Sure," Ed said, "it means to destroy something."

"My people invented that phrase," Dmitri said with pride. "It came from the industrialization period in the Soviet Union when resisters would actually throw a wrench into machinery and destroy it. It was impossible to know which worker did it. And it would take weeks to fix the machinery. This cost the system a tremendous amount and also stopped production for weeks. All for the price of a wrench, thrown into a machine anonymously."

Ed said, "We don't have any machines like that anymore in America, so what are our monkey wrenches?"

"Electricity," Dmitri said. "America needs electricity to function, Disable the electricity and you have thrown in the monkey wrench. The final rule is keeping a mental file on everyone you meet," Dmitri said. "Figure out which side everyone is on. When the time is right, you can deal with the people who support the government. But be sure they are really supporters. This takes time and patient observation. You'll know who to target for that day when you have an opportunity to – how you say – take them out."

Now, on the day after New Year's, Ed was putting Dmitri's

lessons to use. He decided not to involve him because he didn't want to get him in trouble. News had been trickling in that the Patriots had launched an offensive in Olympia on New Year's Eve. This might be the time for Ed to strike, but only if the Patriots attacked Seattle. He was far too outnumbered to take on all the Limas in Seattle on his own. He could support a Patriot attack on his city, but he needed them to be on the gates of Seattle before his lone-wolf work would be effective.

Ed's first idea was, when the time was right, to take his shotgun and use one of his rifled slug shells to shoot the electrical transformer at the nearby police station right about at the time they changed shifts. Then he was reminded of Dmitri's second rule of gray manning: "It's not up to you alone to bring the system down." Shooting the transformer would be loud and he would have to travel by foot to get there and back with a shotgun in his hands. Bad idea.

Ed came up with a second plan. He realized that he had plenty of information on three of his neighbors. Most people in his neighborhood didn't give a crap about politics. They just mouthed the correct things and put up the stupid "We Support the Recovery!" yard signs. But three neighbors were hardcore Limas. They were the FCorps block captains.

Ed got to know them and even did some home repairs for them for free. He wanted to be sure that they were truly Limas before he put them on his list. During his visits to their homes, he was doing more than repairing their homes. He was casing the places, figuring out where the locks were. He even replaced a lock for one of them, and managed to keep the second key. Now he could get in whenever he wanted.

Ed still had his shotgun. Now all he needed was for the Patriots to attack Seattle.

Chapter 314

Reaction in Pierce Point

(January 2)

In Pierce Point, New Year's Day had been a big deal. People were stunned that at least one hundred Patriot guerillas had been training right under their noses and had gone into Olympia as part of the offensive. Right under their noses! Who knew?

Quite a few people, as it turned out. Before New Year's, there were a lot of people whispering about the "rental team." It was amazing that it had remained a secret as long as it did.

Dr. Lisa Matson was thoroughly depressed. She didn't even go into work for several days. Her husband had left her for ... some stupid war. A war? Leaving her for another woman she could sort of understand; men did that sometimes. But playing army with his little buddies? Leaving her for that was insulting.

The worst part was that everyone was telling her what a great hero Grant was. She just nodded, went along, and tried to smile. She was too humiliated to admit that he had left her, but the fact that everyone thought Grant was the greatest thing since sliced bread made the humiliation even worse.

On top of all this was Lisa's constant worrying that Grant, as much as she hated him, would get killed or wounded or captured. She didn't really care about him anymore, but she didn't want her kids to lose their dad. She didn't want them to lose him again, like when he'd left them in Olympia. Then she'd realize that he voluntarily left them and would get furious at him again.

Security at Pierce Point was going well. Rich and Dan had things under control. In the several months they'd been doing it, security had become a well-oiled machine. The gate guards were still doing a great job. They received several new volunteers to replace the guards who left with the 17th. The new volunteers, however, were either a little too young or too old to keep up with the others. That was okay; it was nice to have extra people on the gate and to rotate in and out to keep the better guards rested. The beach patrol was in full swing. They even shot some people trying to steal oysters, but only after the thieves started shooting first. It was sad: dying over oysters.

Crime was increasing in Pierce Point, but was still manageable. It was mostly shitbags stealing little things when they thought they could get away with it. There were no gangs of any kind in the community. Almost every home was well-armed.

The Crew, the backup people to the Team who did perimeter security for Team raids and handled the dogs, were now doing the SWAT work in Pierce Point. They had trained with the Team, and Rich and Dan were giving them lots of great training. They were pretty good. Pierce Point was lucky to have them.

Food and illness were starting to become a problem, though. The New Year's Eve battle in Frederickson stopped the FCard food coming in, although it was dwindling down to a low level before the battle. There were no gardens this time of year. Hunting was very poor because most animals were hibernating or tucked away in their sleeping areas. Besides, the area had been heavily hunted for the past few months. Even rabbits, which were considered pests a few months before, were nowhere to be found. Fishing and gathering shellfish was not yielding anywhere near the amount of food it had even a few weeks ago.

One important source of food was the cattle raised by the private farmers. They were called "private farmers" because they grew livestock and crops for sale, instead of donating them to the Grange. At the beginning of the Collapse, most people didn't resent them for selling for profit because there was an adequate amount of food. But now, in the winter, things were getting tighter and more people started questioning the farmers' "gouging" on food prices. The private farmers hired some of the community as security but realized they couldn't hold back a mass invasion of hungry neighbors. Besides, most of the people in Pierce Point were out of anything they could barter for food, so there was no point to trying to sell the food. The private farmers held a meeting with Rich and Dan and decided to donate half of their cattle and even a few old horses to the Grange kitchen.

Luckily, many people in Pierce Point had been storing food in the summer and especially the fall. Smoked salmon became a staple. Canned clams and oysters became the base ingredient of soups and chowders with a rotating supporting cast of canned vegetables. Those who had been "preppers" before the Collapse were using more and more of their beans and rice, and other foundational foods like oatmeal, dried mashed potatoes, and pancake mix. But these supplies were getting low.

A few more people volunteered to work for the community in

order to get a meal card. Some of the new volunteers felt a little guilty that they hadn't thought volunteering for the community was important until after they needed the food. Some of the long-time volunteers resented them, which caused some tension.

Cries to open up Gideon's semi-trailer of food were getting louder. Grant, the main political force behind the effort to stave off opening the trailer, was gone and no one knew when, or if, he would return. The people who wanted free food were getting bolder and louder. Things weren't desperate yet, especially with the private farmers donating half their livestock, but everyone could see that it was a matter of time before the semi-trailer needed to be opened up.

Chapter 315

Sheriff Bennington

(January 3)

It was sunrise on the third day of the new year in Frederickson and Sheriff Bennington—he named himself Sheriff and no one seemed to mind—was working hard to bring the county under control. His posse of former law enforcement, the ones who left the force when it was getting corrupt, and their volunteers were doing a nice job of cleaning things up.

The population was incredibly receptive to the new Sheriff. They had suffered enough from Winters and the gangs. They were turning in people left and right. Bennington's posse was overwhelmed with leads and citizen arrests of cops, FCorps, and the remaining gang members hiding out. Bennington had more volunteers than he could handle. This was, he reminded himself, a good problem to have.

Some citizens in Frederickson weren't content with just turning in the bad guys. Instead, they became paras and were going after them on their own. The paras didn't trust the police to prosecute bad guys, which was understandable given the Winters' administration. The paras were even going after the bad guys' families. Some of the paras' brutality was shocking and if it didn't stop soon, would hurt Bennington's efforts to win the hearts and minds of the population. He was trying to keep the worst of the para activity under control, but his primary concern was rooting out the Winters people and gangs. In a breakdown of society, there are always regrettable things that happen, but Bennington would have to focus on the paras after Winters' people were gone. He had to prioritize. Then again, the more of Winters' people Bennington's men killed or captured, the less there was for the paras to do, so focusing on Winters' people indirectly eased the para problem.

In addition to dealing with the remnants of the Winters administration and the paras, Bennington also tried to do whatever he could to support the Patriots. Even though Olympia had been taken, it was only a few miles away. The Patriot ham radio network warned the areas surrounding Olympia to expect fleeing Limas to try to hide out there. Bennington responded by alerting his volunteer gate guards at the city limits, who replaced the corrupt Blue Ribbon Boys, to be on the lookout for people in cars with government license plates or strange stories about why they were suddenly coming to Frederickson. Sure enough, a carload of SWAT officers from the Olympia area rolled up to the Frederickson gate. They were arrested without incident. Bennington, wanting to show the population that his way was better than the para way, made sure to use valuable jail space for the SWAT officers instead of shooting them in the street. Their trials would be the first ones when the courthouse opened back up.

Bennington wanted to do more for the Patriots than just hold Frederickson. He wanted to help the statewide Patriot effort. It was the 17th Irregulars, after all, whose massive presence on New Year's Eve made it possible for Bennington to clean out Winters and his minions. Bennington had limited resources because he had to focus on the holdouts and paras, but he decided he would do two things to help the Patriots. The first was to care for their wounded scout, and to make sure the two Pierce Point scouts who were killed in action got a proper burial. It was the least he could do.

The second thing he did was announce to his posse that after Frederickson was stabilized, any of them wanting to join the Patriots in Olympia were free to do so and dozens volunteered.

Chapter 316

One Armored Car

(January 3)

Joe Tantori couldn't keep his eyes open any longer. As the sun was coming up on … he had no idea what day it was … he fell soundly asleep in the passenger seat of one of his company's armored cars. The past few days had been a blur, but they were the most exciting days of his life.

It started on New Year's Eve morning when he and about fifty of his men, most of whom were FUSA Marines, boarded a barge at his facility. They had precious cargo on board: one of his armored cars from his pre-Collapse security business. With a Patriot tugboat to pull them and another as an escort, Joe and his men on the barge spent New Year's Eve puttering down the Puget Sound toward their objective: Olympia.

In the pre-mission briefing by Lt. Cmdr. Dibble, Joe questioned the wisdom of landing a very small force right in the middle of the enemy's location, the port of Olympia. He didn't want to sound like a coward, but he had the lives of his men to think about. "Is this a good idea, landing my men right under their noses?" he asked.

"Normally, no," Dibble said. "But in these circumstances, yes."

"Okay," Joe said, "tell me these circumstances so I can tell my men."

"Sure," Dibble said. "First of all, Olympia is hollowed out. Our intel shows they have been evacuating their key people for a few weeks. All that are left are some poor National Guard kids. You should hear the radio traffic from them. Those kids are terrified and they know they're on their own. We expect mass surrenders."

Joe nodded. He knew how unreliable intel could be, but he had seen with his own eyes the uptick in evacuations by sea on the Puget Sound from areas outside of Seattle into Seattle. The Limas were obviously abandoning their outlying areas and concentrating on Seattle. But the evacuations stopped about a week ago, apparently because they got all their key people into Seattle.

"Second," Dibble said, "we have assets at the port facility itself. We know for a fact that the port employees are taking New Year's Eve off. There will literally be no one there when you land." He smiled. He was very proud that they had this level of information.

"Okay," Joe said. He could sell this mission to his men. They were, after all, privateers operating under a letter of marque, which meant they could technically decline the mission. But there was no way Joe or his men would miss out on an amphibious landing in the Lima's capitol city.

Joe was worried about being intercepted on the Puget Sound as they sailed south toward Olympia. They had to get past the Bremerton shipyards, Seattle, and Tacoma, all of which, theoretically, had significant maritime defenses. It was true that these facilities had potent defenses like mines and harbor boats to counter a close-range force directly attacking them, but several months into the Collapse they didn't have many ships that controlled the open waters. FUSA naval assets needed an enormous amount of spare parts and fuel – and sailors, who were quickly going AWOL or joining the Patriots. So, while the Lima naval presence in the Puget Sound was significant a few months ago when Joe's men were out patrolling on the outskirts of the sound, it had dropped off significantly by now.

Besides, there wasn't much for Lima naval assets to do now, anyway. Except for the recent evacuations to Seattle, there was much less ship traffic in general than there had been before the Collapse. Before everything started, ships with goods from all over the world, especially China, clogged the waterways around Seattle. There was no more international trade now that the dollar had officially tanked and was virtually worthless. No country in its right mind would sell things to Americans for dollars and America had almost no reserves of foreign currency to pay for goods with money that other countries would accept. Fuel was very hard to come by, and this put even more of a dent in ship traffic. Finally, the FUSA Navy and Coast Guard were a small fraction of what they used to be. They no longer had the support of the rest of the American military because many states had "opted out" and weren't supporting FUSA military operations.

The Limas still had a few maritime patrol aircraft. To lower any suspicion if they were spotted from the air, Joe's men filled the barge with garbage, which worked out well because garbage had been piling up at Joe's facility and he needed to get rid of it anyway. They put the men in two small shipping containers. The armored car was covered by a large tarp. The barge looked like a load of garbage with some ancillary cargo; perfectly normal to be on the water. They had some fake papers for the load, but the quality of the forgery wasn't that good. If they were stopped, they'd have to shoot their way out of it. They could easily repel an attack from a patrol boat because the Marines brought some of their anti-tank rockets and they had quite a few .50 machine guns on board. But if a patrol boat or plane radioed in their location, a larger vessel could easily intercept them. They couldn't outrun a real naval vessel. "Die with your boots on," Joe said to himself, which was one of his favorite Iron Maiden songs.

As they were about to land in Olympia, Dibble pulled Joe aside on the bridge of the tug and said with a smile, "Hey, you wonder why no one stopped us on the water?"

"Yes, I sure did."

"We have someone on the inside at the FUSA Coast Guard in Seattle," Dibble said with a huge grin. "She's at the Coast Guard Maritime Control Center. She's one of the radar people that tells ship and planes where to go."

"Or not go," Joe said with a huge sigh of relief. The Patriots never could have won without inside help like this, Joe realized.

The Patriot tug radioed the barge to let them know that they were entering Budd Inlet, the final leg of the journey. It was just before midnight on New Year's and the gunfire and explosions had just started near the capitol. The sounds of war got Joe's men pumped up and ready to land.

Joe was on the bridge of the tug with his binoculars. He was stunned to see the lights on at the port but no one around. It was exactly like Dibble said it would be: abandoned. The gunfire and explosions were still far away, about two miles north of them at the capitol campus.

Landing at night was scary, not because of enemy gunfire but just because it was a landing in an unknown port, and barges aren't easy to steer. The tugboat was manned by an excellent tug crew of volunteers who had landed at the port of Olympia before. They put the barge exactly where it needed to be.

Joe remembered that they had some trouble getting the armored car off the barge and onto the dock. They couldn't drive the armored car off the barge because it would crush the wooden dock. They needed to use the crane to lift it up and onto the cement staging area onshore. They knew where the keys to the crane were because the tugboat captain had hung out with the crane operators before the Collapse. They went to the control center where the keys were, but it was locked. A special 12 gauge breaching round, which shot metal powder out the barrel, took care of the locked door. A minute later, the tug captain was unloading the armored car. It was an ugly crane job, with the armored car swinging wildly, but it got the job done.

By now, the landing party was out of the shipping containers and doing a final coms and gear check. Once the armored car was operational, the men took up positions behind it. Commercial armored cars were the poor man's armored personnel carrier.

Joe's landing party went slowly up the street toward the capitol campus. They first encountered an F Corp checkpoint in downtown Olympia. The FCorps guards, an old man and a young teenager, put up their hands without a word and were zip tied after Joe's men took their radios.

The next checkpoint, manned by about a dozen FCorps, decided to shoot when the armored car disobeyed their loudspeaker order to halt. Their bullets bounced right off Joe's armored car, causing the occupants to laugh out loud. The Marines behind the armored car patiently saw where the F Corp muzzle flashes were coming from and demonstrated the marksmanship skills the Marine Corps was known for.

But, as could be expected, the FCorps checkpoint that shot at them had radios.

"There's an armored car and a bunch of soldiers coming straight up Capitol Boulevard!" one of the FCorps screamed into his radio.

The dispatcher coordinating the response to the gunfire all over the city was overwhelmed. Besides, there was no way an armored car could have driven downtown; all the roads and streets leading to the capitol had checkpoints so it was impossible that an armored car was downtown. The dispatcher assumed this was a mistake or that some teabaggers had stolen a radio and were trying to divert the legitimate authorities, perhaps to an ambush. She disregarded the report of the armored car and moved on to the dozen other emergencies confronting her all at the same time.

Joe remembered how the fire got thicker as they moved toward the capitol campus. Joe's coms guy, Daniel Briggman, was monitoring the Lima frequencies. The Limas had secure channels, but in the chaos of the attack, many of them, especially the untrained FCorps, were freaking out and talking on the unsecure frequencies. This gave Patriots invaluable information.

Joe and Dibble were in the armored car when Briggman came running up and said, with some concern, "Hey, they now know we're here, but some of them still can't believe it. They're trying to get some armor to engage us."

Monitoring the Lima radios wasn't the only source of information Joe's men had. Some of the Marines were scouting ahead of the armored car. One of them turned a corner and saw a tank sitting in an intersection, fully illuminated by the street lights. The engine wasn't running, which seemed strange. He used a silent hand signal to tell his fellow scout, who then ran to the armor car to report it.

"I got it," said Gunnery Sergeant Martin Booth, who was in command of the Marines. He had a plan for this and with a couple of shouts to key personnel, the plan was underway.

Booth pre-determined five Marines to make their way to the corner where the scout had spotted the tank. They had a secret surprise for the tank: a Javelin anti-tank missile. The men made their way to the corner and verified the target was there. It was a block down the street from the corner where the Marines were.

As they were getting ready to fire, the enemy tank crew came running up to the tank, which explained why the engine wasn't running; it was just sitting there, unmanned. Perhaps the Limas were trying to scare people away, but that didn't work on Marines.

"Capture them," the corporal leading the anti-tank party said. "If you can," he added.

Knowing that the tank couldn't fire at them without a crew in it made deciding to take it on much easier.

"Freeze!" the Marines yelled as the first of the tank crew members was climbing on the tank to get into it.

The scared National Guard kids threw their hands up in an instant. One by one, they were ordered to walk down the street to be zip tied.

Once the fifth member of the tank crew was secured, the corporal called in the good news.

"Looks like we captured an Abrams," referring to the M1 tank in the intersection. "Betcha that'll come in handy."

Just as those words left the corporal's mouth, machine gun fire came from the second story of the building just behind the tank.

"Oh, well," he said, and gave the signal to his two-man Javelin crew. After a few bursts of fire from the Marines, the machine gun stopped. But, to the Marines' surprise, a new tank crew came running out and started to get into the tank.

The Javelin crew was in place and gave one last look to the corporal in case anything had changed.

"Light 'em up," the corporal yelled, and a second later the

Javelin exploded out of its launcher and rocked the intersection. The concussion knocked some of the Marines down. The Abrams was still in one piece, but on fire. The secondary explosions from the tank rounds inside started to go off.

The Marine anti-tank crew ran back to the armored car. The corporal reported to Booth about trying to capture the tank. Joe remembered Booth saying, "Shit happens, Corporal" and shrugging.

The Patriot field commanders at the battle of Olympia wondered why one of their biggest problems, a tank in the middle of a key intersection, just exploded. Joe swelled with pride when Briggman got on the radio and told the Patriot commanders that they had taken it out.

The rest of the night, Joe's men slowly went up the street and probed each intersection in the surrounding area. They encountered heavier and heavier fire as they did so. Finally, it was apparent that one armored car and fifty Marines wasn't enough to push through the increasingly strong defenses ringing the immediate boundaries of the capitol. Besides, Joe's men had captured so many Limas it was getting hard to keep moving with all of them in tow. Eventually, Joe's men linked up with Patriot regular forces and started to run heavy patrols in the areas they'd secured, intercepting fleeing Limas. They captured even more of them, almost of all them were scared National Guard kids, but some nasty FCorps, too. They killed several of them who wouldn't surrender, having learned from their prisoners that the hardcore Limas were shooting deserters. This might have explained some of the fire the Marines took when capturing enemy soldiers; the Marines had no choice but to fire back.

On the second day – although Joe's memory was hazy because he hadn't slept – his armored car was in high demand. It proved to be the perfect way to safely ferry high-value personnel. The armored car was the only armored vehicle the Patriots had; they couldn't move tanks or armored personnel carriers up and down I-5 to Olympia.

Joe's Marines were also highly valued; they were assigned to the Delta Company of the Second Battalion of the Washington State Guard. The Marines used their last remaining Javelin on a Lima tank parked at the entrance to the capitol building.

Blowing up the second tank was just about the end for the Limas. After a thunderous tirade of fire from the windows of the capitol buildings, Joe and the others felt and heard an earth-shaking explosion. Joe thought an exploding tank was loud, but this was a hundred times bigger. Later, they found out that this was the Lima's ammunition bunker that they detonated to prevent the ammunition from falling into Patriot hands.

Joe was given the great honor of having his armored car used to bring the Patriot commanders into the capitol to receive the surrender of the last handful of Limas. Using his car was partially thanks for the fifty Marines and taking out two tanks, but was also because it was the only armored vehicle the Patriots had.

Joe started to cry when he saw a soldier bring the new Patriot flag out of his armored car and hoist it up the flagpole over the capitol. It was silent as the flag flew, except for some of the secondary explosions from the ammunition bunker. As he was looking up at the new flag on the old capitol, Joe noticed his Marines were slowly making their way to his armored car. Once they were there, he went into the vehicle and got out three wooden boxes of cigars they'd captured from pirates a few months ago. He motioned for Booth to come over and told him to hand a cigar to every man in the unit. Once they all had one, Joe lit his cigar and said, "Well done, gentlemen. Well done."

Chapter 317

Prisoner Herself

(January 3)

It had been twenty-four hours since she was arrested. Nancy Ringman was remembering what happened.

It all started when Otter said to her back at Clover Park, "Nancy, I bet your arms are getting tired, right?"

She nodded. Her arms had been out at her sides for a few minutes and were starting to hurt. She was pleasantly surprised that Otter cared about her comfort. Maybe he wasn't a teabagger; maybe he had been sent by Linda to rescue her.

"Go ahead and slowly put your arms behind your back, Nancy," Otter said. "And for everyone's safety, one of these guys is going to put something on your wrists."

Nancy nodded slowly, still looking down at the ground. She realized that if they were handcuffing her, they probably hadn't been sent by Linda. Now she was starting to get really scared, but Otter seemed so nice. Her expectation that all teabaggers were mean assholes was wrong and she felt like she could trust him, even if he was arresting her.

She started to put her arms behind her back, but she couldn't because they were so sore. Her knees were hurting, too, she noticed. She struggled to get her hands back. They were wobbling.

"Tell you what, Nancy," Otter said. "One of these guys is going to help you move your arms. First your left one, then your right one, okay?"

Nancy nodded. What a relief. She felt so helpless, not being able to move her arms. She was starting to realize that, on top of all of this, she was still half-drunk from the wine.

Someone came up behind her and gently moved her left arm behind her back and then her right arm. She felt a thin plastic strap go on her wrist. The man tightened it, but not so tight that it hurt.

"Okay, Nancy," Otter said, "Now I need you to stand up."

She nodded but started to cry. "I can't," she said softly. She was humiliated that she couldn't even stand up, but she knew she'd be more humiliated if she tried and fell down.

"Okay," Otter said, "we'll help you."

A man came up behind her and each one gently lifted one of her arms until she was standing.

"Can you walk?" Otter asked.

Nancy, now looking up at Otter, nodded. She looked in his eyes. He didn't look like the monster she expected.

Seeing that she was having a hard time walking, one of the soldiers said, "I'll have the truck brought over here." He got on the radio and soon she heard the sound of an approaching truck.

"Now, Nancy," Otter said, "I've been good to you, haven't I?"

Still looking at him, she nodded.

"Nancy," he said sincerely, "I need you to tell me if anyone else is here."

She stared at him.

"Nancy," he said very seriously, "I really need to know if anyone else is here, okay?"

That made sense to Nancy.

"I'm pretty sure I'm the only one."

"Pretty sure?" he asked.

"Yes, I don't know of anyone else who is here."

"Okay, Nancy," Otter said, "I believe you." He actually did, but he wasn't going to completely rely on it.

The truck came up to them and Otter motioned for her to get inside.

"Where are we going?" she asked.

"To jail, Nancy," he said. "You did some horrible things."

Chapter 318

Pancakes II

(January 3)

Grant couldn't believe what he was seeing. Wes' body was laid out, motionless, in the back of the truck. He ran over hoping to see that it was someone else, but as he ran toward Mark's truck, he saw Ryan's face. From his expression, Grant knew that it was Wes in the back of the truck.

Suddenly, Grant stopped running. He didn't actually want to see Wes. He didn't want to erase all the memories he had of an alive, active Wes. Of a warrior. Of a kind and gentle man to the innocent, and a skilled fighter to the guilty. Of a quiet man who did what needed to be done like when he announced "Lima down." Of a strong Patriot.

Grant forced himself to go over to the truck. He didn't give himself the luxury of closing his eyes. A weak man would close his eyes and run, and Grant was not a weak man, even though he wanted to be.

Grant slowly approached Wes and he noticed two things: the rope burn around his neck and that smile. Grant wondered how a man could be smiling after being hung. It was simultaneously eerie and joyous. That smile communicated perfectly that Wes was happy with his life, he died a happy man, having done as much as humanly possible in his short twenty-two years. He had been a husband and created a new life, even though he would never meet his child. He had fought for his country. More importantly, he had fought for his friends.

Wes was a loyal friend. He was the kind of friend a person never forgets. Grant recalled all the times Wes could jump in the back of Mark's truck to go out on patrol, always wearing that big smile, and joking around in his Southern drawl. Grant remembered the first time he heard Wes talk, and how Wes had said, "We believe in diversity. Fords, Chevies, and Dodges."

Kellie. She would be devastated. The father of her unborn child, her true love was gone. Oh God. This was horrible. Kellie had finally met a decent man, and he was killed a few months later. Grant thought of her and their unborn child as innocent victims of this whole stupid war.

"You can judge a man by the size of his funeral," Grant remembered his dad saying. It was one of the few decent things that guy ever said. Grant thought about all the lives Wes had touched, and how huge his funeral would be. They would have a gigantic funeral, and celebration of Wes' life, back at Pierce Point when they were done with this shit and could go back home.

Grant knew they needed to get Wes' body to the makeshift morgue, but he couldn't say the word "morgue." He wanted to buy time before someone took Wes away from them forever. Forever, at least, down on Earth. Grant knew he'd see Wes again in a perfect and healthy body and with that same smile.

"Let the rest of the unit come by and pay their respects," Grant said. "There is no use having them crowd into the morgue. Let them come by the truck."

Grant told Scotty to grab Wes' "membership cards," like his Raven Concealment holster and pistol, and his AR with the SKT sling. All those would be keepsakes for the Team to remember their fallen brother. They were special items no one else would get to have.

Scotty pulled Wes' bloody Zero Tolerance out of his pocket and started crying. "They took his ZT, man," Scotty sobbed. "Fucking animals. You don't take a man's knife. Animals." Scotty got ahold of himself. He was a soldier, and a member of the Team. He stopped crying and said, "I took care of the guy who took his knife." He wanted everyone to know that.

"You keep it," Grant said to Scotty. "You are the keeper of Wes' knife." Scotty nodded. He would literally kill again if anyone tried to take that knife. It was his last link to Wes. Grant had to pay his final respects to Wes. He didn't want to touch a dead body, but this wasn't just a dead body; it was Wes. He got up his strength and walked over to the bed of the truck and squeezed Wes' arm. There. That was it.

Pancakes. A soldier near them was eating pancakes on a paper plate. Grant remembered that Wes ate pancakes right before they went out. Then all the blood drained out of Grant's face.

Pancakes.

Grant remembered one of the first mornings out at the cabin after Lisa and the kids came out. Wes said one time over breakfast that his last meal would probably be pancakes. That comment had bothered Grant since that day and he never knew why. Now he did.

This was all Grant's fault. If Grant had remembered Wes saying that months ago, then he could have stopped Wes from eating the pancakes and Wes would have lived.

Grant thought about that. Was it his fault? Because of pancakes? That was insane. Grant realized that absolutely irrational guilt comes from losses like this. The lack of sleep didn't help either when it came to thinking straight. Grant took a deep breath. It wasn't the pancakes or Grant that killed Wes.

He had to get back to business, as hard as that was. For the first time, he noticed that Ryan, Pow, and Scotty had blood all over their clothes and gear. He started to say they needed to clean up, but what clothes would they change into? What extra set of kit did they have?

Besides, Grant wanted the rest of the 17th to see that war was serious fucking business. They needed to see the blood and to understand what it was they were doing out there.

"Gotta get back to work," Grant said to the Team, ashamed that he had to leave Wes. They nodded. They understood. They, too, needed to go back out. They would go and help Bravo Company seal off the exits from the park. They wanted to be there when those fucking animals were flushed out of the woods. They wanted to see if no one was looking and then do some more ZT work. They would even use Wes' knife, just for the symbolism of it. This was personal now.

Grant walked back to the area where the 17th was. He tried to look at his pamphlet that he was so proud of, but it didn't mean anything anymore. All the strategy, all the thinking, all the planning, all the … everything was a joke. Meaningless. Words. What mattered was in the back of that truck.

Grant pulled his black knit cap off and looked at the lieutenant's bar stapled onto it. What a stupid piece of cloth that insignia was. Stapled on, not even sewn. What a joke. A piece of cloth. All of this was stupid.

Grant wanted to be back on the range with Wes and the guys before all this started. Back when Grant had a wife and kids he could go home to. Back when he had a real job. Back when sick people had simple medicines to keep them alive and back before all this killing and dying and good people going insane. Like Mark. Poor Mark. And Luke. And Tammy. And especially Missy.

The list went on. The list needed to stop. Everything needed to stop. It was out of control. Grant felt like he was physically spinning, thinking about all the things that needed to stop. He had to sit down. He was starting to pass out from exhaustion and hunger and stress.

He abruptly sat down on the concrete outside the brewery. Sitting there, he realized that he needed to be back in control of things, which meant getting back to Pierce Point. Things were normal there.

Wes wouldn't have died there. They would still be riding around in a truck there and saying, "This never gets old" with big smiles on their faces. He could go home to his family there, too.

Grant took off his black knit cap. He looked at the lieutenant's bar on it. He tore it off. Grant had just resigned his commission. He and the Team were volunteers. Irregulars. They could go home at any time. That was what Grant would do. He'd done plenty. He was done. He went to go gather up the guys before they went out again.

Grant got up off the concrete and took that first step toward the truck. He knew that if he walked up to it and said, "We're done, guys. Let's go back home," that things would truly be over. Even if the guys didn't come back to Pierce Point with him, it would be over for him. Over. He walked quickly to the truck, wanting to say something that couldn't be taken back. He wanted this to be over with.

He was two steps from the truck. The Team looked at him and realized he had something important to say. Grant opened his mouth and said, "Guys…"

Just then, someone came up and grabbed Grant's left arm. He swung around, reaching for his pistol with his right hand.

Grant turned and saw a female soldier was grabbing him. Fortunately, he hadn't drawn his pistol yet.

The soldier exclaimed, "Lt. Matson! The Governor wants to talk to you."

Chapter 319

"We Know Everything. Everything."

(January 3)

She must be telling the truth, Ron Spencer thought as he was looking at Judy Kilmer. There was no faking that kind of shuddering, body-shaking crying.

Ron hugged Judy. She needed that. She needed to know that she wasn't a monster, that there was still some forgiveness and decency left in this world. Ron hugged her as she finished crying. He wasn't hurrying her; he wanted her to get it all out.

When she was done crying, she meekly asked, "What are you going to do, Ron?"

Time to lie, he thought. As horrible as that was, he had to play it safe. After all, until five minutes ago, Judy was a Lima. She was very emotional and scared. For all Ron knew, Judy might run out and naively try to tell Carlos, Rex, and Scott that everything was okay and no one had to do anything like shoot someone. Ron knew otherwise.

"You can stay here for a while," Ron said, looking at the clock and noticing it was now after midnight, officially January third. Three days into the new year and look at how much had changed. A sobbing and apparently confessing Lima, like "Judge" Judy was there on Ron's couch begging for forgiveness.

"Sherri and the kids will take care of you," Ron said. He knew that Judy loved his kids. She had a son of her own, but he never liked her. She had been so focused on her career that she never spent much time with him. He became a left-wing activist, which pleased Judy at the time, and moved to Washington, DC to work for a big union at the beginning of the last presidency. She hadn't heard from him since. This ended up meaning that Ron's adorable kids were Judy's window into the world of functional families and happy kids.

"Oh, the kids!" Judy said, suddenly happy. "Yes, yes, that would be nice. I can stay here tonight. It's best not to be out there tonight. There have been some shooting sounds." That was quite an understatement.

"You bet," Ron said, half feeling guilty about using his kids to keep Judy put, and half proud that he thought of it.

Ron put his shotgun down and said, "I'm going to go talk to Carlos and the others. Unarmed. I just feel like we can work this out."

Judy clapped her hands like a little girl. "Oh yes!" she said. "That would be so great. Violence only begets more violence." She thought that was in the Bible or something. That was the only part of the Bible she ever remembered.

"No need for that," Ron said, pointing toward the shotgun. "I'm going to go warn Len."

Judy nodded. Awesome, she thought. This really is working out. Without violence and guns. What a relief.

"Sherri," Ron called up the stairs to his wife. He went upstairs to explain why Judy would be staying at their house that night.

Ron explained that Judy had told him about Carlos and them wanting to burn down their house and Len's. He told her not to worry, and then explained his plan. Ron told the kids everything was okay and he'd be back in the morning.

He went back downstairs with a coat on. "See you in the morning when everything's been worked out," he said to Judy.

She gave him the thumbs up, feeling so glad this could be worked out peacefully.

Ron walked out of his house and headed to Len's. He wondered if that had been the last time he would ever leave his house. He quickly got there and did their secret knock on the door. It was kind of childish, but it was effective. A "daa daa, da da da, daa daa" knock.

Len came to the door with a shotgun, but also knowing it was Ron. Len asked who was at the door and, when he heard Ron's voice, opened it.

"We have some work to do tonight," Ron said. He told Len what had happened. Len was stunned, but not that surprised at the same time. He wouldn't put anything past the Carlos Cabal, but this? Wow.

Ron told Len the plan and asked to borrow a shotgun. Len nodded and they quickly headed out.

They waited a few hours—long, long hours out in the cold and occasional drizzle—at the one point in the neighborhood on the route to both Ron's and Len's house. A chokepoint.

Sure enough, at 4:35 a.m. Carlos, Rex, and Scott came walking into the neighborhood. Scott had a rifle or shotgun and Carlos had a gas can.

Ron and Len silently watched as the three walked—they thought they were being so stealthy—to a place about twenty-five yards away. It was a pre-planned place Ron and Len came up with where there were no houses directly in front of them.

Ron raised his borrowed shotgun. Len raised his, too. Each of them put three rounds of 00 buck into the three men. Just like they'd planned, Ron put one round in each of the three men from left to right and Len did the same from right to left. That would avoid confusion and make sure each target got two rounds of 00 buckshot.

It was hard for Ron to shoot his last two targets because Len's round had basically torn them in half. Fortunately, the spread on 00 pellets at twenty-five yards is pretty forgiving.

Their ears were ringing as they reloaded. They had duck hunter guns that only held three rounds to make them legal under the game laws.

Ron and Len waited a minute to see if Carlos had any back-up coming, which was very unlikely, but it was a reasonable precaution to take. People starting stirring in nearby houses. Six 12-gauge blasts in a subdivision was pretty hard not to notice, even when the surrounding city was in the middle of a battle.

As part of the plan, Len kept his shotgun pointed at the bodies and in the direction any bad guys would come. Ron started knocking on the doors nearby. He was waking people up telling them to come out and see what had happened.

There was Carlos with a full gas can—well, it was punctured with buck shot and the gas had leaked. There was Rex. Ron hoped Rex was wearing that stupid Che Guevara t-shirt when he died, but Rex's chest was so blown apart and blood soaked that Ron couldn't tell what shirt he had on. Ron really, really hated that shirt. Scott was dead and holding a shotgun. All three were blown to pieces. Blood was everywhere and was flowing in the street.

Ron started to scream out, "These men were coming to my house and to Len's to burn us down. Judy Kilmer told us so." Ron wanted everyone to know what had happened and why.

When another crowd of people timidly came out to see the commotion, Ron repeated what he'd previously said about Carlos and the others and what they were planning to do.

Then he added, to the now-larger crowd, "They said they were going to show us that the 'legitimate authorities were still in charge.'"

Ron pointed down at the dead bodies and yelled, "There you have it, folks. The 'legitimate authorities' with a can of gas coming to burn out two families. That's your 'legitimate authorities' for you. That's what they do. But they're 'legitimate' so it must be okay –

right?"

Everyone was silent. It was time for Ron to yell out what he'd been wishing he could say for months.

"The Patriots have won!" he screamed. "We have taken the city. And our intelligence is telling us about things like what these guys planned to do, how they planned, and when they were going to do it," he said pointing down at the bodies. "We know about everything. Everything."

He paused. He wanted the word "everything" to settle into them.

"So this is your chance, your only chance, to come clean," he yelled, looking each of them in the eye. "Come and tell me all the things you were forced to do for the 'legitimate authorities' and you will be pardoned. I will see to it that you are pardoned. Work with us and we'll take care of you. No revenge. Forgive and forget. Forgive and forget."

Ron paused and then yelled, "But if you continue to fight us, you'll end up like them. We know everything. *Everything*."

Later that morning, people came over to Ron's house and wanted to talk to him privately. Ron had a notebook of paper and took notes as people confessed what they'd done for the government. They were ashamed. The most common thing they admitted was turning in neighbors in an attempt to get extra FCard credits. No one did anything that led to anyone dying or going to a TDF, but still. People were tattling on, or outright lying about, their neighbors to gain favor with Carlos so they could get extra little things and not be a target themselves.

Everyone stressed that to Ron. "We just did this so they wouldn't come after us," they said. Exactly, Ron thought. Help out the system that you know is doing terrible things, just so you will be left alone. So you will keep your privileges. So no one will think you're a "right-winger." Helping the system so they don't come after you. That's how it had been for a long time.

Ron looked at his notes. Confession after confession of shameful and regrettable things. Friends betraying friends. What he read bothered him, disturbed him. This was sick and stuff like this wasn't supposed to happen in America. But this wasn't America anymore.

Chapter 320

Reconciliation

(January 3)

"The Governor?" Grant asked the soldier who had grabbed his arm. The governor of the old state? The Lima governor? Huh?

"The Interim Governor," the soldier said. "Gov. Trenton."

What?

"Ben Trenton?" Grant asked, jokingly.

"Yes, sir," the soldier said. "That's his first name. I'm pretty sure."

No way. How could this soldier know that Grant and Ben were old friends? Or that they had talked about how crazy it would be if Ben ever were the governor. Grant thought he was hallucinating from the sleep deprivation.

"Are you kidding me, soldier?" Grant asked, in his lieutenant's voice. "I'm not in a laughing mood right now," he said, looking over at Wes.

"No, sir," the soldier said confidently. "Gov. Trenton's office wants to see you. A security detail will be arriving in a few minutes to take you there."

This must be real, Grant thought. Shit. Ben was really the governor—or Interim Governor or whatever he was. What are the odds?

You should know by now.

Hearing the outside voice gave Grant goose bumps. It comforted him, too, because he knew the things that were happening, especially Wes' death, were supposed to happen.

Grant still couldn't fully believe that Ben was the Governor. All the evidence pointed toward that—especially if a security detail came soon and took Grant. But ... Grant couldn't really comprehend it all. He had slowly come to understand and accept all the "coincidences." Getting the cabin, knowing Ted and Chip, Gideon's semi, having all the food and guns out at Pierce Point. But Ben as Governor was just too much. It made all the things out at Pierce Point and with the 17th seem like they were mere preparations for something truly big.

Yes.

Grant's goose bumps came back when he heard the outside thought confirm his assumptions. Grant had thought things were already pretty amazing, but this was an order of magnitude more amazing.

This got Grant thinking. He tried to suspend his normal thought process which looked at things in terms of what is likely to happen, instead of what miracles could possibly happen. Okay, he told himself as he waited for the security detail to pick him, anything is possible. Anything. Think big. Don't limit yourself to the likely.

What should Grant try to do at the Governor's Office? What would be considered thinking big?

Blank. Grant's mind was blank. He had no idea. He didn't know what to ask the Governor for or what he needed to accomplish. Blank.

Reconciliation.

That was it! Avoiding a French Revolution outcome. Preventing the people of this state from tearing each other apart for decades with reprisals and blood feuds. Getting people to reconcile with their former enemies and to move on and make things livable again in this place.

A pick-up full of contractor-looking guys pulled up to the vehicle checkpoint at the intersection in front of the brewery. The driver showed something to the guards, they pointed toward Grant and Grant signaled that he was coming over.

Grant started walking toward the truck. He came up to the driver, who had a State Patrol badge out. The old state badge. It was pretty obvious he wasn't a Lima, though.

"Looks like you're my ride," Grant said to him. He noticed that many of the contractor guys had "Wash. State Guard" name tapes on their jackets.

"Your name, sir?" the driver asked.

"Lt. Grant Matson," Grant said.

"Then we are your ride, sir," the driver replied.

One of the occupants of the cab, who was in standard State Guard fatigues with name tapes and all, got out and made room for Grant.

"No," Grant said to the soldier, who he noticed had captain's bars on his uniform. "No, sir," Grant added, seeing the bars. "I ride in the back. I'm used to it."

Grant had a surge of cockiness come over him, so he added, "I'm a 17th Irregular, sir. It's how we roll." He had no idea why he said

136

that, except that he was thoroughly enjoying this moment. He knew nothing bad could happen to him, not if the Governor wanted to see him.

The captain smiled and got back into the cab. He was happy to stay warm while their guest rode in the back.

Grant climbed in the back of the truck with three other guys and the truck took off. Grant was happy that the rain had finally stopped. Grant asked the guys what unit they were in.

"We're assigned to SOC," one of them said, referring to the Special Operations Command.

"Let me guess," Grant said, "You used to work with Lt. Col. Hammond at Ft. Lewis back in the day."

The contractors smiled. "Yes, sir," one of them answered.

"Ted Malloy is my First Sergeant," Grant said. They all knew Ted. Some of them knew Sap, too. They talked about how many former Special Forces guys were Oath Keepers and had come over to the Patriot side. Knowing how many SF guys were at Boston Harbor shed light on why HQ was able to do all the amazing things it had been doing. They talked until the truck pulled up at the old WAB building.

Grant was shocked to see his old office. It was trashed, partially burned with broken windows. But it was full of soldiers and civilians and the lights were on. It was full of activity.

He was also surprised to be taken to the WAB offices instead of the capitol itself. He basically trusted these guys who had taken him, but he was always on guard for a trap. He wondered if this was one.

"This where we're supposed to be?" Grant asked the driver with the State Patrol badge.

"Yes, sir," the driver said. "This is where the Governor is. That's classified, of course."

"Of course," Grant said. Okay, if this was a trap, it was so elaborate that it probably wasn't a trap. No one would go to this much trouble just to capture little ole' Grant Matson.

The driver led Grant into the building. Two uniformed State Patrol troopers were at the reception area. . They were in old state uniforms and had a piece of tape on their badges that said something, probably with the name of the new state on it. The new state? That sounded weird. Grant wondered what the name of his new state even was.

The troopers saw Grant with his AR, kit, and pistol and started to stop him. One of them said, "No weapons past this point, sir."

Then Grant heard a very familiar voice, a wonderful and joyous sound.

"He's cool, gentlemen," Ben said to the guards. Ben came over and hugged Grant. He had to lean into it to get an above-the-arms hug because Grant had his AR slung across his front.

"That won't do," Grant said, referring to the partial hug. He took off his rifle, which caused the troopers to put their hands on their pistols. Grant handed his AR to the captain.

"Now we can do this," Grant said as he held out his arms. He hugged Ben. It wasn't a mere bro hug. It was a full-on "haven't seen you in years, dude, thought you were dead," hug.

Things were normal. Ben was alive. Grant was at the WAB building, just like the old days. Except Ben was the Governor and Grant was a soldier. That was definitely not normal, though it was going to be the new norm now.

"I have some people for you to see," Ben said. He led Grant into office where Grant found Tom and Brian and even Carly!

Hugs all around. Grant was tearing up. So were they.

They all shared their fears that the other had been killed.

They caught up on how they'd escaped and hidden out as POIs, giving the short versions of each story because they didn't have much time. Grant had the strongest feeling that everyone in that room had been protected by a mighty hand. It was an unmistakable feeling.

When the catching up was over, Grant asked, "How did you know I was in Olympia?"

"That's actually why you're here," Ben said. "Send in General Roswell, please," Ben said to Tom and Brian, who were sitting at the table in Ben's office. Brian got up and went out of the office.

Ben said, "We have some business to talk about, Grant."

This was it. The reason for the cabin, Pierce Point, the 17th. All of it. They were the prerequisites necessary to put Grant and Ben in this office to talk about this topic. Grant could feel the goose bumps. He knew, with absolute certainty that all the "coincidences" had led up to this office meeting. There had been a plan, a roadmap. None of this was happening by chance.

Grant hoped reconciliation would be the topic. If not, he would make it the topic, even if it meant angering Ben and losing a friend. He knew what he was supposed to do and he knew it would happen. He expected a miracle. The odds no longer applied to Grant. That wasn't arrogant, it was humbling. He was part of something huge, a little tiny player in a vast, magnificent theatrical production that happened to be real life.

A distinguished looking military man walked in with Lt. Col. Hammond. They both came to attention when they got near Ben.

"At ease, gentlemen," Ben said. It sounded weird to Grant, hearing Ben talk in military lingo, but someone had told Ben that saying "at ease" was what the Governor does, so Ben obliged. And he did it well, just like a real Governor. He *was* a real Governor, Grant kept telling himself.

"General Roswell and Colonel Hammond," Ben said, "this is Lieutenant Grant Matson." They exchanged pleasantries. Grant wanted to high five Hammond, but that wouldn't exactly be protocol.

"General Roswell tells me," Ben said, again sounding just like a Governor, "that we're having some trouble with what to do with prisoners and collaborators. He and Colonel Hammond had an idea that just happened to be along the lines of what I was already thinking, and I thought of you, Grant, as maybe the person who could do it."

Grant knew exactly what it was, but he listened patiently anyway. He needed to hear the Governor and General out.

"From a humanitarian and political perspective," Ben began, "we can't have a bloody twenty-year simmering civil war. We just can't. We have to get this behind us. We have a state to rebuild. We can't get the economy back up and running if neighbors are killing each other over old grudges about who collaborated with which side. We just can't have it."

Ben added, "Obviously, from a military perspective, to which I defer to General Roswell, we can't have a long fight like this. So we need..." Ben struggled for just the right word.

"Reconciliation," Grant said confidently.

"Yes, reconciliation," Ben said. "Thanks, Grant."

"So," Ben continued, "there's a political and military need for reconciliation. I have brought together my political and military people to try to solve it. Suggestions?" He looked at General Roswell, Lt. Col. Hammond, Tom, and Brian.

General Roswell spoke up. "Sir, from a military perspective, we need to have a plan and issue orders down to every soldier and our civilian sympathizers making it clear that we won't kill prisoners and collaborators. We then need to have a method for processing prisoners and collaborators, to find out which ones are truly bad guys and which ones don't need to be punished. We have a system in place for collecting and interrogating prisoners; that's standard military protocol. But we need a way to take it one step further: punish the bad ones and let the good ones go, but with some conditions."

"On the political side," Tom said after a brief pause, "we need this reconciliation process to be fair. The public has to believe in it. We can't be too harsh on the Loyalists or too lenient. We can't favor Patriots who committed war crimes, either. People will be expecting us to let 'our guys' go even if they did bad things. But we can't be too harsh on our guys who were put in tough situations."

"And," Ben said, "on the legal side, the Governor has the power to pardon under the old constitution. I'm sure we'll keep that part in the con con." Grant quietly assumed that "Con con" must be a constitutional convention. Before the war, Ben and Grant had dreamed about a con con to fix all the bad things that were being done.

"Yes, sir," Gen. Roswell said, "You can pardon people. Everything that was done was a state crime. I guess they were federal crimes, too, but we're not part of that federal union anymore, if it even still exists. You have the power to pardon state crimes. That's how we can do this."

"We set up a Governor's commission of some kind," Brian said "that determines who should be pardoned and who should be prosecuted. Civil prosecutions, I presume?"

Gen. Roswell nodded. "Technically, we might be able to do this with military tribunals, but..." he paused, "look how the Limas used those. Everyone they disagreed with was an 'enemy combatant,' even American citizens whose only crime was disagreeing with them. I highly recommend against military tribunals, sir," Gen. Roswell said, as he looked at Ben.

"No military tribunals," Ben confirmed. "Nope. Not after what those turned in to. I can't reassure the population that I'm a constitutional reformer and then do something like that. Nope. Civilian trials only."

Ben paused and thought about what all that entailed. Juries, court rooms, prosecutors, defense attorneys, rules of evidence. "Civilian trials will be a big pain in the ass, but it will be constitutional. We have to be the models of decency, gentlemen. Everyone will be expecting us to be just like the old guys. They'll be chomping at the bit to call us hypocrites. We won't give them that chance. We didn't fight this war and go through all this crap only to end up being just like them."

It was silent in the room. Grant felt so grateful Ben had just made such a statement. Thank God.

"So a civilian commission to recommend pardons of state

crimes is what we're thinking?" Brian asked.

Everyone thought about it.

Gen. Roswell was the first to speak up. "I can see that working," he said. "Obviously, our military people will have a role in getting prisoners and collaborators to a secure setting. Then the civilian commission people can work with our military intelligence units to figure out who the bad guys are. Then the civilian commission can do its thing and have trials for the really bad ones. The not so bad ones can be given pardons. It should work."

"I foresee lots of pardons," Grant said. "It will be hard to prove many of these crimes. If we have a full-blown trial for every crime, we would have to have hundreds of judges and thousands of jurors going at any given time. When, instead, people should be working to rebuild the economy. There's a huge 'forgive and forget' factor to all of this. Many pardons will foster that."

"But not too many," Tom said. "The bastards who did this," he said pointing to some burn marks along the window frames of his former office, "they shouldn't get off scot free."

"True," Grant said, arguing a little with his old boss. "But how many resources do you devote to figuring out who did this and then giving them a jury trial? Wouldn't those resources be better spent on fixing the window frames?"

Everyone nodded. Grant used the perfect analogy at the perfect time. He knew that brilliant thought didn't come from him. He was just the medium through which brilliant things were happening right now. It felt awesome.

"That's exactly the spirit I need," Ben said. "Grant, you will chair the Reconciliation Commission."

What? Grant felt a surge of surprise come over him although the announcement was also what he was expecting would happen.

"Of course, Governor," Grant said matter-of-factly. The biggest honor of his life was just a simple, "You bet, Ben" kind of answer.

"From what I've heard about Lt. Matson's past performance in his little community," Gen. Roswell said, looking over at Lt. Col. Hammond, who was nodding, "I think he'll do a fine job. He obviously has your trust, Governor."

Ben nodded. "That's an understatement," he said.

"When do I get started?" Grant asked Ben, knowing the answer.

"Now," Ben said.

"I kinda thought so," Grant said.

"We'll work out the details," Gen. Roswell said. "Lt. Matson will have all the military assets he needs." Grant had a rough idea how he would take up the General on that offer. Grant's reconciliation commission staff would be fed, housed, and protected by the military. Grant would have a personal security detail made up of … who else? The Team.

Ben stood up at his desk, signaling that it was time to go. That's what powerful people do and Ben fit the role perfectly. Everyone who was sitting stood up. Gen. Roswell and Lt. Col. Hammond snapped to attention.

"Hate to end this, gentlemen," Ben said, "but I have a bunch of other meetings right now. Not as enjoyable as this one, I might add." Everyone was shuffling out of the office, except Tom and Brian who seemed to have permanent seats on the couch there.

Ben turned to Grant and said, "Hey, Grant, you remember the 2005 Super Bowl?"

"Of course," Grant said with a huge smile. "Never thought it would happen … Governor."

Chapter 321

New Washington

(January 3)

As Grant left Ben's office after that amazing experience he felt naked. He realized why. He didn't have his rifle. He'd had it twenty-four hours a day for days now. He sought out the captain who was holding it by the reception area, and was happy to be reunited with it.

"We have some things to talk about," Gen. Roswell said to Grant, and motioned for him to go into a nearby conference room. Grant followed him with his rifle. Ah. It felt so good to have it back. His right thumb could rest on that safety which was very calming.

Once they were in the conference room, Grant stood until Gen. Roswell said, "At ease." Gen. Roswell was deferential in Ben's office, but was in full command in that conference room.

"Glad to have you on board," he began. "Seriously. Colonel Hammond has told me some great things. And you have a long history with Gov. Trenton, so you'll be perfect for this job. This very difficult job, I might add."

Grant nodded. It was slowly sinking into him just how hard this reconciliation thing would be, but he knew he needed to do it. So much groundwork had been laid to make this happen that it was unthinkable to not go ahead and do it. Grant couldn't disappoint the outside thought. Plus, he knew that he could expect miracles. Grant couldn't possibly pull off this reconciliation thing alone, but God could. It would be a piece of cake for Him.

Gen. Roswell and Lt. Col. Hammond talked to Grant about logistics and chain of command. There weren't a lot of organizational charts in a fluid situation like this. Basically, Grant would be in charge of the 17th and would use it to do his preliminary Reconciliation Commission work like investigating the crimes of prisoners until the Commission was formally established by the Interim Legislature. Once that happened, Grant and the Team would resign from the Washington State Guard and become civilian Commission staff acting under the authority of the Governor to help him carry out his pardon powers.

In the meantime, Grant would report directly to the General. However, he would have the unusual power of working directly with the Governor's staff. It was unheard of for a lieutenant to have direct access to the commander in chief like the Governor, but in this case, it made sense. Grant working with the Governor's staff, while still reporting directly to the General, allowed Gen. Roswell to stay in the loop when Grant interacted with the General's boss, the Governor. It was a perfect arrangement in this situation.

Grant saw the existence of Seattle as a huge factor in the reconciliation work. "I take it, General," Grant said, "that the plan is not to immediately take Seattle."

Gen. Roswell laughed. "Oh, hell no," he said. "Maybe never. Let that place rot. I'm not wasting a single soldier on that pile of shit."

"We have enough on our hands in the rest of New Washington," Lt. Col. Hammond said.

New Washington? What was that?

"New Washington, sir?" Grant asked.

Hammond smiled. "Oh, you haven't heard? That's the name of the state you're in right now. We were calling it 'Free Washington,' but now it's 'New Washington.' New Washington is old Washington minus the Seattle area. It's ours now."

New Washington. That said it all. It was "new." And "Washington," as in George Washington, who had to rebuild after a war that divided the people.

"New Washington" was even more symbolic of the times and what was needed now. A new person was needed to rebuild after this latest war dividing people. Grant wasn't the new George Washington — Grant did not provide the military strategy for victory like Washington did — but maybe Ben would be the new George Washington. Grant could at least help Ben be the new George Washington.

Grant needed to get back to business. He didn't want to waste the General's time with history or philosophy.

"From my limited perspective," Grant said, "I love the fact that Seattle is there and the bad guys will go there. Get them the hell out of here, especially the gangs. Let them go do their thing in Seattle. It will cause Seattle to collapse even quicker." Grant felt bad basically wishing another wave of murder, rape, and thuggery on the people of Seattle, but they'd had plenty of chances to leave there in the past. For whatever reasons, they stayed and didn't overthrow that government. People get the governments they deserve.

"I don't want enemy assets to escape," Gen. Roswell said and Lt. Col. Hammond nodded. Letting a weakened enemy just leave went against all their military training.

"Could we open up I-5 and let them just leave?" Grant asked. "I know that's unorthodox, sir, but it would make things go a lot smoother here in..." Grant paused to say it, "New Washington." It sounded so weird.

"I'll have to think about it, Lieutenant," Gen. Roswell said. "I see your point, but it's been drilled into me not to let the enemy escape." Grant could tell that his suggestion was going to be disregarded. Oh well. Grant's job was to give suggestions, and he never claimed to be an expert in military strategy. If the enemy wasn't allowed to retreat to Seattle, Grant would just deal with the increase in bad guys for him to process on the Reconciliation Commission.

"Anything else I need to think about?" Gen. Roswell asked.

"I have experienced some initial resistance among some regular military officers to the reconciliation approach," Grant said.

Lt. Col. Hammond nodded his head, "Lt. Col. Brussels, CO of 3rd Battalion, didn't like the pamphlet Grant made about people turning themselves in and being considered for pardons."

"You issued that pamphlet before our meeting with the Governor?" Gen. Roswell asked.

"Yes, sir," Grant said, as confidently as possible.

"Lucky for you," Gen. Roswell said with a smile, "that ended up being the Governor's policy." He paused and said, "I recognize that you're new to the military." He said because it was true and to remind Grant not to do something like that while he was under his command.

"Sir," Grant asked, "could you let the leadership of the regular military know that reconciliation is the policy?"

"I will issue a very explicit order," Gen. Roswell said. "All my orders are explicit, but they are especially so when they detail something the Governor wants to have happen."

Gen. Roswell stood up. Grant and Lt. Col. Hammond stood up, too.

"Anything else?" Gen. Roswell asked. It was obviously time to go.

"No, sir," Grant said.

"We're adjourned here," Gen. Roswell said and started to walk out. He suddenly stopped and turned to Grant.

"Lt. Matson, you know how important this reconciliation thing is, don't you?"

"Yes, sir," Grant said.

"So do I," Gen. Roswell said. "For months now, my staff and I, including Colonel Hammond here, have been talking about the French Revolution and how to prevent that outcome here. I just about fell over when I was chatting with the Governor a few minutes before you arrived and he said you and he had talked about the French Revolution before the Collapse. Right then I knew you were the right man for this job."

Grant felt those "coincidence" goose bumps again. He was getting used them, although they still amazed him.

"Let's go out and fix New Washington," Gen. Roswell said, as he walked out of the room.

Grant stood and thought about that. Let's fix New Washington.

And on to fix it they went.

Chapter 322

Reconciliation Commission

(January 17)

"This never gets old," Pow said, as the Team piled into Mark's truck nearly two weeks after they took Olympia. Hearing this reminded Grant about Pierce Point, which reminded him of Lisa. For about two seconds. Then he put her out of his mind, which he was getting better and better at. He'd had lots of practice. He knew Manda and Cole were fine. Cole probably missed his tucking, but he was almost fourteen now. He needed to be more independent. Instead of being a kid with autism, Cole needed to be a teenager with autism. Grant had work to do so he needed to focus. He always amazed himself at how he could compartmentalize his family situation and get on to the work he needed to do. Being surrounded by his guys 24/7 made that much easier for him. Grant wasn't lonely out there on the still-dangerous battlefield. There were still Lima hold-outs around.

The Team was still using that beat up truck. Might as well. It worked fine, despite the shot-out windshield from the Watershed Park engagement. By now, New Washington was trading with Texas so there was plenty of diesel in Olympia so that was another reason to keep using it. There wasn't any diesel for civilians, but lots for the military.

Well, technically, for State Police units like the Team. They had been deactivated from being part of the 17th Irregulars to a special detachment of the State Police. Except Grant. He was not technically in the State Police. He had to be neutral, given that he was heading the Reconciliation Commission. He couldn't be "enforcing" the laws when it was his job to decide who should or shouldn't have the laws enforced against them.

Despite technically being cops, the Team didn't do anything differently now. They didn't have badges yet. At least, not official ones. They still had their pre-Collapse "Concealed Weapons Permit" badges so they wouldn't get shot by actual cops when detaining a bad guy. Now everyone on the Team was a real cop.

New State Police badges were on the way, at least, temporary ones. The temporary badges would be a patch with intricate stitching that would be very hard to counterfeit. A small shop in nearby Centralia run by Patriots was able to make them. They would work fine to serve as an identifier that only the State Police had.

Everyone in the truck had their familiar roles. Bobby drove. He had to dress warmer now that the windshield was gone and had to wear goggles for when they got up to speed so the wind wouldn't get in his eyes. They were military-issue goggles from the Iraq war. At first, Bobby looked a little odd with goggles up around his black fleece cap, but it pretty quickly looked normal.

Scotty was still up front working coms. He also was the makeshift medic, although he hadn't had to patch anyone up yet. Thank goodness.

Scotty's kit was still blood-stained from hoisting up that kid who killed Wes. His kit had the most blood on it. They tried to clean it off with some pretty harsh detergents which got most of the blood out, but the stains were still there. The Team wore the blood stains as a badge of honor. It showed everyone that these guys had killed and would do it again. Every drop of blood on their kit was justice for Wes.

Kellie was devastated when she got the news at Pierce Point. At first she didn't believe it. Then she cried for two days. Lisa was concerned she might lose the baby with all the stress. When Lisa told her this, Kellie almost instantly calmed down. She told Lisa, "I won't do anything to harm this baby. He or she is my only link to Wes. If calming down is what I need to do, I'll do it." After that, she was much better, but she missed Wes almost every waking minute of the day. She had the Team Chicks and lots of others to support her. They reduced a horrible situation to simply bad, mostly sad.

The Team had come up with a plan to not only have at least one of them spend every New Year's Day in the future with Kellie, but also to take care of her and their little soon-to-be child. The Team would make sure she always had a good job and everything else she needed, including lots of company and friends around. The Team had made a vow way back before the Collapse to take care of each other's families. It meant that a man could go into danger and fight because he knew his teammates would take one of his biggest fears off his mind: taking care of his family.

Kellie got to Olympia for the funeral. They had to bury Wes in Olympia because they had no good way to preserve him for burial in Pierce Point. Wes was buried, along with way too many others, in a new cemetery in Olympia called Patriot's Cemetery. Wes was laid to rest with full military honors. By some miracle, Wes' dad was there. He was a retired Ranger from Ft. Lewis and had joined a Patriot irregular unit in Enumclaw. He cried at the funeral and screamed out that he was proud of his son. Grant knew that Wes had known this. Wes knew the importance of the work he was doing. Grant went up to Wes' dad at the funeral and told him all the brave and heroic things Wes had done. Grant even fibbed a little and told his dad that Wes had said that he knew his dad would be proud. That would comfort Wes' dad for the rest of his life.

Grant refocused on the task at hand: going to a town to informally hear evidence about some prisoners. Pow was in the back of the extended cab with Grant, windows down to shoot out of if necessary. "That's what a heater is for," they always said. Pow was really developing into a tactical commander, even more than before. He was now leading more than just the Team. He was looked to for his advice on tactical matters by other police and military leaders.

Ryan still rode in the back, which he insisted upon. He didn't want to change his routine. He was always in the back with Wes and that was where he wanted to stay. It was his version of mourning mixed with normalcy bias. It was fine.

They used the back of the truck to haul a few high-priority parcels from point to point. Grant's job had him going all over New Washington. If a load of medicine needed to get to Aberdeen and Grant was going there anyway to a Reconciliation Commission event, then they'd take the load with them.

Grant's main job was to set the tone of the ReconComm, as it became known, and to recruit good people to work on it. He had a flood of volunteers for the ReconComm, many of them Patriot lawyers. Most of them had done tax protestor and other liberty work before the Collapse. It wasn't hard to determine who was a real pre-Collapse Patriot and who was just saying they were for the sake of career advancement. Since there were so few Patriot lawyers before the Collapse, Grant knew most of them. He had about two dozen of them and about two hundred investigators. They were all volunteers who didn't get paid. They did receive meals and a place to stay.

Grant didn't actually decide cases—there were too many for one person to do—but he read all the reports his staff produced. Instead of deciding cases, he was the driving force behind the ReconComm. He was basically going out and giving speeches about the reason why reconciliation was important. He was there to show people that a real person—a fair and decent person—was the "face" of the ReconComm. It helped that Grant was a "war hero" (although he didn't think so). The 17th Irregulars quickly became famous, not for pure military feats—the regular military units did all the hard work—but because they were a largely a bunch of regular civilians who did some important things, especially in the first few hours of the attack on Olympia. The stories about Olympia were exaggerated, as were the stories that Grant had single-handedly turned Pierce Point into a paradise, but the Patriots needed heroes so the population would believe in them. Grant was happy to oblige and it made it easier for him to accomplish what he wanted to accomplish, which was reconciliation.

Grant viewed every speech he gave, every group he talked to, and every small article he wrote for the new independent newspapers as an opportunity to go out and persuade people about reconciliation.

Most people were initially skeptical about why they should forgive and forget when Limas had done terrible things. Grant was good at explaining this. He got lots of practice.

There were still small pockets of Lima insurgents. Grant was a big, fat juicy target, so the Team was there to protect him. He had to stop carrying his AR and kit everywhere because it wouldn't send the right message if he had those. If the war was over and this guy is telling everyone to forgive and forget, why does he have a rifle and full kit? Grant still wore his pistol and extra magazines, though. He had to protect himself at all times. He continued to wear "contractor" clothes as they became known. His 5.11 pants, "hillbilly slippers," earth-tone shirts and jackets.

The Team also wore contractor clothes and, like just about all soldiers and police, had beards. Like the beards, the knit caps became part of the Team's "look" during that winter.

Grant didn't want to wear a business suit which would send a message to people that Grant was a technocrat or a politician. And Grant needed people to believe the "war hero" stories in order for him to have credibility with them so they would be open to reconciliation. Grant wearing contractor clothes reinforced the impression that he was an irregular unit citizen-soldier. Besides, Grant didn't have any suits, and if he did, they wouldn't fit anyway, given all the weight he'd lost.

On this particular day, Grant and the Team were going on a long trip. Across the mountain pass—Highway 12, the only one open because the main pass, I-90, went through Seattle and was Lima-held—to Yakima in eastern Washington. A trip that took four hours before the Collapse now took a whole day. There was a lot of traffic clogged up the one open mountain pass, and lots of precautions for staying out of an ambush. There weren't too many because the Limas were very weak in New Washington, but there was always that threat. Grant and the Team had a military Humvee in front of them and behind them during this trip.

On the rides, Grant would read hundreds of pages of reports and recommendations on pardons or prosecutions for various people. He signed off on them. He couldn't possibly know the details of all the cases. He had to rely on his commission staff. These reports were chock full of interesting stories.

Chapter 323

Reports and Letters

From all the reports he was reading, a pattern was emerging. There were two kinds of Limas: involuntary and voluntary. The involuntary ones, which were the vast majority of them, were people "just doing their job." They were government employees or government contractors and their business was doing what government wanted. And before the Collapse, government was the majority of the business in the state, so the majority of people did business in some way with the government.

The involuntary Limas weren't angels. They profited — handsomely, in most cases — from the government. Leading up to the Collapse, they got things that were taken from other people. Whether it was tax money or property seized, or whether it was a competing business that was regulated out of existence, these people got things that were taken from other people. It was that simple.

The theft accelerated during the Collapse. The involuntary Limas were the ones with big fat FCards and gas. They had the power to potentially put their neighbors in jail with one "report" to the authorities. Some of them abused this power, but many did not. Most abused this power a little but usually, they would say, only to take care of their families.

"I didn't have a choice" they would say. That might be true, or at least partially true, in most cases.

The involuntary Limas would be pardoned. There were several reasons for this. First, and most disturbing, was because it would be impossible to execute them all. Not that killing them all was what anyone wanted — except some hardcore "retributionist" Patriots as they became known. But, with the limited resources the New Washington government had, there weren't enough firing squads or jails for all the involuntary Limas. Most of the pre-Collapse economy was tied to government. Most people had done business in some way with government. Grant remembered that for a while, he too, was a government employee at the State Auditor's Office. He technically "profited" from government, too. Should people like him be killed?

There were just too many involuntary Limas to do anything about.

Second, mass killings and revenge was exactly what Grant was there to prevent. In fact, Grant spent most of his time fighting the retributionists. Not physically, although he and the Team were expecting a retributionist para group to try to take him out, but politically. There were retributionist legislators and even a few judges. Politics was helping Grant, though. While most average citizens hated the Limas and wouldn't mind if they all died, they were so tired of war and hunger and dying that they wanted it to stop. They wanted the economy to get back on its feet and for life to quit being so damned hard. Therefore, there was little political support for the retributionists. Especially if the ReconComm was being fair and punishing the truly bad people, which was Grant's job.

The third reason for not killing all the Limas was that the economy needed these people. The majority of educated people were Limas, if not active ones, then Lima sympathizers in the past. This was because, once again, most of the economy was government. The well-educated Limas were the white-collar people who ran things. The managers. They were managing and running things that didn't need to be run like a giant government. However, they were the ones who would be necessary to make things run smoothly in the new economy where a former government manager wouldn't have a new government job, but he or she might be a great manager for a manufacturing plant that wanted to open.

Voluntary Limas, however, were a different story. These were the people who weren't just "doing their job." They sought out the power and money and abused it. And they loved it. They were the Commissioner Winters of the world, the Nancy Ringmans. They did horrible things and ordered the involuntary Limas to do them, too.

The FCorps kept coming up in the reports Grant was reading. People who just joined it to get some extra FCard credits, like Ron Spencer who volunteered to do accounting for the FCorps, were not the problem. It was the people who joined the FCorps and actively went out and hurt people. All the sex offenders and other criminals who joined up because they were now immune from the law. Grant read reports about the "bumfucks" the FCorps did. Grant ordered hundreds of those people to be prosecuted, which meant they would probably be hung. It was literally a box to check on a form and then initial. It was easy to order the probable death of these people. Technically, Grant did not order their deaths. By checking the box, he was recommending against the governor granting a pardon. They would then be given a jury trial and almost certainly convicted. It was impossible to be in the FCorps for months and not leave behind proof of it. Most of them bragged about all the things they'd done. They loved bragging about how they weren't subject to the laws. And they loved telling people how important they were, which meant gloating about all their crimes. That hubris ended up being the death of them, literally.

Grant would pray that he was doing the right thing. He essentially had the power of life and death in his hands which was an enormous responsibility. He prayed that he exercised it wisely. He would stop doing what he was doing and just close his eyes and listen for the outside thought to guide him. The outside thought never told him he was making a mistake. The only thing he heard from it, and he heard it often, was *forgiveness*. It was hard to forgive, especially after hours of reading those reports. But then he would hear it again. *Forgiveness.*

Grant wondered if Lisa was forgiving him. He was so busy with life and death matters that, he hated to admit, he didn't think about her that often. Why do it, though? He'd just get more depressed. Then he'd feel sorry for himself. It did no good for Grant to constantly think about how doing what he was supposed to do during the Collapse, war, and Restoration, as they were calling it, had cost him his marriage. No good whatsoever.

"Lives, fortunes, and sacred honor" he kept telling himself. That put his sacrifice in context and helped him get through it.

But still, he wondered. He would tell himself that she was missing him, which was probably true, but would she be able to admit that? Would the fact that Grant and the 17th Irregulars were now almost legends in New Washington sway her? Would she realize that if thousands of people thought what he did was awesome, that maybe she should think so, too?

Would Manda and Cole sway her? The kids certainly missed their dad. Manda would understand why Grant was doing what he was doing. On some level, Cole understood, too; he knew that his dad was putting the bad people in jail. Funny, an autistic kid had a better understanding of the situation than a grown-up doctor.

Grant tried to call the kids, though the phones were a complete mess. The Limas took them down on their way out. The internet was spotty and Grant didn't want to use it even when it worked because, for all he knew, he would be giving away his position to someone in Seattle who could get a Lima hit team out to his location.

No, Grant would just sit there and wonder about his family

from afar. Whether they loved him or hated him, or a combination of both. All he could do was write letters and give them to people who were going in the direction of Pierce Point. Since he was well known, and, although he hated to admit, because he had the power of life and death as the chair of the ReconComm, he could get letters through that others couldn't.

Grant wrote letters to his family describing all the good things that he was doing. He constantly downplayed the danger and aimed the letters primarily at the kids. He would tell Lisa that he loved her and missed her. He wondered if that just made her angrier.

"Oh, if you love me so much," he could hear her saying, "then why did you leave? And why haven't you come home?"

Every time he wrote a letter back home, he felt terrible. Those letters reminded him how he had left, how letters were necessary because he wasn't there to say the things he was writing.

He never got a letter back from them. Never, though he kept waiting for one.

He would start to feel alone, like he was totally alone, the only person in the world. Then the Team would be there and would remind him that he wasn't alone. He had the best friends in the world around him. He had dozens of people a day tell him how much good he was doing with the ReconComm. He would meet a few people each day for whom he had obtained pardons and they thanked him for literally saving their lives. It was powerful.

And empty. He didn't want strangers telling him how awesome he was. He wanted to be a dad again. He really wanted to be a husband again. He wanted the appreciation coming from his family.

Lives, fortunes, and sacred honor. It all kept coming back to that. Grant was making a sacrifice. It was the price he was paying to do the things he needed to do.

As the Team was taking a break at a rest stop on the way to Yakima and standing around Mark's truck, a soldier came up to Pow.

"This is a letter for Lt. Matson," the soldier said.

"It's Commissioner Matson, but I'll get it to him," Pow said. "Thanks." He looked and saw the letter was from Lisa. It was likely the most important piece of mail Grant would ever receive.

Chapter 324

Nightmares

(January 17)

Nancy Ringman heard someone coming down the hall. She perked up. She had only been in prison for two weeks – two long, agonizing weeks – and already missed human contact. That was because she was segregated in the old High School building in Olympia, which now served as a makeshift prison for high-value prisoners. It was directly across the street from the Olympia State Guard Armory, formerly the National Guard Armory. It was extremely secure.

She was segregated from other prisoners because word got out that she was the Clover Park Butcher. Most of the other prisoners were hardcore Limas, but some were Patriots who had committed war crimes. Nancy couldn't be anywhere near them or they would kill her with their bare hands. And, as much as the guards and warden hated her for what she'd done, they wanted to her to stay alive for the trial. Televising that trial would be very important for the Patriots to win the hearts and minds of any remaining Undecideds. Nancy had confessed on video so the trial would be short and the outcome certain. But having her confess again on the stand was extremely important to the Patriots. The Governor personally called the warden and reminded him of this.

Nancy had been having nightmares. In them, she saw the faces of the prisoners from Clover Park. They would ask her, "Nancy, why did you do this?" They would say, "Tell my daughter her daddy won't be coming home, Nancy." Sometimes they would ask, "Nancy, do you want another glass of wine?" Other times they said, "You were a coward for not shooting yourself."

Nancy's mind had essentially shut down. She couldn't cope with what was happening. She couldn't eat or sleep. She knew she'd be hung soon. but she wanted to have her trial and the opportunity to publicly tell everyone how sorry she was. She had radically transformed from a month ago when she hated teabaggers and actually enjoyed killing them. A switch had gone off in her head. She didn't hate anymore; she just felt guilty.

"More letters for you, Ringman," the female guard said. She pitched them under the locked classroom door that held Nancy inside, except for the three times a day she was handcuffed and let out to use the bathroom and eat.

At first, Nancy tore open the letters and read them intently. But they were from victims of Clover Park and told her they hoped she died a painful death. She couldn't read the letters anymore. She just stared at the envelopes on the floor of the classroom. She knew what they said. They said the same things in her nightmares.

Once again, she looked throughout the classroom for a way to kill herself. Some rope, something sharp. Nothing. They had removed all of those things, of course. But it eased her mind for her to spend hours thinking of ways she could kill herself. It made the nightmares go away. For a while.

Chapter 325

The Aftermath

(January 17)

Pow was running to Grant full speed to get him the letter from Lisa. As he came up on Grant, Pow got the code word in his earpiece, "Tillamook!" It was the name of the Team's favorite local brand of cheese and also the code for an immediate attack.

"Tillamook!" Pow yelled as he grabbed Grant's arm. "Now! Move!"

Grant knew he was serious. They had practiced this. The Team instantly formed a small perimeter around the truck. As soon as Grant was in the truck, they jumped in, too. Bobby was already in the truck idling it, of course. The State Guard escort vehicles were scrambling around too, getting ready for a firefight or to take off.

Dying at a crappy rest stop, Grant thought. What a shitty way to go. Not very glamorous, especially after all he'd been through.

Grant had his AR, which he kept in the truck since a peace loving and forgiving public figure like the chair of the ReconComm shouldn't be seen slinging a rifle. Grant was ready to fight it out.

Silence.

More silence.

The radio crackled. "False alarm," the familiar voice of the dispatcher said excitedly. "False alarm."

No one relaxed. The dispatcher could be wrong or, conceivably, could be in on a hit.

"Marco Polo," another voice said on the radio, and everyone relaxed. That was a code word for a true false alarm.

In the all the excitement of the possible ambush, and because he hadn't slept more than three hours in a row in the past few weeks, Pow shoved the letter in his pocket and forgot to give it to Grant.

Grant went back to work. He was so used to reading reports when he was in the rear cab of the truck that he just went back to doing that.

Grant had been saving a batch of reports for a time when he could really concentrate on them because they were reports about people he knew. This meant he couldn't approve or disapprove the suggested action on their cases because he had a conflict of interest. His assistant, John Bollinger, did that. Regardless, he was really curious about what had happened to the people he knew. Now was the time he had to read them, so he dove right in.

The first report was on Jeanie Thompson. Grant had always liked her. He felt sorry for her because she had compromised her beliefs to be a big shot in politics. It turned out she had been at Camp Murray all along with the old governor and then the new governor, Rick Menlow. He was the governor of Seattle now. How sad. Grant knew he was trouble when Menlow swept into power as a "reformer" and then wouldn't fire any of the old people who were doing bad things. Whatever. That was typical.

Jeanie had made it out of Camp Murray to a Patriot unit on the bridge on I-5 south of JBLM and north of Olympia. She brought some friends with her.

The report detailed how she had been taken out of any position of power because she was a Facebook friend with a POI, Grant Matson. She was relegated to menial jobs. Right before the attack on Olympia, all the important people fled Camp Murray and only people like Jeanie were left. She described in the report how she was approached by numerous people similarly left behind at Camp Murray and got them out to the Patriot lines.

The people Jeanie brought with her were a treasure trove of intelligence nuggets. Code phrases, frequencies, locations of equipment and key communications facilities. And the defectors Jeanie led also confirmed several rumors about an impending counter attack. They also had information on Patriot prisoners the Limas had and described the crimes some of them had allegedly committed.

Grant looked down at the recommendation box on the report. He knew what it would say. "Full Pardon" was checked and initialed by John Bollinger. Good.

The next name that caught Grant's eye was Nancy Ringman. Given that she had beaten Grant's son back in Olympia, attacked his wife, and trashed his house, Grant was definitely not going to judge her case. He wanted to, though. He had assumed she was just a low-level Lima who probably wouldn't be punished. He was relieved to read the report on her. It was sickening, but at least he knew she would be dealt with.

The report detailed the Clover Park massacre and how she had admitted she ordered it. Grant knew she was a horrible person, but the football field incident was more than he imagined she was capable of.

Then again, she always had the ability to insist that she was 100% correct and hate anyone who disagreed with her or questioned her. That mindset was necessary to follow orders like that, to never question them. The report said she was in the old Olympia High School prison awaiting trial and execution. Good, Grant thought.

The next report he read was that of another person he knew, Eric Benson, a former WAB staff member, who was also, strangely enough, in custody in the old Olympia High School prison. Grant had to know what had happened to Eric and why he was in custody. Eric was a Patriot, Grant remembered, so why was he being held in the same prison with Nancy Ringman?

It turns out Eric was a little too much of a "Patriot" – so much so that he could no longer be called one. He had always been hardcore, even angrier at the old government than Grant had been. Grant remembered the last time he saw Eric. It was at the WAB building when the riots were starting and all the WAB employees were evacuating. Eric came into Tom Foster's office and yelled that WAB guys needed to go out and beat on the protestors. When no one would follow up, Eric stormed out.

Eric had gone ahead and taken matters in his own hands. In the report, Eric admitted that he formed a small group. Grant didn't recognize any of the names and wondered how Eric recruited them.

Eric and his group started doing "overpass jobs," according the report. In the first week of the Collapse, one of the members of Eric's group would ride in a car down the highway with a little Motorola radio. The car would look for cars with liberal bumper stickers. The radio car would tell Eric, who was hiding on an overpass, the description of the lib car and its distance from the overpass. When the lib car got near the overpass, Eric would shoot the driver with a hunting rifle. Even if Eric missed, which was most of the time, the exploding windshield would cause the lib car to crash and either kill or injure the driver. They did four "overpass jobs." Just having a bumper sticker, even a stupid one, should not be a reason to kill people, Grant thought. Grant felt a twinge of guilt because he had wished he could shoot some people with those bumper stickers, but Eric took it way too far and actually did it. At least four times.

Later, about two months into the Collapse, Eric and his group hit gang gas stations. They would start to fill up and, when no one was looking, tie down the latch on the nozzle so the gas kept flowing. They would walk away with the gas nozzle with gas gushing out. Then they would shoot a flare gun at the spilled gas. The gas station would go up

160

in a fireball. Grant wasn't opposed to killing the gangbangers selling gas, but many innocent people were killed, too. Blowing up gang gas stations, Grant had to give Eric credit, did reduce demand for gang gas. But too many innocent people got hurt.

Eric also admitted to a crime that Grant was silently cheering about. He had killed Bart Sellarman, the corrupt real estate licensing board monster that terrorized Ed Oleo in one of Grant's and Eric's cases back at WAB. The killing was a gruesome carwash slaying. Grant was ready to buy Eric a steak dinner for that one. Then Grant realized that this kind of vengeance was exactly what Grant was supposed to prevent, but Grant could smile. And the way Eric killed Sellarman. It was pure genius. Grant wished he could have seen that. Grant would never go into a carwash again.

The final thing Eric did was attempt to infiltrate the Red Brigade. Grant was fine with that because the Red Brigade were communist terrorists who thought the FUSA wasn't socialist enough. But it was how Eric did it.

Right before the Collapse, Eric found out that the local leader of the various left-wing causes was a student named Maddy Popovich. She went to the left-wing nut job college in Olympia, the Evergreen State College. Eric started following her around. He even enrolled at Evergreen. He was determined to get her.

Eric found out Maddy had a roommate, a young woman named Michele Tarrant. Eric found out where Michele hung out and got to know her. Pretty soon, Eric was sleeping with her. She introduced Eric to Maddy and he got to know both of them.

Eric said he suspected, but admitted during interrogations that he could never prove, that Maddy was the leader of the local Red Brigade. Michele was not involved. She hated politics, as a matter of fact.

One night, in Michele's bedroom, Eric slit Michele's throat. He admitted in the report that he really enjoyed it. He went into Maddy's room and did the same thing. He really loved that, too, he admitted.

It turns out that Maddy was a left-wing lunatic but not a Red Brigade member. When the interrogators proved to Eric that she was not a Red Brigade member, he shrugged to the interrogator and said, the report stated, "Whatever. A dead hippie. I did everyone a favor." Eric fully expected to get a medal from the Patriots for slitting the throats of two innocent women.

That wasn't going to happen, Grant decided.

Grant hated to see what had happened to Eric. For whatever reason, Eric had decided that the Collapse gave him a license to kill people he hated—some of whom he didn't even know. The reports told of his confession about a "good Eric" and an "angry Eric," his dual personality, showing he was obviously mentally ill. The people who were killed by the angry version of Eric were not Lima military or police or FCorps. They just had a bumper sticker of a politician he hated, or he suspected they were terrorists. Hating and then killing people based on their politics or suspecting, but not verifying, they were terrorists was what the Limas did. But so did Eric. In a sense, he became a Lima.

The bottom line was that Eric had admitted to killing innocent people. Sellarman had it coming, but the drivers with liberal stickers didn't. Maddy didn't, and Michele Tarrant certainly didn't.

Eric, a so-called Patriot, had been the one who killed innocent people instead of the Limas, who were usually the ones who did. Eric needed to hang just like the Limas who did that. He would. The box "Deny Pardon" was checked and initialed on Eric's report. Grant hated to see that because he knew Eric. Grant wondered if he had spent more time with Eric whether he wouldn't have turned out that way. No, Grant told himself, Eric had some hatred of a certain kind of people and when society broke down Eric decided this was his chance to go out and kill people. Eric was just as guilty as the Limas, and in some ways, more guilty. As a person with at least some Patriot beliefs, Eric should have known better. Now he was going to die.

Grant realized the political importance of hanging Eric. The population had to see the Patriots would not tolerate atrocities from their own side. The law applied equally. No matter if the guy you used to work with at WAB was the chair of ReconComm or not. The guilty hanged. Period.

Then Grant got a brilliant idea. Evil, but brilliant.

Chapter 326

Leaving Seattle

(January 21)

Prof. Carol Matson was living her merry little socialist life in Seattle … for a while. A few days after New Year's Day, she noticed more and more harsh measures by the government. She also noticed the gangs seemed to be out more. Things were getting scarce again in the stores. But luckily, there were laws against hoarding, so Carol was confident that people wouldn't be hogging things up for themselves. That's what set Seattle apart from the barbarians in "New Washington": people in Seattle cared about others, not just themselves.

Then she got a knock at her door one night. She answered the door, which was dangerous with all the crime. But she could see through the peephole that the men at her door had yellow FCorps helmets. Whew. They were safe to let in, so she did.

Once the three FCorps men were in her house, one of them asked, "Are you Carol Matson?"

"Yes," she said.

"Is your brother Grant Matson?" he asked.

Carol felt all the blood drain out of her face. Oh no. They were after her because of him. "Yes," she said, meekly.

"You need to come with us," he said, as the other two grabbed her by each arm. They were hurting her arms and were yelling at her. She hadn't even done anything wrong. Having a stupid hillbilly brother wasn't a crime. Was it?

They took her to a prison, an awful, dark, overcrowded, filthy place. She found out that she was being held because her brother was the head of the New Washington "Reconciliation Commission." He therefore had the power of life and death over many important government officials who had been trapped in New Washington.

"We are proposing a trade," her interrogator told her. "You for him."

Carol wanted to get out of that awful place. She didn't want the authorities to get her brother, though. But she realized that she had no power over the situation. Either she would be traded for him or not. It wasn't her decision.

Then Carol started to think about how awful it would be even if she were released. Everyone would know that her brother was some high-ranking teabagger. She could never show her face again.

After days and days of waiting, word came back that there would be a trade. Of sorts. She was released and allowed to go to Olympia.

When she got there, Grant was waiting.

"Welcome home, sister," Grant said as he hugged her. She hugged him, too. He looked different and she almost didn't recognize him. He was thinner, had a beard, and had a gun. Everyone around him had guns. Didn't they know that guns were illegal? And could get them sent to prison forever? Then she would remember she was no longer in Seattle.

Olympia, now under Patriot control, was fundamentally different than Seattle. Carol marveled at how there were no lines for things. In Seattle, she stood in line at every store and paid for things with an FCard. In Olympia, there were small businesses springing up. People paid with New Dollars, which was the currency of the southern and western states, and with some weird local currencies. They still bartered, but it was weird for Carol to watch people buy things with cash. It was all cards in Seattle.

Being in a Patriot city was very strange for Carol. She was in teabagger central. She expected to see Klansmen running around hanging blacks. That's what she had been led to believe. She actually expected to see that.

After the initial shock of not seeing Klansmen, Carol's next emotion was extreme indecisiveness. On one hand, she still feared the Klansman that she expected to see in that teabagger town. On the other hand, she was thankful for being out of jail and out of Seattle, which, she now had to admit, was crumbling. She could see with her own eyes, from the conditions in New Washington, that things were much better here.

However, she could not instantly feel comfortable in Olympia. She thought people would mock her, or would preach to her some fundamentalist Christianity, or wanted to hurt her because she was from "evil" Seattle. Yet, she knew it was better here. She could not decide if she belonged in New Washington, especially since she couldn't feel comfortable in New Washington. She didn't need permission to do things here. Everything was legal. There were so few police and soldiers around. People were making decisions for themselves.

Carol found this very hard. She had difficulty making decisions, even about little things. It was frustrating to make decisions. It seemed like too much work to make her own decisions. Then she would realize that making decisions was normal and having them made for you was not normal. She was slowly adjusting. Grant realized that his sister was suffering from what newly released prisoners often struggled with. They had had decisions made for them for so long that freedom was hard to adjust to.

Grant told Carol about the deal that got her out. A straight one-for-one swap of Carol for Grant was laughed at by the New Washington leadership. A war hero and head of the ReconComm for … a Spanish literature professor? The New Washington leadership never told Grant about the situation in case he did something stupid like turn himself in to Seattle to save his sister. Later, after he found out, Grant had to admit that he never would have done that. He barely knew his sister and she had made repeated choices to stay in Seattle. He didn't want her in jail, but she chose to live in a place where people went to jail for no reason.

Just as the New Washington leadership suspected, Carol was the opening bid in a negotiation. When it was all over with, the Patriots and Limas traded prisoners. Equal numbers for equal numbers. The Patriots bent their own rules and counted Carol as a Lima prisoner to be swapped. So they got her out, but it only cost them a random Lima, not a prize like Grant's capture.

As Carol settled into New Washington, she had to hide her identity because, as a family member of the chair of the ReconComm, she was a target for Lima attacks. She would also be a big target for a kidnapper because she could be used to get pardons from Grant. So New Washington issued her a new identity and she found a job working at a small bookstore. No one needed a Simon Bolivar-era Spanish literature professor anymore.

Chapter 327

Reconciliation Starts ... Tomorrow

(January 29)

Grant was in Olympia for a few days between speaking engagements for the ReconComm. He still hadn't heard from Lisa. He had written her off and had other things on his mind.

Grant needed to visit someone. The Team was enjoying some R&R in Olympia, so he arranged for a State Patrol EPU detail to take him where he needed to go.

"Sorry to trouble you guys," he said to the EPU agents, "but I gotta have a political discussion. It's all hush-hush."

"No problem at all, Commissioner Matson," the senior agent said. "It's an honor to be on your detail."

The younger agent, who was driving, asked, "Where to, sir?"

"Meconni's," Grant said, "You know, the sandwich shop."

"You got it, sir," the younger agent said.

When they got to the Meconni's parking lot, Grant said, "Hey, guys, I'm trying to lay low in town here. Do you mind if I have someone in the car. It's sensitive and we don't want to be seen in the restaurant."

"We'll be outside the vehicle, sir," the senior agent said. Maybe Commissioner Matson was meeting a girlfriend. He didn't seem like that kind of guy, but maybe.

"Thanks, guys," Grant said, "I appreciate it." He added, "I'm very well armed so I can handle anything, unless of course, I can't and that's when you guys jump on in."

"Roger that, sir," the senior agent said as he and the younger agent took up positions in the Meconni's parking lot.

Grant got into the driver's seat and put the keys in the ignition. At exactly 2:00 p.m., a man came walking up to the parking lot. Grant rolled down the window to the unmarked State Patrol car.

"Hey, Jason, need a date?"

The man looked stunned and then recognized that it was Grant.

"Get in," Grant said as he unlocked the passenger door.

The man got in.

"Okay," Jason Wallace said, "to what do I owe the pleasure of this unusual rendezvous?"

"I need a favor, warden."

Grant proceeded to make his request.

"I dunno," Jason said after hearing it. "This is super illegal."

"Oh," Grant said. "I know. Not only is it illegal, but it destroys my credibility and the Governor's – if I get caught."

"You won't get caught," Jason said as he sat up straight, "I have total control over everything that happens at the old Olympia High School prison." He was proud of that fact and he was going to prove it by doing Grant that favor. That hugely illegal and politically destructive favor. Because it was something Jason had wanted to do for a long time.

"Thanks, Jason," Grant said. "I owe you, man."

"No, you don't," Jason said, "Pardoning my cousin repaid me in full."

"I would have recommended his pardon anyway, Jason."

"I know," Jason said, "but it makes it easier for me to justify what I'm about to do."

Grant smiled.

He remembered the speech he gave at the Delphi Road overpass when they caught that teenage kid texting their position to the Limas. Instead of shooting the little bastard, like they were perfectly entitled to do, Grant told the 17th and the Delphi guards, "Reconciliation starts today," and then he proceeded to merely hammer and tag the kid.

Well, Grant admitted to himself, given what he did today, reconciliation starts tomorrow. He was taking this day off from reconciliation and letting revenge have just one day. He owed it to all those poor souls under the Clover Park football field.

Chapter 328

New What?

(February 1)

"Vehicle approaching," the CB radio said in the Forks City Hall, where Steve Briggs was sitting around talking to some other guys about how to fix a broken water heater.

"Lots of them approaching," the scared voice on the CB said. Steve and the others grabbed their rifles and headed to the city gate.

Steve was terrified. Two pickup trucks with armed men and a small military fuel truck were parked right outside the city gate. It was probably a gang fuel run to supply Port Angeles that got lost. They'd fight to death to protect that treasure in their fuel truck. Then a larger bunch of that gang would come looking for what happened to their treasure and kill everyone in Forks. This was the exact nightmare scenario the Forks guards had been talking about for months and now it was coming true.

A military looking man got out of the first pick-up. Maybe this was a gang of AWOL soldiers, Steve thought. The military man put his arms out like he was hugging everyone. Great, they were high.

The man was smiling. Another man got out with a yellow Gadsen flag, but it had an evergreen tree on it. What?

"Welcome to New Washington," the man exclaimed.

New what?

Steve went up to the man, wanting to get these stoned AWOL gangbangers back on the road and the hell away from Forks.

"Can I help you find where you're going?" Steve yelled.

"I'm where I'm going," the man said with another huge smile. "I'm in Forks. And you're in New Washington."

What was this "New Washington" thing? Oh wait, Steve thought. Don Watson, the Forks ham radio guy, had said that the state, except for Seattle, was calling itself that. Steve hadn't really paid attention to that. Politics from the outside world didn't matter in Forks, which had been forgotten by the outside world.

Pretty soon, more men got out of the trucks and came walking up to the gate with their arms out. They seemed really happy about something.

The flag. Doc Watson's ham radio reports about the Patriots taking over most of the state. Now it was starting to make sense.

The Patriots won? It took Steve a few seconds to process that.

"What the hell is 'New Washington'?" Steve yelled back. He thought he knew, but wanted to make sure.

"The new state you live in," the military man replied. "The Patriots won. We have the whole state, except Seattle. You're free and we have gasoline and a medic."

A warm wave went over Steve. Gas and a medic. Freedom. A new state. Patriots won. Gas and a medic.

The Forks guards started to jump up and down and whoop and holler. The realization was hitting people at different speeds and they reacted at different intervals.

Pretty soon, it was a full-on party at the gate. People were hugging the soldiers, asking about news from New Washington — which sounded so weird to say. "New Washington." It would take some getting used to, but thank God the Patriots won.

Steve spent the next two days distributing the gas and arranging for medical treatments. He made sure the soldiers radioed their base with a list of additional needed supplies. Pretty soon, another convoy arrived with blankets, some antibiotics (but not enough), biscuit mix, and a precious, precious item: a newspaper. *The Olympia Patriot*, it was called. A new newspaper. Independent. It actually seemed believable, what all the stories were saying. The internet was still spotty and the Limas hacked Patriot sites to put in Lima propaganda so, amazingly, actual hard copy newspapers were getting the real news out.

Steve devoured the paper. He read every single word in it. He almost fell over when he saw a long story about Grant Matson. Grant was a war hero and heading some Reconciliation Commission. Thank God he was okay, Steve thought. As Steve read the story, he got goose bumps. All those things about Grant's past that Steve knew about seemed to have been planned long ago. The miracle of getting the cabin and of knowing that Special Forces guy who trained them. All those weird things in Grant's life, Steve could now see, had been planned and allowed Grant to do what he'd done.

"Here for a reason," Steve said out loud. That's what Steve always told Grant when Grant was down. "You're here for a reason, dude," Steve would say, and as it turned out, Steve was right.

Steve went on to become the mayor of Forks. He refused to take a salary. He was living just fine on fish and deer, although he was glad

169

to see that first semi of food come to Forks about two weeks after the first soldiers arrived. A few weeks after that, someone from Steve's old company showed up and started to take orders for car parts. Many vehicles were not running and now, with a little gas being available, people wanted to drive again. Boy, did they want to drive again. And now Forks could sell timber again because that was a "critical industry" under the new laws, which meant that they cut the red tape to get it moving. People had jobs again in Forks. It was a miracle.

The Collapse had changed Forks. It had brought them together as a town. They had fed each other and saved each other's' lives. The churches stayed strong. So many people had experienced tragedies and miracles and there was only one explanation to many people. Thanksgiving would never again be about overeating and watching football. Thanksgiving was real in Forks now. It was about giving thanks. Everyone who lived through the Collapse in Forks knew why they should be thankful.

Later, when Steve got to Olympia to visit Grant, he couldn't believe how much that place had really changed. For the better. He and Grant had a grand old time, telling stories about their upbringing and the Collapse and all the "coincidences" in their lives. "Here for a reason," they would both say time after time.

Chapter 329

Remembered for a Hundred Years

(February 2)

Warden Jason Wallace walked onto the second floor of the old Olympia High School prison.

"I need to speak with Eric Benson," he told the guard.

"Yes, sir," the guard said.

The warden was let into the classroom housing Eric.

"You're dismissed," he said to the guard. The guard left.

"We need to talk," the warden said to Eric.

"Whatever," Eric said. He was still stunned that the Patriots were holding him as a prisoner when his only crime was working too hard to help them. He could not understand why they didn't give him a medal for killing so many Limas.

"You know who Grant Matson is?" Jason asked him.

"Yes," Eric said. "He's the guy who isn't giving me a pardon."

"Grant asked me give you a message," Jason said. Eric was silent. He could care less what Grant Matson had to say. "Don't you want to know what he said?" Jason asked.

"Okay," Eric said sarcastically, "What did he say?"

Jason whispered, "Nice work at the carwash."

Eric smiled and briefly relived the thrill of killing Bart Sellerman. He could see the blood and the sudsy carwash foam on the cement when he was done with Sellarman.

"He wanted to ask you a favor," Jason said. "And I know you're gonna love doing it."

Eric's curiosity was piqued. "Yes?" he said.

Jason told him the plan.

"I'm in," said Eric. "Let's go."

"Okay" Jason said as he took a knife wrapped in cloth out of his suit jacket.

"How do you know you can trust me?" Eric asked.

"Because you asked that question," Jason said. "If you were going to kill me, you'd enjoy it more by surprising me."

"Excellent point," Eric said with a laugh.

"Besides," Jason said, "you want to be a Patriot hero. I'm giving

171

you the chance, and if you kill me, you won't be a hero. You want to be a hero, don't you, Eric?"

Eric nodded like a child.

"Remembered for a hundred years as a man who did a great, great thing?"

Eric nodded again and let out a slight guttural sound.

"Okay," Jason said, "make it good."

Eric, feeling like a giddy child, gave Jason the thumbs up.

Jason handed Eric the knife, careful not to touch it so his fingerprints wouldn't get on it. The only fingerprints on it would be Eric's.

"Oh God!" Jason screamed. "He's got a knife! Help! Guards!"

The guard came running to the door but was afraid to open it.

"Open that door or I kill him!" Eric screamed. He felt a rush of pleasure just screaming those words. He felt alive again, like he hadn't felt in months. He was going to get to kill someone. And not just anyone.

The guard unlocked the door and watched in horror as Eric held the knife up to Jason's throat and slowly walked out of his classroom cell.

Eric took Jason down the hall. By now, several guards stood petrified, unable to believe that a prisoner had taken the warden hostage. When he came to classroom 210, Eric screamed, "Open the door!"

The guards were still frozen.

"Open the damned door!" Jason screamed.

A guard slowly came up and opened the door. The prisoner in room 210 started to scream, too.

A second or two later, the screams turned to shrieks of agony, shock, and slaughter. The shrieks got quieter and quieter as the slashing sounds got louder and louder. Eric was started to cry out with pleasure and Jason cried out in horror.

And Nancy Ringman lay dead.

Chapter 330

Smiley Faces

(February 3)

Grant and the Team were in Mark's truck, driving to Yakima. He was in the back cab with Pow, as usual. Pow was checking his kit to make sure he had everything. He looked stunned. He had everything all right; he had something he forgot he had.

He looked sheepishly at Grant and said, "Oh, dude, I totally forgot I had this," as he handed Grant the letter from Lisa.

Grant looked at it in disbelief. "How long?" he started to ask.

"Like, two weeks," Pow said. "Oh, I'm super sorry, bro. Super sorry. Things got crazy. That Tillimook at the rest stop, going on R&R, all the stuff that's going on. I put in it my kit so I wouldn't lose it, then I forgot. I'm sorry, Grant."

"No, it's not your fault," Grant said, politely. Because it really *was* his fault that Grant had lived two weeks or so without knowing what Lisa really thought.

"If it's bad news," Grant said to Pow, "then thanks for two weeks of me not worrying."

"But if it's good news?" Pow asked.

"Then I hate you," Grant said with a slight smile. He had far more important things on his mind now than being mad at Pow. The future of his marriage was in that envelope. He could see it going either way.

Grant carefully opened Lisa's letter. It was written in her familiar handwriting, her crappy chicken scratch doctor handwriting that no one but Grant, and a handful of pharmacists, could read.

This was the divorce letter, Grant kept thinking. He didn't want to read it, but he also could barely wait to learn what it contained. He had to know where he stood. He had been getting hit on by many attractive women — there were an abundance of widows and broken marriages from the war — and wondered if it was time to start saying yes to inquiries.

"I don't hate you anymore," Lisa wrote. "I'm still pissed. But I don't hate you." Grant felt his heart warm up. He felt a surge of joy and relief. He felt a comfort, like things were going to be okay.

The letter went on to describe the hug that he never gave her when he left Olympia. The hug that, if he would have given her, would have gotten her to come out with him instead of having the Team bring her out. "I need you back. As pissed as I am at you." She drew a frowny face, which made Grant laugh. Grant had always said how much he hated smiley faces and frowny faces in emails. Lisa would draw them on little notes to him just to watch him freak out. It was all in good fun. Seeing that frowny face on the letter was hysterical. It meant they were back to normal, or at least, headed in that direction. Then her letter said, "This letter is my hug" and she drew a smiley face. That smiley face was the most important thing Grant had ever seen. A tear rolled down his check.

Lisa gave Grant an update on the kids. Manda and Jordan were engaged to be married in a year. She wondered if Grant would be back by then for the wedding. She said Manda was having fewer nightmares after shooting Greene, but she still had difficulties. Their bubbly red headed teenage daughter wasn't as bubbly any more. She worked hard feeding people and taking care of kids for the community. Her carefree teen years had been taken from her. "She still wants a real prom," Lisa wrote. "Can you pull some strings?" she asked.

Grant had an idea about that. It would blow Manda's mind. Grant would talk to Ben about that.

"You better be nice to me the rest of our lives," Lisa wrote. With another one of those damned smiley faces. Grant laughed and laughed and laughed. Pow, Scotty, and Bobby looked at him like he was on drugs or had finally gone insane. Grant laughed until his sides hurt. It was a huge release. He had bottled all his emotions for months. Grant knew what to do.

"Hey, Scotty," he said, "can you get on the radio and have some EPU agents go to Pierce Point and pick up my wife and kids and bring them to my quarters in Olympia?"

Scotty just smiled. He knew that this must mean Grant's family was back together. "Roger that, Commissioner," he said with great relief and joy.

Grant could hardly concentrate on the work he had to do in Yakima. He gave some speeches about reconciliation, met with the regional ReconComm staff, and talked to local troops and dignitaries. He loved doing this, especially talking to the troops, but his mind was focused on the reunion with his family. Finally. The reunion.

They spent two days in Yakima, two really long days. As they left, Scotty told Grant that his family would be at the Olympia guesthouse where Grant was staying. Grant was silent for the entire ride back to Olympia, which took a full day. He was just thinking about his family. All they'd done. All they'd gone through. All the emotions about being reunited at Pierce Point right after the Collapse, and then all the emotions about having to leave to go to war. All the worrying Grant had done during the war.

Scotty gave him an update, saying that Grant's family had arrived in Olympia at Grant's guesthouse. Grant could hardly wait. He just about drew his pistol on a checkpoint guard on I-5 at the southern entrance to Olympia. He wanted to be home so badly.

Bobby didn't even have to ask Grant if they would go directly to Grant's guesthouse. He just drove there. As they pulled up to the guesthouse, there was a military Humvee and three pick-ups of contractor-looking guys. Security for the family of the chair of the ReconComm was a high priority. In fact, a few days after the fall of Olympia, Ben sent a small detachment of State Guard to Pierce Point to guard Grant's family. That was one of the things that led Lisa to write her letter. If Grant didn't care about them and was only thinking about himself, she thought, he wouldn't have sent a military unit to guard them.

When Mark's truck pulled into the driveway of the guesthouse, Grant had his door open before they came to a complete stop. He jumped out and ran into the house. If this was a Lima ambush, he had just fallen for it, he thought.

Luckily, the guard at the front door knew from Scotty's radio dispatch a few minutes earlier that Grant would be coming soon. The guard stepped aside, saluted and said, "Welcome home, sir."

That sounded so sweet to Grant. "Welcome home."

Home.

Lisa and the kids were there in the entryway jumping up and down. The kids seemed so old now. Not that they had aged in the past five weeks since Grant saw them last, just that in his mind they were still little kids. Over the past five weeks, he had seen them in his mind as the little kids he had remembered. Now, in the entryway of the guesthouse, he was seeing them as the teenagers they really were.

And Lisa. She looked beautiful. Magnificent, in fact. Smiling. That big "not that I'm wrong, but glad to see you" smile. And sexy. Grant had gone quite a while without any. It was hard to think about that when you're fighting a war and you're trying to prevent the state from sliding into decades of revenge killings and misery. It took something huge like that to crowd out Grant's usual thoughts about his gorgeous wife.

Grant hugged Lisa and the kids so hard they thought he would squish them. Joyous wasn't a strong enough word to describe how Grant and the kids felt, yet Lisa was a little bit distant. She was happy and smiling and hugged Grant, but he could tell that things were not like they had been before the war. She was holding back her full joy at seeing him and being reunited.

Lisa's faith in Grant had been broken. He had left her. Twice. She was proud of him and knew with her head why he had done it. But in her heart, she felt like he had left her. Twice. She couldn't help thinking that Grant was okay with the prospect of never fully reconciling with her, that he was happy to go off and fight a war and meet some other woman if Lisa hadn't let him come back. She wondered if he had been faithful while he was in Olympia and all those crowds told him how great he was.

Grant, too, was a little distant with Lisa. She had put him through such unnecessary misery. Twice.

What the hell was wrong with her? Why couldn't she let Grant go off and do the things he needed to do—even Lisa had to admit that they were important—without telling him their marriage was over? She was so lucky, Grant thought, that he hadn't taken up some of those offers from women who wanted to meet a war hero ... or get a pardon for someone.

So this would be it, Grant thought. He and Lisa would be together again, but a little distant. Overall, things turned out spectacularly well. But still.

"Lives, fortunes, and sacred honor," Grant thought. This was his sacrifice.

Chapter 331

A Weird Truce

(February 28)

Things didn't turn out in Seattle like Ed Oleo, or anyone else, thought they would. Ed was glad he never killed those people. He had been ready to use his hidden shotgun on the Lima ringleaders in his neighborhood, but they just took off one day, a few days before the big battles in Seattle in February. It wasn't a Patriot invasion like everyone thought it would be. Some of the Lima soldiers, or cops, or whatever, started to fight with other ones. It was like there was a civil war in Seattle, at least among the government. The civilians just sat it out — they didn't have any guns anyway. In the end, military, police, FCorps, and various gangs went street-to-street killing each other. They were largely leaving civilians alone; this was a fight among government people and their associated gangs. None of the civilians, like Ed, even knew who was on whose side, or even cared. It was over pretty soon. Ed didn't notice a difference in anything. Food was still scarce.

But then, in the spring, things started to get better. The government — Ed lost track of which side won the battles — was still basically in control, but people were starting to do business again. Not just the hand-to-mouth bartering like the little home repairs Ed was doing, but real business. The reason was the New Dollar.

It was technically a crime in Seattle and the rest of the FUSA to use New Dollars, but everyone did anyway. It was technically a crime in Seattle to do a bunch of things that people now were openly doing. It was weird: the military, police, FCorps, and gangs still ran things; it was just that a free or semi-free market was tolerated. The government and gangs still took a cut, but a cut of a much bigger pie. The Limas weren't stupid. They knew that their thefts were destroying the goose that was laying the golden eggs. They knew that they couldn't get through another few months without a real economy providing things like food. All the corporate farms in eastern Washington that had been providing food to Seattle were now in Patriot hands, so the people running Seattle needed a new plan. They did what many collapsing socialist economies had always done: allowed a little capitalism.

Ed realized something weird, and good, was happening when

he got his first inquiry about buying a house. What? Someone wanted to buy a house? That hadn't happened for over a year, but it made sense that there would be demand. People were relocating. There wouldn't be any new home construction for probably two decades. All that abandoned existing housing coupled with all those people who needed a home in the new place they had settled in meant people would start buying and selling real estate again.

But buy and sell with what? Ed wondered. FCards? Nope. New Dollars were the answer. Ed looked into it and found that the escrow company would do transactions in New Dollars. Ed did the sale, got a commission in New Dollars, and went out and bought some fresh vegetables with them. He couldn't believe it, though it did make sense when he thought about it. It took a long time for the Collapse to build and it would take a long time for it to unwind, at least in Seattle where the government and gangs still tried to control things to the greatest extent they could. Ed noticed more and more economic activity and all of it being done in New Dollars. The military and police were letting all of this happen. They were even cracking down on the gangs. Some of the gangs must have been becoming liabilities or, maybe, the military and police were actually listening to people. Ed couldn't really believe it, but the evidence pointed in that direction. Most of the really bad people in the government and gangs had been killed. That intra-government civil war and the resulting assassinations and gang wars had thinned out the hard core Limas pretty well.

At first, most people in Seattle had been silently hoping the Patriots would come in and take over. But now that sentiment was waning. Sure, people wanted things back to normal and no one would deny that the economy and freedom were booming in New Washington. But, with the healthy New Dollar economy in Seattle, things weren't so bad that it was worth fighting another war over. Besides, just about everyone in Seattle had collaborated with the former legitimate authorities so the Patriots coming in would mean lots and lots of hangings and jailing.

A weird truce developed. Seattle was still technically in the FUSA and a kinder, gentler group of Limas was running it. But Seattle had essentially integrated into the New Washington economy and, by extension, the southern and western states' economies because New Washington was part of that economic bloc. All while everything like New Dollars were theoretically illegal.

New Washington, too, didn't want to fight a war with Seattle. There was no reason to. Seattle wasn't trying to invade New

Washington and the Lima terrorist attacks had gone down to almost none. New Washington was actually trading with Seattle. In fact, New Washington agriculture was feeding Seattle, and New Washington manufacturing was rebuilding Seattle. In turn, Seattle had lots of smart business people and even squirreled-away money to invest in New Washington.

In the end, New Washington and Seattle developed a relationship like the one between the Revolutionary War colonies and Canada. Many Loyalists during the First Revolutionary War fled to Canada, just like many Loyalists fled New Washington into Seattle. But the two countries—technically different countries with different currencies, but speaking the same language and economically intertwined—were at peace with each other. After a few years, it was as absurd for New Washington to invade Seattle as it would have been for the old America to invade Canada.

Which was why Ed was so glad he didn't have to kill anyone back when the Patriots took Olympia. He didn't want blood on his hands. He just wanted all the bad things to stop. And they slowly did.

Chapter 332

Fixing New Washington I

(February – December)

In the year after taking Olympia, the New Washington government did several things. The very first thing they did was establish a structure for doing everything that needed to be done. This had been developed in exile at the Think Farm.

The basic structure, which wasn't fancy and was made up as they went along, was that there would be an Interim Governor for a year, along with an Interim House of Representatives and Interim Senate. They also had interim judges.

There was one basic requirement to be an interim official: no prior ties to the old government. Every single one of the officials for the old state, especially the judges, was compromised, having done the Limas' dirty work. Some were outright corrupt; others just went along with things that they knew were unconstitutional. Either way, they were done. New Washington didn't need them. New Washington didn't need their "experience," which was basically experience at screwing people.

The Interim Government, as it was called, eventually convened a constitutional convention, or "con con," where constitutional delegates met, drafted a new constitution and then submitted it to the people for a vote. Grant was honored—truly honored, once-in-a-lifetime honored—to be one of the constitutional delegates. It was a lot of work being both a constitutional delegate and running the Reconciliation Commission but, as Grant used to say when the Team was getting into Mark's truck, "Is there any place you'd rather be?" When Grant was tired and stressed out over the latest problems he was confronting, he would smile. He was doing was exactly what he wanted to be doing: fixing things. He knew all the "coincidences" that had fallen in place to make it possible for him to be doing this work.

"Anything is possible when miracles are popping off all around you," he would say.

The old Washington Constitution, which was a magnificent document of liberty if it ever had been enforced, served as the first draft of the new state Constitution. In fact, most of the Bill of Rights from the old constitution was adopted word for word in the draft of the new one. The main debates were whether to have a "pure" libertarian constitution with almost no government or a "practical" libertarian constitution with a very small amount of government.

The Interim Legislature met in the stately old House and Senate chambers, which now had bullet holes in places from the fighting, and quickly passed a handful of laws necessary to carry out the Restoration. Grant had been offered a spot in the Interim Legislature, but he thought that it would look bad if he were a "politician" and also heading up the Reconciliation Commission, which was deciding who should live or die or go to prison. Life or death decisions should not be made by politicians up for re-election. Instead, Grant took a less political spot as a Constitutional Convention delegate, which was a one-term position with no re-election.

The Interim Legislature passed laws setting a date for the first election in one year. They also passed some laws necessary to establish the framework for the rest of the Restoration, such as laws about the State Guard, newly re-formed State Police, and the Reconciliation Commission. The Interim Senate confirmed Grant as the Chair of the new Reconciliation Commission, which was not a surprise. The Interim Legislature also repealed every other law in the state to give the new Legislature a clean slate. Besides, no one was enforcing the old laws, so what was the point in having them? It was time for a clean slate. It was what people wanted, and what they had fought and died for.

Once the new Interim Government was formed, they immediately started on all the problems facing New Washington following decades of creeping socialism and then a war. It was a war that was still going on because there were constant skirmishes on the Seattle/New Washington boundaries, although those were diminishing. New Washington had security problems and economic ones, especially when it came to getting food to the population. Medical problems persisted because the hospitals had largely ceased to function and it was nearly impossible to get medicines and medical supplies.

New Washington also had political problems, largely centered on the reconciliation issues. Some wanted to forgive and forget, but most wanted to hunt down the Limas and kill them and collaborators, too. That was the hard part: the collaborators. How far would that go? To anyone who had a stupid "We Support Recovery Now!" yard sign? Many old personal disputes, like divorces, rivalries, business competitors, and family squabbles, were now dressed up as rooting out

Limas. Someone who had always hated someone else would claim he or she was a Lima collaborator. Grant was determined that his Reconciliation Commission would not be turned into the hangmen for personal disputes that had nothing to do with actual Lima crimes.

Last, but not least, the new state also had infrastructure problems from all the war damage. There was actually very little damage from the fighting because there had been very little physical battling. A few small patches of Olympia, especially around the capitol, had been shot up. But the war was fought almost exclusively with rifles instead of aerial bombs, artillery, helicopters, and other weapons that busted up cities and caused massive infrastructure damage. Thank God, Grant thought, that all the super high-tech weapons the FUSA military had were useless when the semi-trucks stopped rolling with spare parts and the computers went down. And thank God, the FUSA military was so dependent on technical people, most of whom went AWOL or defected to the Patriots. The mightiest military in the history of the earth was shut down by just-in-time inventory and Oath Keepers.

However, there was still massive infrastructure damage, but it was from socialism, not war. Over the past five years in particular, when the politicians were fully out of control with taxing and regulating, the economy ground to a halt. No one was spending money to maintain things. Businesses were closing shop left and right. This hurt infrastructure. Roads were an example of how socialism destroyed the infrastructure. Roads were in disrepair because all the money that had historically gone to their repair had instead been siphoned off to pay interest on government debt. The small companies that supplied the things needed to rebuild infrastructure had gone out of business. Now there were shortages of all the parts and equipment needed to fix things, and a shortage of money to buy them and make the repairs.

A great example of this that came to Grant's mind was Hoffman Rentals, Wes' employer before he came out to the cabin. In the past, if small bulldozers were needed to fix an Olympia street and a repair crew needed an extra bulldozer, they could just go rent one from Hoffman's, but not now. Hoffman's had been closed for over a year. Its bulldozers had been stolen and were rusting in some parking lot somewhere with no keys.

New Washington was careful not to repeat the infrastructure mistakes of the past. Old Washington had used infrastructure as an excuse to spend gobs of money and give jobs to union workers. New Washington treated infrastructure improvements as something that needed to be done to get commerce moving. New Washington was repairing roads, damaged utilities, and railroads.

What was New Washington's solution to all this? Governor Trenton never got tired of talking about the answer.

"The solutions are less government and following the Constitution. Period." That summarized the Interim Government's approach to problem solving. Use the minimal amount of government necessary and follow the old Constitution until the new one, which would be pro-liberty, could be ratified.

First and foremost, the Interim Government restored order. Seattle was actually helping the Patriots. Even though I-5 remained almost entirely sealed off, thousands of Limas and gangbangers streamed into Seattle and its suburbs. That place was a basket case of violence and oppression, but whatever. At least the Limas were all concentrated in one place where they couldn't continue to hurt people except themselves. But hey, they were living the dream of a socialist paradise! Even with most of the Limas gone, New Washington wasn't all sunshine and lollipops. It took weeks to root out all the holed up Limas. Throughout New Washington, especially in Olympia, small bands of diehard Limas and some gangbangers who didn't escape to Seattle went underground and attacked Patriot soldiers, police, and civilians at night. It was bloody.

Most people were so tired of all the violence. They turned in Limas and gangbangers in droves. There was no popular support for Limas. Everyone in the new state was either a Patriot or an Undecided who just wanted to get back to work and have a safe neighborhood for their families. The only Lima sympathizers were the actual Lima insurgents.

There were pockets of Limas in some rural parts of the new state. Patriots weren't the only ones who went out to the country, grouped up, and fought. A handful of Lima bands did, too. One of them was on Hartstine Island, the location of the first cabin Grant looked at and almost bought. Grant always had a bad vibe about that place, especially with all the libs who lived out there. He knew his instinctual reaction was right when he learned that those libs invited their Lima friends over to stay.

The Limas out on Hartstine Island became pirates, real life twenty-first century pirates. No eye patches or parrots, but they attacked ships and stole and killed. They used Hartstine Island, which became known as "Pirate Island," to stage their raids. It took Joe Tantori's men, "Tantori's Raiders" as they became known, landing on the north and south ends of the island and driving an armored car down the only road on the island to clean out that place. Joe lost a dozen men, most of them Marines. Gunnery Sergeant Martin Booth was one of them.

Police departments were cleaned up in New Washington. The majority of the former cops were decent. They had left their departments as the Collapse approached, like Rich Gentry. The ones still on active duty during the war were the problem. After the Patriots took over, most police forces fired or arrested all the active duty cops and replaced them with former cops and new recruits. They used lots of citizen posses, too. In Frederickson, Sheriff Bennington was an example of what was happening all across New Washington.

Crime was a big problem when the Patriots took over. People were hungry and saw that police forces were stretched thin. You didn't rob someone in a gang's territory; that was the exclusive privilege of each gang. The newly re-constituted local police forces concentrated on street crimes and didn't focus too much on rounding up Limas.

The State Guard was doing that. Well, not technically the State Guard. Having the military enforcing civilian laws is a bad idea everywhere in the world it has been tried. Early leaders of America knew this and therefore passed the Posse Comitatus Act, which outlawed the military from enforcing civilian laws. The FUSA government repealed the Posse Comitatus Act before the Collapse, but the Interim Legislature in New Washington, and other newly free states, reinstated it. So, technically, the State Guard military units that once hunted Limas were deactivated and turned into state police units. Same guns, same ranks, same everything, just not a military unit. Because the Patriots were nervous about a militarized police force, they limited the commissions given to the new state police officers to six months. They could be renewed, but on a case-by-case basis. Besides, most State Guard enlistments were only a year, so six months or so of training and military fighting around the New Year's offensive, and then six months of policing, usually finished out an enlistment. Most State Guardsmen were glad to be done with their stint after a year. They had families to get back to and the economy was rebounding.

That was because, at least for that first year, there were no taxes or regulations on commerce. None. Every law had been repealed. Business exploded. No more permits, licenses, environmental studies, or even taxes. That's right: no more taxes. The Interim Government repealed all of them. They couldn't collect them even if they wanted to; people were feeding themselves and that was about it. What would the new government, the freedom-loving Patriots, do? Seize a family's food as "taxes." That wasn't the Patriot way.

The Interim Government basically ran on donations and captured goods. There was so little government that it wasn't hard to do so. The only significant expense was the State Police. Donations were informal. Much like the Grange had just fed guards in Pierce Point, citizens who had extra food fed the security forces. Donations weren't enough to live on, but they did help a lot.

The Interim Government primarily ran captured supplies. Limas' property was seized with a judge overseeing things, but most of the Limas just took off to Seattle or elsewhere and there was no one there to claim the property. Seized Lima property supplied the State Police with food, ammunition, and fuel, which was about all they needed. Things were so broken down that the necessities were all people had or used.

Seized Lima houses, called "guesthouses," were used temporarily by Interim Government officials. Grant used a seized Lima house in Olympia as his "guesthouse," while his real house in Olympia was on a long list waiting to be repaired after Nancy Ringman trashed it.

The plan for after the elections was for the Legislature to pass very, very low taxes and cap them in the new Constitution. By capping taxes to a small percentage of the state's gross domestic product, government could never grow like it did in the past. Yet, at the same time, government would have enough money to only do the one thing it was supposed to do: protect individual liberties. That was it. This was a shock to most people: the new government would only protect individual liberties. This wasn't just the right thing to do; it was all that could be done. The New Washington government didn't have enough resources to do anything else. Good.

"Critical industries" were another economic solution used by the Legislature after the interim period of no taxes and regulations expired. Industries essential to an economically independent and prosperous state, like agriculture, manufacturing, energy, and natural resources, were designated "critical industries," which meant the government got the hell out of their way. The taxes and regulation did not return for these industries. Software, filling out government forms, and making lattes were not "critical industries" in New Washington.

Manufacturing, farming, fishing, and logging took off overnight. There were plenty of good jobs and lots of products. Prices were reasonable because there wasn't layer upon layer of taxes and regulation artificially driving up the price.

In the southern and western states, which had broken away from the FUSA and were having booms of their own, domestic energy production shot up. Gasoline from there was plentiful and cheap in New Washington. And no more wars in the Middle East to fight, at least not with Americans fighting them, because the need for oil was gone. Grant would shake his head and wonder why in the world this hadn't been done sooner.

New Washington rebuilt infrastructure much differently than the old state had done it. New Washington did it much more cheaply after the repeal of "prevailing wage" laws that ensured unions got all work, and the repeal of the layers and layers of complete overkill environmental regulations. And, of course, New Washington contracted out almost all of the work. There was now transparent and fair contracting; no inside deals. Total and complete disclosure of everything about the contracting. Corruption in contracting carried the death penalty. The past theft by contractors for the old state would not be tolerated.

Civil liberties were a huge part of the plan. Not "civil liberties" in the ACLU sense of the term, which they turned into meaning a "right" to welfare. No, real civil liberties, which meant protecting individual liberties, all the time, not just when it served a political agenda.

The New Washington government's "plan" for civil liberties was extremely simple: follow the Constitution. Grant would laugh when people asked him if such a simple plan could work. He would ask them, "How did the Limas' 'sophisticated' plans work out?"

A very good constitution to follow already existed. As good as the United States Constitution was, the old Washington State Constitution was actually better. Written in 1889, it had all the good stuff from the 1789 U.S. Constitution, but a hundred years of more wisdom in it. The old Washington State Constitution had amazing rights in it, but they were never actually followed by the old state. That was the problem: magnificent rights that were never followed. From the first few meetings of the Constitutional Convention Grant attended as a delegate, the general consensus was that the new Constitution would tweak the old one to make sure it didn't slowly get whittled away, but all the good stuff would remain in the new version.

Now that they had a chance to start over and draft a constitution that truly protected civil liberties, and now that they had graphically seen what a few hundred years of chipping away at those rights led to, the people in New Washington had a very clear idea of what their new Constitution would say.

Government could no longer take things. Laws against takings without just compensation were strengthened. And takings through taxation was addressed by limiting taxes.

Not only would taxes be capped at a low rate, but the new Constitution would prohibit differing tax rates. New Washington would have flat taxes. The old system of huge tax rates for productive people while no one else effectively paying any led to a small percentage of productive people paying the freight for the large majority.

Another improvement in the new Constitution was that due process of law would actually mean something. No more "administrative hearings" that were kangaroo courts to rubber stamp the government's decisions. Grant had seen plenty of those in the past. Now, juries would decide almost all things. Just like at Pierce Point, Grant thought. Under the new Constitution, it would take a jury to decide whether the state could take away people's kids, not some social worker filling out a form. It was the same for mental illness commitments. And, in criminal cases, juries would get to hear the accused describe why he or she thought the law being enforced was unjust. The jury could decide to acquit if the law was indeed unjust. That would be a big deterrent to malicious prosecutions and a huge check on government power. What a tremendous power to let twelve people veto the application of an unjust law. It would be back in the new Constitution.

The new state Constitution had a few "no, really" clauses, as Grant called them. They laid out a civil liberty and then emphasized how important they were by basically saying "no, really don't infringe this right."

One of the "no, really" clauses — perhaps the most important and effective one — appeared in the sections on the judiciary. After describing that judges' only obligation is to protect individual liberties and to neutrally apply constitutional laws duly passed by the Legislature and signed by the Governor, this was added: "Any decision of a judge in derogation of these obligations subjects that judge to a recall vote of the people." Grant, having been an informal judge out at Pierce Point could understand how effective this would be. Now a bad decision infringing on civil liberties, coupled with a reasonably significant number of signatures on a petition, would put that judge on the ballot to keep his or her job. An enormous incentive to not do what the old state's judges did.

Drugs were decriminalized, but truly scary drugs, like meth, could be criminalized, though it would take a two-thirds vote of both houses of the Legislature and the signature of the Governor. This was a compromise because many people wanted total drug decriminalization.

This showed the debate among the pure libertarians and the "practical" libertarians. Grant considered himself one of the "practical" ones. He had basically run a small community and saw things slightly differently than the "pure" libertarians, but not too differently.

"Civil forfeiture," which was where the police and prosecutors got to keep whatever it was they seized in a case would be eliminated. Getting the cash had been the prime motive in many prosecutions. That was over now.

Searches would be curtailed. A warrant would be required in almost every case. Searches would be rare, as they were intended to be by the Founders of the country.

This did not mean that crime was made easier with the new Constitution. A one-strike law was authorized for rape. One time and that person went to prison for life. Egregious cases, such as rape of a child, got the offender the death penalty. However, conviction required the testimony of two witnesses. Gone were the days of an ex-wife in a divorce case sending a man to jail and ruining his life with no evidence.

Restraining orders were changed. Grant was shocked to learn that, right up until the Collapse, a person could go to a kiosk—a little ATM-like machine—in a mall and simply say a person was harassing them and then a restraining order would be signed by a judge back in a court room. It was that easy: get mad at someone, go to a kiosk in the mall, and then get a restraining order against them, thereby ruining their life. There had been no need to even go to a court and look a judge in the eye, let alone have a jury decide if this person was really a harasser. That ended. In New Washington, the way to prevent people from harassing you was now to exercise your right to keep and bear arms.

The new state Constitution had a "no, really" clause in its version of the Second Amendment. The new version stated that the right to have and use weapons could not be limited by registration, permits, taxes, or licenses of any kind. The new Constitution provided that this right was not only for personal defense, but "to equip the people to ensure, as a practical matter, that the government honors its obligation to protect individual liberties," and added that:

"Infringements on the right to keep and bear arms, however seemingly slight at the time, will not be tolerated by the people, who have the right to overthrow any government attempting to infringe their rights." That was a not-so-subtle threat.

To keep the government honest and to protect citizens, New Washington needed a militia, but not with that name, which had too many negative connotations. The new state constitution provided for the "Civil Guard," which was voluntary and open to all men and women of a certain age. The officers of the Civil Guard would be elected by the members of the unit. The Civil Guard would answer to the people, not the government. The name "Civil Guard" was intentionally picked to contrast it from the "State Guard," which answered to the state. The Civil Guard was specifically described in the new state Constitution as a check on the power of the government, which would prevent the Civil Guard from becoming a political goon squad like the FCorps had become. The State Guard would maintain a small full-time force that largely existed to be able to train and equip the Civil Guard in times of emergency.

Chapter 333

Fixing New Washington II

(February – December)

Of course, the FUSA no longer existed except for on paper. The FUSA issued proclamations, demands, and pathetic court orders to the wayward states, but had no power to tell the free states what to do. It was limited to bossing around California, which was still in the FUSA, as well as the east coast states. Many states in the Midwest had broken into two parts, like New Washington: a Patriot new state and a Lima old state. The FUSA was a patchwork of little states and territories.

This made sense to Grant. The FUSA, with over three hundred million people, half a continent of land, and some extremely different cultures (Texas versus New York) had become too big to be one country. Grant thought about all the free republics of the past in Greece and the middle ages in Europe. They had a few million people at most and one basic culture. It worked just fine for a republic that small. Look at the original thirteen colonies; a small population and roughly similar culture.

New Washington was the same way. It had a reasonable-sized population and a similar culture since Seattle was not included. New Washington had a good chance of succeeding as a small republic, like Pierce Point did on a mini scale.

New Washington would consider being part of a union with the other free states and it was a decision that would be weighed for quite some time. There was no rush; New Washington was doing well on its own. It traded with the southern and western states. Business was booming. It was still small compared to the pre-Collapse economy, but was growing every day. People could feel that a real economic recovery was happening and they got to keep the money they earned for a change.

There were several currencies in use. Many local areas had Free Dollars, which were redeemable in gold or silver by free banks, like the ones issued by Joe Tantori's bank.

In addition to local free bank currencies, the people of New Washington had quickly adopted the southern and western states' currency, the New Dollar. There was no government decision on what currency to use; people just starting using the New Dollar because it made sense. That was the magic of a free market.

The New Dollar was actually backed by gold, silver, and, indirectly, oil. A person could take a New Dollar into any bank in the southern and western states, and eventually a New Washington bank, and walk out with gold or silver. They couldn't walk out with a barrel of oil, but oil was indirectly backing the New Dollar. The southern and western states had plenty of oil and used it to buy gold and silver that was then used to back the New Dollar.

There was no inflation wherever the New Dollar was in circulation and people flocked to the New Dollar for that reason. This increased the economic and political influence of the southern and western states. Everyone wanted to hitch their cart to the economic powerhouse of these states.

There was no burning reason for New Washington to formally join a union of the southern or western states, however. That certainly might eventually happen, but New Washington had a stable currency courtesy of the New Dollar, so joining a union of states wasn't necessary to have a currency. No one was trying to invade New Washington, so they didn't need military alliances, which could suck New Washington into a war it didn't want. Why get dragged into some border dispute between Wyoming and Nebraska or whatever just to be in a union of states with Wyoming? No, joining a union of states had to make sense to the people of New Washington. They were thinking about it. It was a big decision and any treaty to join a union of states would be voted on by the people. They had seen what being part of a too-large union of states ended up getting them.

A much bigger debate among the people of New Washington than whether to join the southern and western states was what to do about the "Seattle question," as it became known. Should New Washington force Seattle to join it? To reunite the state so it had its old borders?

Most people in New Washington initially wanted a forceful reunification with Seattle. There was something mesmerizing about the old borders of the state. The whole state had to be under one flag.

But then most people thought about it and decided Seattle, rotting, dying, and gasping for life, could remain a part of the FUSA for as long as it wanted. Most people realized that with free and prosperous New Washington as a shining example, people in Seattle would start to voluntarily come to New Washington. That's how New Washington would eventually regain Seattle: when everyone in Seattle wanted back into a functioning state like New Washington. The Patriots weren't in a hurry. They had lots to fix in New Washington.

Religion was another topic that needed some reform, or, actually, just some freedom. There was a massive return to religion after the Collapse. So many people had experiences that led them to believe in a higher power. Most of the people from Pierce Point and the 17th fit into this category.

The New Washington Constitution created a very clear separation of church and state. Government was not to be in the religion business; that was a purely private affair, but the New Washington Constitution would not allow silly bans on religious life. No more suspending kindergartners for saying "Merry Christmas." The New Washington Constitution would do what the federal Constitution was supposed to do before judges perverted it, which was to ban the government from "establishing" an official government-sanctioned religion, not to ban people from exercising their religions. Government allowing kids to say "Merry Christmas" was not "establishing" a religion; it was allowing people to exercise them. But requiring kids in public schools to pray was forcing religion on people, so that would not be tolerated.

Government exists to protect liberty, including everyone's ability for free exercise of religion. This included non-Christian religions and atheism. Religion must be protected for two reasons, Grant had always thought. First, free exercise of religion is a fundamental liberty and government exists to protect liberty. Second, and a very practical reason, is that a healthy religious life means a healthy society. Charity flourishes and takes care of people the government can't take care of, and private charity does a much better job. Religion often means people feel accountable to a higher power, not just to bureaucrats. There was no downside to a society when religion was healthy, provided that people could be truly free to worship, or not worship, as they pleased.

In addition to more religion, another social phenomenon after the Collapse was the reversal of the wussification of the American male. (New Washingtonians and others in the FUSA still called themselves "Americans.") The government couldn't do much to reverse wussification, except to get out of the way of society. By virtually eliminating taxes, now both parents in a family didn't have to work. This was huge. Men and women could have their traditional roles without having to worry about a second wage earner to pay the taxes. If men and women didn't want to have traditional roles, that was fine, too. It was just that the majority of Americans did want the traditional roles. Now, without crushing taxes, they could have them if they wanted them.

Men had been vilified by the old state. Grant thought of all the TV ads and sitcoms in which the man was the stupid idiot and the woman saved the day. Over and over again. All threats to decency were from men. They were all wife beaters and gun-toting nuts. Grant had always thought that the reason for this was that the old government didn't want strong families to be a check on government power. Government wanted full control over people. And, to do that, government needed to eliminate the family. That was actually in the Communist Manifesto.

Gov. Trenton would use his bully pulpit to remind society that men actually have some worth. They need to be strong and work hard. Men have an obligation to provide for a family. Men cannot be lazy and expect the government to take care of their families. If a man were injured or disabled that was a different situation, of course, and a charity should help. And in some families it made more sense for the woman to work and the man to take care of the kids. That was all fine. It was just that the era of men getting to be overgrown boys, shirk their responsibilities, and have the government take care of their families was over. Over for good.

The war, in which many regular suburban men had picked up a gun for the first time and used it, had also taught both men and women that men have some worth as protectors of their families. There hadn't been a need to do this for several generations. People were reminded of the unique role men have in a properly functioning society, in a free society.

Stopping the vilification of men didn't mean that women had to stay at home and cater to men. Not at all. Just as the war meant many suburban men picked up a gun and used it for the first time, many women did the same. People realized just how incredibly important women are to a society and especially to families when times got bad, even more so when many men weren't around because they were off fighting a war. Many families saw with their own eyes that women canning and growing gardens saved the family. And women are usually better at comforting and nurturing. There was plenty of that which needed to be done. Almost everyone suffered a tragedy of some kind; there was a lot of comforting necessary. Grant kept thinking about Anne Sherryton and how she had read the brewery orphans those stories after doing some very brutal and tough work that few men could. There was no denying how important women were.

Thinking about the vilification of men got Grant thinking about race. Just like the old government had divided up society along gender lines and pitted people against each other, with government riding in to save the day, the old government had done the same with race. It was so apparent, especially after the war. Before the war, the old government tried to scare minorities about all those evil white teabaggers who wanted to kill them and enslave them. Just like they'd told women that men were evil and needed to be controlled by ... the government.

The government used race to get support from whites, too. While never saying it, the government was hinting pretty clearly to whites that all these new security measures were necessary to protect people from "crime," which often meant ethnic gangs. The common denominator in all this was that government was the only fair and powerful thing that could protect one group from the evils of the other group.

It would be impossible to be a racist after going through the Collapse and war. People of every race did bad things and good things. Grant thought about his own experience. There were Mexican gangs in Frederickson. On the other hand, there was Gideon and all the Hispanic soldiers in the 17th. Race didn't fit into any rigid "good" or "bad" category.

Almost all people in New Washington had similar experiences. They had seen minorities do bad things and good things. Minorities had seen whites do bad things and good things, too. It was not lost on most minorities that the politicians and bureaucrats who had destroyed everything were white. Well educated, upper income whites.

Grant thought about all that the Patriots had done. He was very proud. Not cocky proud, but deep-breath-and-smile proud for a job well done. Grant was just a small piece in this whole thing. He had always thought that the only way things would get fixed was for the old system to collapse. People, who could start over on a clean slate instead of being trapped in the old system, would do what made sense, and that was freedom.

Chapter 334

(February 24, year after Collapse)

His pants were falling down. Damn it. Stay up.

Grant Matson hated wearing a suit, and he hated a tuxedo even more. A tuxedo that was too big was even worse. His pants were several inches too big and his shirt was baggy and had about two inches too much collar. His bow tie looked silly cinched up in an attempt to hide the fact that the collar was too big. Oh well. Almost everyone else was in the same boat.

No one had clothes that fit anymore. It was a mixed blessing. Everyone lost some weight they probably didn't need. The old way of living, like having plenty of food to make those clothes fit, was a thing of the past. But, things were getting back to a new kind of normal and there was enough to eat now. Things were getting better. Much better than they had been 299 days ago.

Two hundred ninety-nine days. His son, who loved to count days and could tell anyone how many were between any two given dates like he was a computer, told him earlier today that it had been 299 days since May 1. That was the day it all started. And now, just 299 days later, it was wrapping up, as symbolized by the event he was attending tonight. Thank God it hadn't lasted longer.

There he was in their new house. "New house" used to be a happy term as in "we just bought a new house and it's great." It used to mean the fun of moving up and getting something better. That was the old America.

This new house, a "guesthouse", wasn't like that. It was a fine house; in fact, it was a little nicer than his old one. But it wasn't his. It wasn't the house his kids spent most of their childhood in. His wife didn't like it. She missed the old house, but understood why they had the new one. Tonight, she was dropping the kids off at her parents' who would be babysitting while they were out. He was all alone. He chuckled at how lucky he had been throughout this whole thing. He had almost been alone forever. In fact, twice he had almost been alone forever.

Tonight, Grant wasn't alone. There were some plainclothes soldiers outside the guesthouse in inconspicuous places, guarding him. But no one was inside the house. Just him. It was so quiet. He felt alone.

In the downstairs bathroom of the guesthouse, Grant looked in the mirror to adjust his bow tie. He was the same guy in his mid-forties with brown hair. But wow. Look at that. His face looked so much thinner than just a few months ago. Grant barely recognized himself because he had finally shaved. He hardly recognized himself without that military "contractor" beard.

Grant had aged quite a bit in the past 299 days. His face was toughened, and he looked confident. Deadly confident; the kind of confidence that it takes to stand up to bullies and help people. His eyes were different than before the Collapse. There was a hint of loss in them. Not a cry-at-the-drop-of-a-hat kind of loss. His eyes showed that there was less of him now, that something had been lost. Taken from him.

Staring at the new him in the mirror, Grant got lost in memories. That was happening a lot lately. He would just lose his train of thought and drift into heavy thoughts, usually triggered by remembering someone or some event. Extremely vivid memories like waking from a realistic dream, in that first moment when the dream is so vivid it feels real, despite it being a crazy and unrealistic dream. The memories he was having were real, however. That's why they were so vivid. And, in this case, reality had been crazy and unrealistic.

Grant looked again in the mirror and examined his tuxedo. It was symbolic of so much going on that night. He bought it about five years ago when he was climbing the ladder of law and politics in Olympia, the capitol of Washington State, and occasionally had to attend formal events. He would have fit in it just fine 299 days ago.
On this night, Grant was wearing a tuxedo to an event that warranted a tuxedo. It was the kind of night that only happens once in a lifetime, and never happens at all in the lifetimes of most people. Dinner tonight was a victory celebration. It was a victory in the biggest thing in his life or the lives of almost any American. He would be remembered throughout state history, at least as a small figure. He would have a school or something named after him. He should be happy, shouldn't he?

This victory came at an enormous price. "Bittersweet" is a cliché, but it was true in this instance. Bitter because a lot of people died and suffered. Not billions of people like in some over-the-top apocalypse movie, but plenty of people. People Grant knew, some of them very well. Everyone knew many people who were killed, widowed, maimed, went crazy, were ruined, or had their families broken up. Grant thought about sweet Kellie. All she had ever wanted was a good man. He died in the war.

Almost everyone had been hungry and afraid. Grant didn't lose his wife, but they weren't nearly as close as before the Collapse and it would probably stay that way for the rest of their lives. His daughter was no longer the bubbly outgoing teenage girl she had been; now she was quiet and deadly serious most of the time. She had seen and done things that no teenage girl, or anyone for that matter, should have to experience. His son had fared okay as far as Grant knew.

His old home was trashed so he was borrowing this new one, the "guesthouse," from someone who was now in jail. Grant would rebuild his real home but it would take a while. Things like police protection, farming, and rebuilding roads were a higher priority than remodeling. His old home was a symbol of what everyone was going through. It would take years of hard work to rebuild his town, state, and his country. Actually, the countries.

The "sweet" part of bittersweet was that some very bad things ended. Some wrongs were made right, and some guilty people paid for what they did. They couldn't hurt people anymore. Some people who thought they were losers found out they were heroes. People came together and really lived for the first time in their lives. Lifelong friendships were formed between people who just 299 days ago wouldn't have talked to each other. And, Grant felt guilty for thinking about himself, he was absolutely certain that he'd made the most out of his life. He saw dozens of "coincidences" in his life that were planted years ago and then sprang up at just the right time so some absolutely amazing things could be accomplished. He was being used to do great things. Grant was just a guy with no particular skills who didn't exactly lead the perfect life.

All Grant did right was have a little faith and listen to the outside thoughts, even when they said things that seemed crazy at the time. There was no denying that, for nearly forty years, the "coincidences" had been pointing him in the direction of helping people and fixing a bunch of really terrible things that needed to be fixed. He was here for a reason.

Snapping out of the vivid memories and back into getting dressed for the big event, Grant realized that all the bad things that had been fixed were what he needed to focus on tonight. Measures would be put in place to prevent the bad things from happening again, he hoped. That was his new job and the reason for the dinner tonight. I have to get this right, Grant thought. I can't screw this up. Please help me, he thought. Actually, he prayed that.

Grant looked at the invitation on the sink in the bathroom of the guesthouse. The invitation was beautiful, made of parchment paper and written in calligraphy. That was a rare sight nowadays, something ornate like that. He picked it up and soaked it all in. He was holding an invitation to dinner with the Interim Governor before the Inaugural Ball. It was a very select group; just a handful of the Governor's oldest friends and closest advisers. It was a dinner to chart out the future of New Washington State. The inauguration was for "Governor Benjamin Trenton." Ben's name looked so funny like that. More of those vivid memories were coming back.

Like when, years ago, Grant and Ben got drunk at a Super Bowl party and had the half serious, half joking talk about Ben being the Governor someday, and then laughed because that could never happen. But it had actually happened. What a crazy world.

There was a knock at the front door downstairs. Grant grabbed his Glock and carefully poked his head out the bathroom door down the short hall toward the front door. He wasn't alarmed enough to aim his pistol at the door, but he was alarmed enough to have it in his hand.

"Yes. Who is it?" Grant said loudly enough to be heard through the door. There was that command voice he had developed in the past few months. It was not his peacetime voice.

"Sgt. Vasquez and Trooper Timmons," a male voice said. Grant was expecting them. He laughed at himself for having the habit, acquired only recently, of always having his gun with him and assuming every knock on the door could be someone trying to take him away. He put his Glock down on the sink, not wanting the troopers to shoot him by mistake if he were waving it at them. He'd come this far, with so many guns pointed at him recently and was about to be the Governor's dinner guest before the Inaugural Ball; he would be too embarrassed to get shot now by friendly fire.

"Be right there, gentlemen," Grant said casually. He looked at his Glock again. The memories started flooding back like they had been all evening. He knew every detail of that gun. Nothing was more comforting than holding it in his hand. It had comforted him through the absolute worst things in his life. He'd carried it almost constantly the past 299 days, and had used it several times to save his life or the lives of others. There had been that terrifying night in the neighborhood when everything changed forever. There had been that other time...

Grant realized he was keeping the gentlemen at the door waiting while he was remembering all those things. It was impolite to leave people waiting. He wanted to grab his pistol again when he headed toward the door. No. He forced himself to put it down on the sink.

He needed to get his head into the new normal, and the new normal was that he didn't need a gun all the time. In fact, other people had guns and were protecting him. That was such a weird thought. But, so was everything that was happening, so why not throw this weird thing into the big pile of weirdness. Roll with it, Grant thought.

He looked at his Glock on the sink and took a deep breath. He could do this without his gun. He put his beloved pistol in the locking carry case he had intentionally placed in the bathroom because he knew he'd have to stow it there before leaving. He took a deep breath and walked out of the bathroom, unarmed and feeling naked.

Grant opened the door and saw the two plainclothes State Police troopers. They looked so young. Much to Grant's delight, their suits didn't fit too well, either. He didn't feel so poorly dressed now. "Come on in, guys."

"Thank you, Colonel," one of them said to Grant.

That sounded so strange: "Colonel." Grant had acquired that title only a few days ago. His first reaction to hearing people call him "Colonel" was always a little guilt because he hadn't really done anything to get that title. Well, he thought, maybe he did do something but he couldn't get past the feeling that having that title was a little disrespectful to real military men who did real military things to earn their titles. But he knew that "Colonel" was not strictly a military recognition now.

The New Washington Legislature recognized forty-three people from the war who had done various helpful things of a military nature and awarded them the honorary title of "Colonel." Grant was one of them. He chuckled to himself. I'm more like Colonel Sanders, he thought. Except I don't know how to make fried chicken.

The troopers were standing in the entryway with him. Grant still wanted his pistol. He pointed to the bathroom down the hall and said to the troopers, "Let me guess, guys, I can't bring my pistol with me to the Governor's Mansion." "Correct, sir," the older one said.

"That's cool. I have you two," Grant said. He started to get a tear in his eye for no apparent reason, which was happening a lot lately. He tried to control his emotions by distracting them with some conversation.

"Hey," Grant said to the troopers, "I really appreciate what you guys are doing for me. I know the odds of a gunfight are pretty low, but I appreciate..." Grant wanted to say "you risking your lives" but didn't. "I appreciate what you're doing," is all he could get out. The troopers could sense that Grant was seeing in them other young men and women who had volunteered for things and who were no longer with them. Or, they were alive, but messed up.

"No problem, sir," the younger one said.

The older one checked his watch and said, "We need to get going, Colonel."

Grant composed himself again. He was getting better at that as time went on. He was decompressing from the events of the past few weeks and slowly getting his emotions under control. Most of the time.

"Is a separate detail getting Dr. Matson and my daughter?" Grant asked. He knew the answer. He knew the plan well because it involved his wife's and daughter's safety. He always knew where his wife and kids were because there were still isolated instances of Loyalist violence. And given his new job, he and his family would be a juicy prime target.

"Yes, sir," the older trooper said. "At Dr. Matson's parents' house. Another detail will be there at 18:45 to take them to the ball." Grant nodded to them.

Grant's daughter, Manda, was coming, too. Grant had pulled a few strings and got a nice Inaugural Prom for the young people who had been cheated out of their high school proms by the Collapse. Ben, "Governor Trenton" Grant forced himself to call him, had made that happen. Manda was the Queen of the Inaugural Prom.

As they were going out the door, Grant said to the troopers, "Did I ever tell you guys about how Governor Trenton and I got really drunk when the Seahawks were in the Super Bowl and talked about how a guy like him would never be Governor?"

It was going to be a great night.

Epilogue

Most people slowly recovered from the Collapse into a somewhat normal life.

In the Cedars, things mostly bounced back. Ron Spencer was a hero for his Patriot gray man work. He had lots of accounting clients because businesses were forming and Ron was a respected man. He had enjoyed the excitement of all the gray man work he did, but he was glad to return to the ho-hum life of being an accountant.

Judy Killmer sold her home in the Cedars and moved away. No one knew where she went. She was ashamed for being a collaborator, but was still proud of the fact that she told Ron about Carlos and the others coming to get them. Overall, though, she was humiliated by the whole situation. Many people moved to different parts of the state or different states altogether. With all the official records of everything in shambles, people would just pick a new name and start a new life.

Joe Tantori became a businessman with his banking and security firms. He was a war hero; Tantori's Raiders were a legend. He took care of all of his men. Most left to go back home or start new lives. Joe made sure they were paid fairly and had good jobs. He gave each one of them a cigar to remember Tantori's Raiders by.

John Bennington was the Sheriff and a newlywed. He married Julie Mathers and was nursing her back to a more stable mental health. She'd been through a lot. Julie was helped through all of this by Abby, John's daughter from his first marriage. John's ex-wife ran off with someone to Chicago and John was there to take in Abby. Abby and Julie were perfect for each other.

The WAB families were fine. Ben, of course, was the Interim Governor, and then was elected to several more terms. Laura was the perfect First Lady of New Washington.

Tom Foster and Brian Jenkins worked for the Governor's Office. Their families were fine. In fact, they were much closer after their time at Prosser Farm.

The Prossers just wanted to return to their normal lives, but hiding the future governor during the war was too much attention for them to remain anonymous. The Prosser Farm became a historical monument. Visitors constantly came by. Finally, a wealthy Patriot bought out the Prossers and turned the farm into a monument. The Prossers relocated to a new farm. They liked it; the new place had more equipment and was fancier. They still grew their own food and sold it. Business was good.

Dennis, the Prosser's cousin, had some tough times. He had met Angie, a "food ho," which was the Collapse term for a "food whore," or a woman who would live with a man in order to be fed. Angie was gorgeous and a genuinely nice woman. She seemed to be in love with average-looking Dennis, but when the war was over and the economy was better, she left him. It was heartbreaking. Then again, lots of Collapse relationships were ending as things switched from collapse times to normal times.

The EPU agents out at Prosser Farm were heroes for all they did. They gained high positions in the new State Police and provided security details for the new Governor and his family and staff.

Things at Pierce Point turned out well. Rich Gentry was a hero and became the de facto mayor of the community. No surprises there. He and his wife, Amy, finally had the kids they wanted.

Dan Morgan finally got to retire for good. He, too, was a big hero at Pierce Point. Dan trained his dogs and fished. He was very happy.

John and Mary Anne Morrell finally got to retire, too. They had grandkids and Mary Anne still gardened and canned. She was showing young women and a few men how to grow and store their own food. People had learned their lesson about just-in-time inventory. They weren't going to let that happen again.

Special Forces Ted also got to retire. He avoided the limelight. He was a famous war hero, but was done with war forever. He got a homestead about thirty miles from Olympia and tried to forget all the things he'd seen. The highlight of his year was the annual reunion of the 17th Irregulars. Members of the unit started having kids and they often asked Ted to be their kids' godfather.

Sap didn't retire. He stayed in the State Guard for almost two years after the Olympia operation. He then went home to rural New Wisconsin, which was now getting back on its feet like New Washington had. He owned several businesses and did very well.

Chip had found his family at Pierce Point. He married his girlfriend, Liz, and they settled down there. Chip received one of the few Patriot pensions from the Legislature. These were monthly payments for donating property during the war. Chip's basement full of ARs was much appreciated. People in Pierce Point always brought over food, too. Chip couldn't sit still, though. He opened up a gun store in Frederickson where he would tell and retell all the stories from

Pierce Point. He didn't sell too many guns but he had a hell of a good life.

Gideon went back to Philadelphia to try and find his family. Things were a mess back in the FUSA and his family was gone, so he returned to Pierce Point and settled down. He started a trucking company there with Doug Smithson. As a hero of Pierce Point—the story about the semi-trailer was told and retold until it was completely exaggerated—Gideon had no trouble getting business. Doug, too, was a hero for driving the semi full of the 17th Irregulars into Olympia.

The Team did just fine. They all married their Team Chick girlfriends and started families. Pow became the SWAT team captain for the Olympia Police Department. Scotty was Pow's first sergeant on the SWAT team. Bobby went into business with his cousin in a construction company. Bobby's war hero status helped with business. Ryan joined the State Guard and trained new soldiers. He, too, was a hero and received a lot of well-deserved respect. Someone from the Team spent every New Year's with Kellie and the child who Wes never got to meet, telling her stories about Wes' bravery.

Tammy Colson was not doing well. Mark was still insane. He kept thinking Paul would be coming back. Tammy was encouraged to divorce Mark and get on with her life. She couldn't think about that. She would go visit him as often as she could at the mental home run by the local church. She would come back and cry.

Missy Colson was doing better. She was starting to talk again. Cole was helping her by being the quiet autistic kid who could relate to her need for silence.

The more Cole helped Missy, the better he was getting at talking. He was growing up, too. He was a teenage boy now. His voice was changing.

Lisa realized that Cole and Missy were inseparable. But Lisa and Cole and Manda (until she got married) had moved back to Olympia. Lisa thought that Cole needed her fulltime care.

But he actually didn't. He was so independent and talking so well that he didn't need fulltime care. He didn't need his mommy anymore, which was hard for Lisa. Grant, on the other hand, was thrilled that Cole was pretty much independent now.

So Lisa and Tammy talked. They came up with a plan that was good for everyone. Cole would stay out at the cabin in Pierce Point with Manda fulltime. That way, Cole could be with Missy for as long as she needed it. Tammy would oversee them most of the time, but others would help too. Gideon was out there, as were the Morrells. There were plenty of good people who could keep an eye on Cole.

Grant would come out, too, as often as he could with his new job on the state Supreme Court. His ReconComm job had wound down and now, two years after the war, Grant, ironically, had a government job. A justice of the New Washington State Supreme Court.

In fact, coming back to the cabin and relaxing was his favorite thing in life. And so he would come out and check in on Cole.

Lisa still preferred Olympia to Pierce Point. That was okay. She had come out to the cabin at the right time and done quite a bit of good out there. She had earned the right to stay in Olympia if that's what she wanted.

Grant hadn't heard from the outside thought since right after the war. The last time when he heard from it was when Grant thought one time, "Wow, I did a lot for people."

You?